# FROM PENVARRIS, WITH LOVE

# FROM PENVARRIS, WITH LOVE

Rosemary Aitken

This first world edition published 2008
in Great Britain and the USA by
SEVERN HOUSE PUBLISHERS LTD of
9–15 High Street, Sutton, Surrey SM1 1DF.

Copyright © 2008 by Rosemary Aitken.

British Library Cataloguing in Publication Data

Aitken, Rosemary
  From Penvarris with love
  1. Penzance (England) - Social life and customs - Fiction
  2. Great Britain - History - George V, 1910-1936 - Fiction
  3. Love stories
  I. Title
  823.9'14[F]


  ISBN-13: 978-0-7278-6627-1    (cased)

*All Severn House titles are printed on acid-free paper.*


Typeset by Palimpsest Book Production Ltd.,
Grangemouth, Stirlingshire, Scotland.
Printed and bound in Great Britain by
MPG Books Ltd., Bodmin, Cornwall.

# Part One
## August – September 1914

# One

The train was late. Even when you leaned forward and squinted down the track there was no sign of even the faintest wisp of smoke. Maudie straightened her new best bonnet a little on her bouncing light-brown curls, tugged at her shawl and pinched her cheeks to make them pink. Still no approaching train.

She sighed. She couldn't help it. She only had an hour or two. It was half-day closing, so the shop itself was shut, but there was always work to do behind the scenes. So if Stanley didn't get here very soon indeed they would not have time to have this little 'talk' he'd mentioned in his note, before she would be back with Madam, dressing the window, fetching hats and gloves – 'They set off the material simply perfectly' – or pinning hems and marking darts for fussy customers, on clothes that often looked quite perfect as they were. A shame it was sometimes, tinkering with those lovely frocks and coats, but as Madam said, some of their ladies liked to have alterations done so they didn't feel their clothes were wholly 'off the peg'.

Maudie tugged at her own brown skirt impatiently. Serviceable, of course, and warm and nicely cut like all the girls' uniforms in Madam's shop. But chocolate brown did show the dust so round the hems, and the cream blouse with the brown bow at the neck did nothing for her mousy colouring. If she had the chance, she knew the dress she'd buy. Gorgeous it was, all pale blue silk, with little imitation roses on the skirt, and a frilled bodice right up to the neck – though you'd need kid boots to go with it, of course. The sort of thing a bride might wear. She wondered what Stanley would think of her in that – if he was going to ask her what she thought he was. Though she could never have afforded a dress like that.

Half a year's wages it would cost, even now, though she had
finished her second 'improver' year at last and was beginning
to earn a little money of her own, instead of paying Madam
for the privilege of being an apprentice seamstress at the shop.

She was so busy imagining the pleasure of that silk, the
way it swished and rustled as you put it on the dummy, that
she almost forgot to notice that the train was coming in. But
here it was now, and she hadn't even watched it coming round
the bay – you could see it clearly all the way from Marazion
if you looked. There was a hiss, a rush of steam, as though
the engine was sighing to a stop, and general flurry on the
platform too.

There were flags and whistles – 'Pen-zance! This is the
terminus. Pen-zance!' – while porters bustled past, and waiting
friends and servants eyed the clanking carriages. Impatient
young men had already flung the first-class doors open and
were handing down their leather luggage from the rack, while
people with humbler packages were clambering from the third-
class section further down.

And then finally there was Stanley smiling down at her.
'Hello, Maudie.' His eyes were very blue. Bluer than that silk,
and just as beautiful.

She gave him a little smile – somehow she was always
bashful when he spoke to her. ''Lo Stanley.' She need not
have bothered pinching up her cheeks, they were redder than
the apple that he was holding out to her.

'Brought you a little something from the garden up at home.
More of them in my pockets. Thought you'd like them for
your tea. Well, go on, take it then.' He gave his playful grin.
'It's not forbidden fruit. I didn't even have to steal it off the
tree. Pa suggested it. And Mother said I was to send her love.'
He fell into step beside her and they walked along the platform. 'When are you going to come up to Nanvean again and
meet them properly?'

She grinned. 'Get on with you, I know them perfectly.' Of
course she did. She'd got to know them pretty well that time,
five years ago or more, when she was sent up to stay with a
maiden aunt while her own mother was poorly for a month
or two. Turned out she'd developed a fever when little Tully
was born – her second, late and long-awaited child – and both
of them had very nearly died. Not that anyone had told Maudie

what the trouble was. It might have been a very sad and frightening time, if it wasn't for the kindness of Stanley's family next door. Aunt Jane had done her best, but she wasn't used to children; her idea of solace was to pray at you, and administer sharp doses of malt extract and weak tea in her cramped, damp parlour hung with gloomy texts.

But Stan's mum and dad made the newcomer so welcome when she called round at the farm for half a pint of best buttermilk that Maudie still had grateful memories of that cheerful kitchen, where there always seemed to be the smell of baking and warm stew. She could see it now – kindly, plump-cheeked Mum Hoskins up to her ears in flour, and Dad Hoskins' weather-beaten face twinkling as he stamped the farm-muck off his boots. And there was Stan, of course, much younger then, who had made her laugh so much, helped her find the places where the hens had laid their eggs and showed her the treasures turned up by the plough – broken pots and patterned bottle-stoppers which were really old, he said. In the end she'd found excuses to go round every day. Even now the memory of it made her smile.

'You mean to say your parents don't remember me?'

He grinned at her. 'Of course they do. They were thrilled to bits last year when I told them I'd come down here and run into you again. But what they remember is a skinny thing with plaits. I'd love for them to see how pretty you've turned out.'

'Get on with you!' She gave his arm a push and they threaded their way out, through the crowd of passengers awaiting the up-train. There were a large number of young men in uniform, she realized with a surprise, as if half the country was already off to war. She looked around for Father, who worked on the railway and might have been dealing with parcels from this very train, but there was no sign of him this afternoon.

'Now, Maudie Olds, you want walk to Alverton, along beside the sea, like we belong to do, and then up to Mount Misery through the woods and back?' Stan asked as they emerged from the station and out on to the street.

She shook her head. 'I haven't got much time. Let's go up through the town. It's quicker that way and besides, as I was coming down, I thought I heard a band. Sounded like some sort of a parade. I'd dearly like to go and find out what it was.'

'A funeral most likely.' Stan sounded as if he felt there were more things in life than bands, but he did not protest, and they walked up Market Jew Street, not holding hands, of course – someone might have seen them and that would never do. Madam was particularly strict with all her girls about that sort of thing. In fact, when she thought of it, Maudie rather wished she hadn't been so keen to take this route and she found that she was quickening her pace. 'Come on, I don't want Madam catching sight of us.'

Stanley took her by the elbow and gave his easy laugh. 'Oh, come on, Maudie, what's the harm? You've got an hour, you said. She isn't going to eat you, I suppose, for strolling up the street in your free time with someone you have known since you were just a child – no one could object to that, not even your famous Madam Raymond.' He gestured to the sign. 'Not even Madame with an "e" – funny sort of name, when you come to think of it. French or something, did you say it was?'

She giggled. 'Well, it's supposed to be. But Belinda – that's the senior girl – says it's only swank. Madam isn't Madam anything at all.'

'But it says so in gold letters on the window, large as life.' Stanley turned and read it with exaggerated care. 'Madam Raymond, Ladies' Modes. Fittings and Alterations carried out.' And underneath in smaller script: 'Select range of gloves and corsetry also kept in stock.' He said it so loud that a woman with a basket stopped and stared at him.

'Here, don't!' Maud tugged his arm, pink with embarrassment but laughing all the same. 'Someone will hear you – but it's true! Plain Mrs Raymond she ought to be, by rights, but she thought "Madam" was classier for a shop. Belinda says so, and she ought to know. She's been with her since she first began – though no one calls Mrs Raymond anything but Madam now, of course. Proper comical it is at times, to hear them in the shop – her saying "Yes, Madam" to the customers and they calling her the same. Half the time you don't know which is . . . Here, whatever's this?'

They'd reached the corner of the road, where a crowd had formed and a commotion was taking place up ahead – and in the middle of it, when she came to look, what was obviously the band that she had heard before. They had stopped playing now, and were drawn up in a straggling line, blocking the roadway under the town clock, and people were all crowding round to see. So it was not a funeral but something military by the look of it. There were flags and banners, and through the jostling shoulders Maudie caught a glimpse of an imposing-looking officer with lots and lots of braid, who was obviously making some kind of speech, while a red-faced drummer in scarlet uniform struggled to hold up a drum that seemed too big for him.

Maud said suddenly, 'I see what it is: one of those recruiting rallies that you hear about. I didn't know that they were going to have one here this afternoon. Being quite successful by the look of it.' She gestured to a table that had been set up to one side, just in the entrance of a block of offices. Already a longish queue had formed, and presently a stern soldier with moustaches and a cap came and sat at it, took out pen and paper, and started writing names. Maud turned to Stan, excited, but he did not look at her.

Stan was staring at the rally in dismay. Drat! Of all the things to run across this blessed afternoon! It was the last thing he'd expected – though he should have thought of it – and it was confoundedly bad luck. Now Maudie would think that this had influenced his news. He hadn't meant for it to be like this. He had planned to take her up into the woods, ask her if she would be prepared to wait for him and break it to her gently that he was planning to enlist. But now . . .

'You should be signing up yourself, a great strong lad like you.' The voice came from behind him, and made him whirl around. It was the woman with the basket who had stared at them before. 'Instead of larking like a witnick round the streets.' She poked a knobbly finger almost in his face, then turned to point at Maudie. 'And you, young lady – you should tell him so! Teach that ruddy Kaiser a thing or two, that's what.' She hugged her basket to her ample stomach with both hands, and bestowed a light-lipped scowl on both of them.

Maudie turned scarlet and Stan sprang to her defence. The words had stung him on his own account as well. He heard himself saying, as he pulled off his cap, 'You're quite right, madam, and I mean to do it too, soon as harvest's over and they can spare me from the farm. So there isn't any need to speak to Maud like that.'

The woman looked discomfited, and then gave a sniff. 'Well then,' she said, as if she'd somehow scored a point, and she moved away, elbowing a pathway through the crowd. He turned to Maud, ready to turn the moment with a jest, but her expression told him it was too late for that.

'You mean it, Stan, don't you? I can see it in your face. You really plan to go?'

'I'm sorry, Maudie,' he said contritely. 'I didn't mean to blurt it out to you like that. I was going to tell you properly – when we were on our walk.'

'So that was what you were so anxious to talk to me about?' she said, in a very peculiar tone of voice. She sounded really wounded, not just surprised and cross. It rather puzzled him. He'd expected that she would react the way his mother had – half proud and patriotic, half inclined to cry, but ready to support him all the same. Instead Maudie was staring at him, ashen-faced. 'You just wanted to tell me you were going away to war?'

'Well, it was that – partly,' he admitted, wishing to heaven that he had held his tongue just now. If he had only waited till they were walking in the woods, he could have prepared her better, but it was too late now. He decided on the truth.

'Thing is, Maudie, I think I ought to go. Shouldn't feel easy in myself if I didn't try to do my part – fight for King and Country, and all that sort of thing. Mum and Dad can manage, for a month or two; Granfer's on his feet again, near as good as new, and it will all be over by Christmas anyway, so everybody says.' He gave her his most winning smile. 'You wouldn't like to think your Stan was only half a man. Not if we're walking out and planning to get wed – as I hope you will agree to, one of these fine days.'

There, he had said it, but not the way he'd meant to. He'd had a plot to do it at the stepping stones, when he took her hand to help her across the slippery bit. Something about 'taking her hand for ever more' and planting a secret kiss on her lips, there in the private silence of the woods. But somehow it hadn't worked out like that at all. She was standing like a statue, as if she'd turned to stone, right in the middle of the pavement. People were turning round to stare at them again.

'I aren't going to stop you signing up, if you've made your mind to it,' she said, still in that strangled tone of voice.

'But I do think you might have told me first of all, instead of telling total strangers and leaving me to hear.' She gestured to the table where the man was making lists. 'Go and write your name down if that's what you want to do.'

'Oh, Maudie, I aren't wanting to do it straight away!' He tried to take her elbow but she snatched it away. 'Got to wait until the harvest's in and they can spare me from the farm. I've written to the army to ask them for some forms – thought I'd offer in a month or so, after my birthday, if they're still wanting men. They won't take you for service overseas until you are nineteen. Eighteen before they'll sign you up at all.'

Maudie turned away and wouldn't meet his eyes. 'Well then, what's Jim Tregurtha doing in the queue?' She nodded towards the line of people waiting to sign on. 'He was in the babies when I was at school. He can't be more than fifteen or sixteen at the most.'

Stanley looked and saw the boy she meant – conspicuously more childlike than the rest of them, though he was standing up as straight as rods and trying to look grown. With his scrawny body, freckles and thin, straw-coloured hair, he looked even younger than Maudie said he was, but the man with the moustaches was writing down his name and giving him a piece of paper like the rest of them. Stan frowned. 'They always have had boy soldiers for drummer boys, I suppose, and I know they're taking them, if they have special skills. Engineers and signallers and that sort of thing.' He didn't sound convincing, even to himself, and Maud made a scornful sort of face.

'What kind of special skills d'you think Jim Tregurtha's got? Never played an instrument as I ever heard – except maybe a tin Mayhorn, like the rest of us, on Mayday once or twice. And he's no engineer. Works down the cattle-market these days, sweeping out the stalls.'

Stan saw an advantage. 'But you see how it is,' he said quickly. 'Even boys are going. So how can I stop at home? Be ashamed to look myself in the eye when I was shaving, else. And it's not even as if I should be going for very long. Like I said, be home again by Christmas, with a bit of luck.' He felt that she was wavering, so he tried a little smile. 'And you haven't told me what you think about the rest of what I said.'

'You mean about our walking out?' She sounded full of tears. 'I thought that's what we were doing – at least until today. But if you're going away to be a soldier, I don't know how we can.' She turned away and began to walk quite quickly up the street so people had to move aside to let her through.

Stan had to hurry to keep up with her. 'Oh, come on, Maudie. You know what I mean.' He reached her side again and took her by the arm, forcing her to face him. 'About our planning to get wed, some day.'

But it was no use. She wouldn't meet his eyes. 'Well as to that, Stan Hoskins, I will have to think. I don't say I wouldn't like to, one of these fine days, but I can't think about it now. I've had enough surprises for one afternoon. We'll talk about it Christmas, when you come home again.' Then she added briskly, in an artificial tone, 'Now, we going to take a walk up to the park, or not? Too sticky for the field-paths this afternoon, I think.'

So they didn't take the promised stroll into the woods at all. They stuck to public pavements where she couldn't take his hand. And he didn't really have a chance to tell her more about his plans. She kept up a brittle, cheery chatter about Belinda and the shop, as if she was afraid of drawing breath, until it was time for her to go. Stan had some business to do in town before the train, so she left him in the street – though she did squeeze his fingers as she said goodbye.

Maud told Belinda all about it, later on that night, when they had closed the shutters and locked up the shop, and were up in the front attic sitting on their beds. 'I didn't mean to be horrid to him,' she wailed. 'Only I'd been so hoping for . . . something else, you see.'

Belinda was brushing her long, shining chestnut hair. She always did that, night and morning, at least a hundred strokes, never mind how tired or late the pair of them might be. By day she wore it pinned up in a bun, but now she had it all brushed forward so that it screened her face. She glanced up at Maudie from beneath the waterfall of hair, but did not interrupt the rhythmic movement of the brush. 'Hoping that he would propose to you, you mean? Seems to me he did, in spite of everything.'

Maudie put down her own brush with a sigh. She did not

have Belinda's patience with the nightly ritual, and though she envied those lovely, glossy locks, she knew that however much she followed suit her own hair would remain its wayward mousy self. 'Funny sort of way to ask a girl, I think – tell her that some day you'd like to marry her, but first you're going away to war. Probably won't see her for months and months – if then! He doesn't seem to think he might get killed, or hurt.'

Belinda paused in her brushing and pushed back her hair. 'Oh, he'll have thought of that all right. I'm sure they always do – that's what makes them seem so brave. Though they don't dwell on it, as a rule, or they would never go at all.' She caught the length of hair and twisted it, tying a rag around it so it formed a sort of coil. Tomorrow, Maud knew, it would lie in lovely waves, though when she'd tried it with her own hair once, it had only ended in a frizz.

She went over and pulled back the patchwork blanket on her bed. As senior girls they had the whole room to themselves, with an iron bedstead and a rag rug each, and didn't have to share the way the new apprentices did.

She slid between the covers. The sheet was calico and it was cold to touch, but she snuggled into it and pulled the blanket up. 'Talk as if you know all about it, you do. But I suppose you're right. The boys are very brave. I should have told Stanley I would wait for him. But it's very well for you,' she added wickedly. 'You got a stream of fellows knocking at your door. They aren't all likely to go rushing off to the war, I don't suppose.'

There was a little silence and then Belinda sighed. 'But my brother is. In fact he volunteered today. Came into the shop this morning to tell me that he had – though he had to find a pretext, so he said he wanted gloves. You might have seen him. Tall, quite good-looking, with a blue cravat? Madam shooed him off, but not before he'd managed to tell me what he'd done.'

Maudie nodded. Of course she'd noticed him. You couldn't miss the presence of an unaccompanied young man; it was quite a rare occurrence in a shop like theirs. And this one was so handsome that even she'd looked twice. 'I might have guessed that was your brother, if I'd only thought of it. He's got your colouring. That hair and everything. Mind, I thought it was funny when he asked to look at gloves. A present for his mother, so he said, but he didn't know the size.'

Belinda laughed. 'I don't think Madam was very much convinced; I expect she thought he was after one of her new girls. But he managed to give me the message, which was why he came – and he escaped without a pair of gloves he didn't want!' She put the brush down on the wash stand and got into her bed, rubbing her forearms to warm herself. 'Of course, he's a man now, and he feels he has to go off and enlist. But I can't help being anxious – any more than you can.' She said it in an oddly wistful tone of voice, as if Maud had been claiming some sort of privilege.

Maudie felt that she had been a bit unkind. 'I'm sorry, Blin,' she said. 'I didn't know about your brother.' She thumped the pillow to make a hollow for her head. 'I wouldn't have gone on so, if I had realized.'

'Well, we can keep each other company worrying, I suppose. And, Maud . . .'

'What?' Maud said rather warily. Belinda was a great one for giving good advice.

'Next time you see your Stanley, you tell him what you told me. That you will wait for him. I would if I was you. Give him something to hang on to, while he is overseas. Now, we'd better get to sleep or we shan't wake betimes, and there's still that dress to alter before Mrs Knighton comes. Her fitting is booked in for tomorrow, ten o'clock.' Belinda sat up and blew the candle out.

# Two

Despite what she had said to Maudie about being up betimes, Belinda couldn't sleep. She lay awake for a long time staring up into the dark, and it was not only because of the uncomfortable knots of rag wound into her hair. Truth to tell, she was a little jealous of her friend. Here was Maudie, only seventeen, talking about marriage to her famous Stan, while she, Belinda, had no steady beau, though she would be twenty in a week or two.

Of course there had been a number of young men from time to time – Mark the fisherman for one, and more lately that good-looking Jonah Lotts who came round with the coal – but as soon as she hinted about a wedding ring, they'd either lost interest or got the wrong idea. Though she hadn't altogether abandoned hope of Jonah Lotts.

*Mrs Jonah Lotts.* She almost said the words aloud. It would be a fine thing, wouldn't it, to be a wife? To have your own house, or a room or two at least, where you could have things how you wanted them. No more thankless errands and scrubbing endless floors 'to save Gran's aching knees', or sewing hems until your fingers ached. No more of those awkward alterations for the shop, like Mrs Knighton's silk – that bodice would have to be pretty well unpicked to move those pesky darts. And she wasn't naturally nimble-fingered the way that Maudie was, though she couldn't admit that to anyone, of course.

Perhaps she'd been too eager to be apprenticed at the shop, but she'd been so anxious to get a place somewhere, and lucky to have the money for the premium out of what her parents had left for her in trust. After all, as Gran had pointed out a hundred times, after that awful accident when Ma and Pa were killed, not many orphans had a chance like that. She didn't think Belinda appreciated it, she said – meaning she could have found better ways of spending twenty pounds.

Belinda could have thought of better ways as well. If only it had been possible to get a place at once – like her brother Peter, who'd gone in for carpentry – or to have moved to Truro or somewhere else to train. Perhaps she could have learned china-painting, like she'd wanted to, or tinting the portraits for photographers. There were girls who were doing that sort of thing these days. But most people wouldn't take you till you were seventeen, and Gran had insisted that Belinda came to her ('You're not going into service; you'd break your parents' hearts') so when this opportunity arose she simply snatched at it. Perhaps she was lucky to be here at all.

And there were real advantages, in so many ways. Now, for instance. She stretched out her toes, revelling in the luxury of a whole bed to herself, without the fear of encountering

Gran's knobbly form somewhere and earning a sharp, reproving little jab. Of course, she thought dreamily, that was one drawback of getting wed: you'd have to share a bed again, as Ma and Pa had done. She was vaguely aware that most married people did. But once your husband was at work, you could have the pleasure of the whole place to yourself. Or, if you wanted, you could ask the neighbours in, put the kettle on and have a little chat.

She shifted on the pillow, trying to find a spot where she could lie more easily. 'Vain about that hair, you are,' Gran had grumbled more than once, pulling it tightly into horrid corkscrew plaits, and maybe it was true. She did take a lot of trouble with her hair. And people noticed it. 'Your crowning glory,' Jonah Lotts had said one evening when she sneaked out after closing to meet him secretly. There was a little winding alley which led down to the sea, close enough to get to, but away from prying eyes, where he'd paid her lots of compliments about the way she looked. He'd even seemed to like the little freckles on her nose.

So why had he not been waiting, this last day or two? Her thoughts kept coming back to probe at the idea, like a tongue to a sore tooth. He hadn't been there yesterday – or the day before – and there had been no answer to the message she had sent round to the yard. If he wasn't there by Friday she'd go round to look for him. Not at his house perhaps – his mother hadn't liked it when she called there once before – but there was nothing to prevent her from waiting in the street, or outside the depot where he took the cart each night.

Of course he had been hinting lately that he might have to go away and that he mightn't see her for a little while. What did he mean by that? There had been mention, months ago, of going to Plymouth for a horse. Was that all it was? Or was he trying to let her down gently without a painful scene? Or – she sat up sharply – could it mean that he was thinking of going off to the war? That was possible. If Stan had decided to enlist without informing Maud, it had to be admitted that Jonah might have done the same. Strangely, the notion gave her hope.

She wondered if he had been in the crowd at that recruiting rally. Not that Maud could tell her, even if he was. Belinda liked dropping hints about 'admirers' to the other girls, but she took care not to be too specific about exactly who they were. And when there was someone like Jonah, she kept him well away, not only because Madam disapproved of followers, but partly in case he started making eyes at someone else – some of those younger sewing-girls were pretty little things. So Maudie would not have known who Jonah was if he'd walked straight into her, though he was so good-looking you'd think she would notice him. Drat! If only she'd taken her friend into her confidence!

Mind, Maudie was never the best informant in the world – she didn't pick up details the way other people might. If Belinda had managed to get outside herself, and have a proper look – instead of merely getting a quick peep through the windows now and then – she could have told you anything you asked. Who was there, and what was happening. Not that she was a gossip – not a bit of it – but if there were things to know, she hated missing them. And she was very good at holding pictures in her head.

So she couldn't help wondering if Jonah had been there. How could she find out? If he didn't come tomorrow she would drop a little note. He hadn't said that she couldn't write to him – not exactly – and if he had really gone away they'd have to send it on – wouldn't they? – if she stuck a proper stamp on it and put it in the post. She almost hoped he would write back and say he'd gone off to the war, and then she could be like Maud and say she'd wait for him. There was something quite romantic in the whole idea.

But suppose he'd only gone to Plymouth about this dratted horse? Or simply did not want to see her any more? Even in the dark she felt her cheeks ablaze.

'Maudie,' she whispered, but there was no reply. So, what with the worry and the rag-tails, and thinking about the alterations to Mrs Knighton's dress, it was almost daybreak before she drifted off to sleep.

Up at the farmhouse at Nanvean, Stan was waking up. He hadn't slept well either and he struggled out of bed. He had to splash cold water on his face to sting himself alert before he pulled his clothes on and stumped out to the cows, still cursing himself for an idiot as he'd been doing half the night.

It was a fine, clear morning, just the kind he loved, with

the sky still pink and golden with the rising sun, and the dew dancing like little jewelled lanterns in the grass. But today he hardly noticed as he undid the gate and whistled to Jess to come and help him bring the milkers in. How could he have been so stupid? Shocked, she must have been. Poor Maud. He'd sprung it on her badly; no wonder she was hurt.

'Hup, Daisy!' He patted the animal's warm, brown, familiar rump and she lowed back at him, then led her sisters out into the lane, the way she always did. The beasts hardly needed the barking of the dog. Already they were lumbering towards the milking-shed. Dad was there and waiting, his cap on back to front, and his old shirt without a collar fraying at the sleeves. But he nodded in greeting as he caught sight of Stan.

'Nice day for the harvest.' That was all he said. Not a word about Maudie or the events of yesterday. Stan nodded gratefully.

All the way home he'd been dreading having to tell the family what a mess he'd made of it – Mum in particular was very fond of Maud. But he hadn't had to, to his great relief. Not that they weren't interested, because he knew they were – Mum had been dropping wedding hints for months – but more as if they read the situation from his mood and there was no need for words. There had been one question – only one – on the way home from the station. Dad had driven in to pick Stan up from the train, and smiled as his son swung up beside him in the cart. But, though Stan did his best to smile a greeting in return, Dad looked him in the face and said at once, 'You told her then?'

Stan made a performance out of settling on the seat before he said, morosely, 'Did it very badly. Dropped it on her, sudden. She didn't like it much.'

Dad carefully didn't look at him again. 'Anxious for you, because she's fond of you, I 'spect. That's all, Stanley lad; see if I'm not right. Sixpence to a shilling she'll come round to it in time. Now, you got that spare part for the thresher from Bullivant's all right? Mother's got bread and cocoa waiting for us, home.'

And that was all. Conversation about the business of the farm, and the need for the small part which they'd been waiting for. A trip to the shipping agent's office in Penzance was usually Stan's reason for visiting the town – though everyone knew that it was largely an excuse; Bullivant's would gladly have forwarded the goods.

Stan shook the box. 'I got it here,' he said. 'It's the right one, too. I checked.'

Dad grunted. 'Glad of that tomorrow, if the weather holds. Here we are then, home. You get out and see about the gates.' There were two gates between the farmhouse and the lane, and both of them were closed at night to keep the chickens in.

Stan slid down from his perch with some relief. 'Don't worry, I'll see to that, and put the horse away. Just leave it all to me. You go in and let them know that we've arrived.'

Stan took his time unharnessing the horse, and when at last he went inside the house he found that Dad must have said something to the other two, because though there was bread and cocoa round the fire, they talked of anything but Maudie and the war. Once, when Granfer seemed about to ask, Mum shook her head at him.

'Give the lad a bit of peace,' she muttered. 'It's hard enough for him. Here, have your old pipe if you've finished with your tea.'

The old man looked startled but he lit up his pipe, and to Stan's surprise he let the subject rest – it wasn't often anyone could shut Granfer up like that. All the same, the atmosphere was strained – everybody conscious of what wasn't being said – and Stan had gone to bed as soon as possible.

And now here was Granfer hobbling out to help them with the cows, limping as though his feet were killing him, though he swore the trouble was only in his knees. He was wearing his old-fashioned farmer's smock, as usual, but he had got so thin those last few months, when he was ill, that it now hung loose on him and the high-buttoned neck band of his woollen vest was sticking out above the top of it, baggy and faintly yellow like his wrinkled skin.

'Well, if you're going to harvest, Horry, you've got the day for it,' he said to Father now, picking up his milking stool and moving to the shed. Granfer had been a tenant farmer all his life, and he liked to let Dad know that he was still in touch with things. Daisy and Mollie – clever creatures – were already in the stalls, munching on the feeders as though they knew the first-comers got their pick of hay. Granfer paused in the doorway before he went in after them, pulling his shapeless felt hat lower on his head and calling over his shoulder, 'Got that damty steam-thing coming later, I suppose?' He pulled his lips down in a mock grimace, showing the gaps where his bottom teeth had been.

Dad, who was still standing by the gate, looked at Stan and raised his eyebrows high, but he called back cheerfully, 'Spoke to McLeod last night. We can have the machine here for a day or two, at the price that we agreed.' He walloped the last cow on the backside and got her in the yard, then closed the gate behind her. Then he turned to Stan and added in an undertone, 'Not as long as I had wanted it. So let's hope we can get the threshing finished in the time.'

Stan grinned. 'Oh, we'll have willing helpers – they'll want the engine too.' It was true, apart from the casual labourers who came looking for work at this time of year, the family would turn out from the neighbouring farm to help bring in the corn – just as he and Dad and Granfer would do the same for them, since they too had a field or two of corn to see to. Never mind they might be rivals in the market later on: it was a race against nature, and they worked as a team. 'Looks as if the weather will hold for all of us.' He glanced up at the golden glory of the sky.

His father nodded. 'And that steam engine helps. Thresher does the work in half the time, and we can rig a belt to help us rick as well. Even if Granfer isn't much impressed.'

That was an understatement. McLeod had bought a steam engine years ago, and now made a living leasing it to several farms in turn, not only for the threshing but also for helping with the plough. Granfer had never liked McLeod in any case, and the machine was an instrument of Satan in his eyes. He didn't even like Dad's binder – 'damty new-fangled thing – and that was horse-drawn.

'Nothing to beat the old ways,' they heard him grumbling now, as he went into the shed. 'No satisfaction like a proper furrow or a stook you've made yourself. Where's the pleasure in dealing with a soulless old machine? Give me a decent plough horse every time. And what's the matter with a donkey thresher, I should like to know? Good enough for Father, and it's good enough for me. Folks today are idle, that's the truth of it.'

Stan was about to protest, but Dad shook his head. 'No good to argue with him. You know how he is. Remember when I used the steam plough last back-end? On and on for days, he was, how it didn't get into the corners or do up to the edge, just because you need the space to site an engine either end and run the plough between. He can't see the other side – that the steam plough does the work in half the time. Or that it doesn't wear out the man who's taking charge of it.'

Stan nodded. Granfer could plough a perfect furrow with a horse and thought the steam plough was a wretched thing. 'Be the end of farming, all these damned machines. And the end of me, I shouldn't be surprised,' he'd muttered at the time – though it had been a fever which had nearly seen him off.

However, the old fellow looked spry enough today. When Stan and his father got into the shed he was already squatting on his stool, milking Daisy with a practised speed which put Stan to shame – though he was a good milker too, and it was a job he loved to do.

Stan leaned his head on Mollie's rough flank and allowed himself to revel in the pleasure of the task, concentrating on the rhythmic movement of his hands, the satisfying splash of milk into the pail, the warm, thick smell of animals. The old girl trusted him, and let the milk come down, and he forgot his troubles for a moment as he worked.

They didn't have a large herd – just two dozen cows – and between the three of them the task was quickly done, and it was soon time to go back into the house to eat. Delicious breakfast it was too, since it was harvest day. Mum had been out early seeing to the hens, and there were new-laid eggs the way there always were this time of year, and a slice of bacon from the flitch above the fire (from poor old Porky who had met his end this March). Stan thought of Maudie and her slice of bread and scrape, which was all that Madam Raymond provided for her girls, and wished with a fervour that she was here with him. She would have liked to join the other women helping with the corn.

Mum might have been glad of an extra pair of hands as well. It was a busy time for her. She always brought down baskets for all the harvesters – food as well as welcome tea and lemonade. She had been baking already: there were splits and saffron cake out cooling on the rack, and a good smell of buns and jam tarts coming from the range. 'I've got cheese and pickle and that bit of ham,' she said, pouring Stan and Dad a steaming cup of tea. 'I'll bring it down for crowst. And there's the end of last year's cider I've been saving up. Them as aren't chapel will be glad of that.'

Dad nodded. It would be hot work in the cornfields on a day like this. The men would start by scything from the outside in – all done by hand until there was a swathe enough to let the binder work – and when the rabbits and other animals came bolting from the decreasing square, Granfer and his crony would be standing by with guns to pick them off and hang them in the larder for pie. Behind the binder came the women, picking up the sheaves and stacking them neatly into mows or stooks, and last of all came the youngsters, doing what they could to help. By mid-morning they'd all be pleased to rest, passing the cider flask from hand to hand or – in the case of children, Methodists and girls – quenching their thirst with refreshing lemonade gulped from enamel cups. By the time the steam engine arrived to help them rick, there would be many tired arms and aching backs.

Mum went over now to take the jam tarts from the range. It was new, and the envy of many round about who only had a cooking fire and a baking stone. 'Here's Mrs Next-Door now. And everybody else, by the look of it. I'll make some little supper pasties for your tea, if I have time.' She nodded towards the window and the yard beyond, where a gaggle of people in big hats and boots were beginning to assemble at the gate.

Dad pushed back his chair and nodded. 'Time we made a start. Come on then, Stanley lad. And you too, Father.' But Granfer was already on his feet and reaching for his gun.

Stan swallowed his second cup of tea and followed them outside. The day was as hot and busy as he'd known it would be, and he was glad of it. He worked so hard there was no time to think – not even about a certain brown-haired girl and what he should have said.

'Hey. Cheer up, Maudie. What's the matter, then? Your face is like a fiddle, only twice as long.'

Maud looked up from her stitching. Belinda was standing almost at her ear, with a piece of shot-silk bundled in her arms – Mrs Knighton's alterations by the look of it. Obviously, she was on her way downstairs, but she'd paused by Maud a moment to whisper to her friend.

'Mmhemmhem,' Maud mumbled. She was letting out a heavy coat for someone – tacking the new seam and taking out the pins, a little store of which she held between her lips. She took them out, laid down the work, and said – more clearly this time, but softly enough that only Blin could hear, 'It's only Stan. Wishing that I hadn't been so harsh with him. I ought to write him really. I will when I go home. I haven't got pen and paper to do it while I'm here – and anyway I'll never get the time to put it in the post.'

Blin grinned that knowing little grin of hers. 'How don't you do what I do, and use the office here? 'Tisn't as if Madam's ever going to know.'

Maud was startled. 'Blin! You never did!' The 'office', as Blin called it, was a little anteroom where Miss Simms, the cashier, presided over the takings and issued receipts, and where Mr Raymond (Madam's husband, who was so pale and wizened he might have been a ghost in eyeglasses) came for an hour or two a week to 'make up the books', which mostly meant sign letters and take money to the bank, since Miss Simms left nothing else for him to do. She was a tall, thin woman, always dressed in grey, who wore her steely hair piled up on her head with combs, which made her look skinnier than ever – like a human hatpin, Belinda said in joke – but both her mind and tongue were needle-sharp, and she guarded her empire jealously. 'However in the world did you get past Miss Simms?'

Maud had dropped her voice to make sure that no one heard but Belinda didn't seem to care. 'I don't go in when she is there, you goose. I go later, when we're closing up the shop and there's no one here but us. There's a spare key to the office, on the shelf above the door – Mr Raymond uses it when he forgets his own. He doesn't know I've seen him, but of course I did. So it isn't very difficult to get in when they've gone, and they aren't going to miss a piece of paper and some ink, I don't suppose.'

Maud looked round in horror, but no one was paying the slightest attention to herself and Belinda. The second-year improver was using a machine – the shop had only two of them, and the treadle was an honour which you came to very

late – and it made a loud whirring sound. She was showing
the two novices how to handle overlock, while the other
improver was pretending not to care.

'Blin, you can't do that, it's stealing,' Maud began, but she
was interrupted by a shrill voice calling from downstairs.

'Miss Richards, would you bring that dress downstairs at
once? Mrs Knighton's waiting.'

Belinda made a face and slipped away. But the conversation stayed in Maudie's mind. Later that afternoon, when she
had done the coat, she took it down so Madam could have a
look at it. She had done it skilfully, if she said so herself, and
Madam nodded approvingly as she hung the garment up.

'Splendid, Miss Olds.' Madam must be pleased, then, to
have called her that. It was a reminder that she was not an
apprentice any more. She'd been plain 'Maud' until she'd
served her time, and had only fetched and carried in the shop.
But 'Miss Olds' was a person who could help fit customers,
and even serve the less important regulars by herself. That's
what 'Miss Olds' meant. And for Madam to say 'splendid'
was a compliment indeed.

Maud was seized by sudden daring. 'Madam . . .'

Madam stared at her. She was only tiny – neat as folded
cloth – but imposing all the same. There were times when
she could draw herself upright and purse her lips, and you
would think that she was twice the size. Tonight was one of
them. 'Yes, Miss Olds? What is it you want?'

Maudie wished fervently that she had held her tongue, but
there was no going back now. She found herself burbling. 'I
wondered, Madam . . . That is . . . I was going to ask . . . would
it be possible for me to write a letter to a friend? Using your
pen and ink and everything? Only I haven't got none, not till
I get home.'

Madam was looking impassively at her. 'You might get
some at the post office or stationer's, I suppose.'

'Course I could, Madam, and I would do too if I hadn't
already taken my time off this week. Only he might be going
away, you see. He's signed up for the war and I want to catch
him before he has to go. And by the time I get to write this,
it might be too late.'

Madam's face had hardened. '"He", Miss Olds? I thought
you said "a friend".'

Maud could have bitten out her tongue. 'Well, so he is a friend. All his family are. They were very good to me before my mother died. Like relations almost.' She was struck by inspiration. 'The family sent me a little present just a day or two ago.' It was true, in a fashion – the apples could be called a present, couldn't they? 'I'd like to write and thank them, and to wish him well before he goes away.' She had another brainwave. 'I can't call in and see them. They don't live round here.'

'So how are you acquainted?' Madam asked loftily.

'I was sent up to stay there – at my aunt's – when mother was so ill.' She sensed a softening. 'Please, Madam, I wouldn't have asked you, if I could have thought of any other way. You can stop the ink and paper out of my wage this week. The poor lad is going to fight for King and Country, after all.' She was only quoting what everybody said, but it did sound heroic, when you thought of Stan that way.

Madam was actually smiling. 'I see that you are keen. Very well, Miss Olds, I applaud your honesty. You may use the office later. When Miss Simms has gone I will let you in myself. But I will take threehalfpence for the paper and the stamp out of your pay-packet, as you suggest, and you will bring the letter back for me to read before you send it, so I can be sure that it is as you say – a letter to a family friend and not some *billet doux*. And understand that this is to be the one and only time. In future you will buy your own stationery and writing implements.'

'Yes, Madam. I mean, no, Madam,' Maud said, so surprised by her success that she could hardly take it in.

'And, Miss Olds . . .'

'Yes, Madam?' She was rather nervous now.

'Learn not to say "I haven't got none", especially in the shop. Say "I haven't any" like an educated girl. Now, come to me at closing and I will let you in to write your letter when Miss Simms has gone.'

'Yes, Madam,' Maudie said again. But when she was shown in to the office later on, she found Miss Simms still in there, taking so long to pack up her reticule that it was clear she did not want to go. So Madam left them to it, and Miss Simms turned to Maud.

'So you are to write a letter? Well, make the most of it.

I shall see that the opportunity does not arise again – not for you, nor for whichever of your friends has been careless enough to blot their letters on my blotting pad. You sewing-girls must think that I'm completely blind not to notice the nonsense that I find there back-to-front. I've not said anything to Madam up to now, although I should have done – but I will do, I promise, if it occurs again.' And with that she plonked her little bonnet on her bun and whisked out of the room, looking more like a poker than a hatpin, Maudie thought.

She dipped her nib-pen in the inkwell and wrote very carefully. It was hard enough trying to let Stanley know the way she felt in words that would get past Madam's prying eyes, but it was doubly difficult when she didn't dare to blot. But when she'd finished, she was satisfied.

Madam looked at it, and just said, 'Humph! You write a decent hand. Very well. I'll stamp this and put it in the post myself.'

So Maudie had to let her have it – and couldn't add the extra words that she had hoped – before she scuttled off to warn Belinda about the blotting pad.

# Three

Jonah Lotts was whistling as he sauntered up the hill. He always got off at the steepest part, 'to save the horse' he said, but also because he liked to walk past the windows of the big house on the right. There was a dark-haired kitchen maid who sometimes smiled at him.

She wasn't there this evening, but he didn't mind too much. There was still warm sunshine and this was the part of Friday afternoon he liked the best. All downhill from here on, so he could ride the cart, and only a half-dozen deliveries still to make. Only eight more sacks to hoist up on his back and empty into the cellars or coal holes in the street – at some of the bigger houses they took more than one. And there was a choice of pretty women at the end of it.

Though he wouldn't meet Belinda, he had decided that. Not that he didn't like her; she was nice enough, and quite a feast for anybody's eyes. He'd been quite keen to start with – and who wouldn't be? – but she was worse than coal-dust for sticking to a man. They'd only been out walking once or twice and holding hands a bit – well, all right, he might have kissed her and fondled her a little – but nothing that should have made her start hearing wedding bells. And Jonah wasn't ready for anything like that, not by a long chalk. Why would a man settle for one kind of fruit when there is a whole orchard waiting to be picked?

The General, well-trained cart horse that he was, knew where to stop, of course. He'd been doing this round longer than Jonah had himself. He had paused now and was waiting beside the last house in the street. Jonah walked up behind the cart and hoisted off a sack, easing his shoulders so as to balance it, and set off half-bent to the nearby coal chute. He was still bent over, tipping out the coal, when he heard a voice behind him.

''Lo, Mr coalman. Jonah, isn't it?' It was the little kitchen maid from further down the road. She saw his look of mild surprise, and added eagerly, 'I seen it written on the cart, you see. "Jonah Lotts, Coal Merchants".'

She was skinny as a lamppost and her face was pale. Too thin for dimples, but she had a perky smile and big, dark, knowing eyes. She would be pretty if she had more to eat, he thought. He found that he was smiling in return. 'That Jonah is my father, but I'm called after him. So yes, I'm Jonah. And you are . . .?'

She grinned at him. 'Lilian. Lily-Anne, my mother wanted, but they wrote out Lilian. Mind, they call me Lily, down the kitchen where I work.'

'Well, hello, Lily-Anne,' he said. 'I shall call you that. Supposing that I happen to run into you, that is.'

He had meant to be flirtatious and she laughed delightedly. 'Course you will do – if you want to.' She dropped her head and looked up at him from under her long dark eyelashes. 'Like you have tonight.'

It was so brazen that it took him by surprise. 'You mean you were looking out for me?' he asked.

She gave a little giggle. 'Course I was. Seen you coming this way, haven't I, same time every Friday for weeks and weeks and weeks. Used to try to work beside the window so I'd see you when you came. Don't pretend you didn't notice, because I know you did. I seen you get down from the cart and walk along the street, just so you could see me and give me a little smile.'

He'd never met a girl who was so direct and bold, yet when he said, 'So you came out to meet me?' she blushed and dropped her eyes. It was a funny contradiction and an exciting one.

'I used to think,' she murmured, with her gaze fixed on the ground, 'if only I was free on Friday afternoons, I'd go and talk to that good-looking boy. And now they've gone and changed it – the mistress has joined some charity committee for the war so I'm not wanted Fridays – and so here I am.' She raised her head to look him in the face. 'And in my best clothes too.' She ran her hands across her bodice and then down her flannel skirt in a way that managed to be innocent and yet provocative. 'Though I bet you got a girl or two already, haven't you?'

He found that he was grinning. 'Off and on,' he said. 'And you must have admirers, a pretty girl like you.'

She gave him that little upward look again. 'None that you could speak of. Nothing serious.'

He said, so that he should not be misunderstood, 'Don't want to be too serious, at your age, anyway.'

She shook her head. 'Of course not. Bit of company, that's all. But when you are working in the kitchens all day long, you hardly get the chance.'

'And when you do, you have to seize it?' Was that what she meant? It rather looked like it. He took her by the waist, experimentally, and she did not pull away. Indeed, she squirmed around to look at him, and raised her face to his, almost as if she was hoping to be kissed.

Jonah was astounded. He could not believe his luck. Generally it took him weeks and weeks to get as far as this. And the girl was pretty, when you came to look, and though she was skinny there was that hint of pleasing curves under her coarse bodice and tattered petticoat.

He almost bent to kiss her, but she pulled away from him and stepped backwards, laughing. 'Here, whatever am I like? I don't know, Mr Jonah, what you must think of me. I must seem awfully forward, coming up to you like this – but the truth is that I've seen you so often and thought about you for so long, it seems as though we've met. And now we're talking face to face, it's just the same. As if we've really known each other for all this time, I mean. You don't seem like a stranger. It just feels natural-like.'

She said it so earnestly it made him smile again. He felt quite protective and adult suddenly, as if there were dragons to be slain and he was her St George. He reached out and squeezed her hand. 'I know exactly what you mean.'

She smiled at him. 'I knew you'd feel it too.' She pressed his hand against her so it brushed her budding breasts, and he recognized a dragon stirring in his loins.

He released her quickly, and stepped away himself. 'Trouble is, I'm working right now, Lily-Anne. I can't stand here chatting, I've the round to do. And look – there's the General, waiting down the street. I've been neglecting him. My Pa won't half give me what for if he goes wandering off.'

It was quite true; he had forgotten all about the horse. Not for the first time, either. There had been quite a scene one day, when Jonah had stopped to talk to the girl across the street until the General got tired of waiting at an unfamiliar place and simply ambled off and found his own way home. Pa had given Jonah a proper larruping for that, and forbidden him to speak to Annie, or any other girl, while he was supposed to be delivering on the cart – and then Belinda had come and made it worse, by arriving to ask for Jonah at the door, making it clear that he'd stopped on his rounds to talk to her as well.

'I'll have to go.' Jonah tried to tear his hand away, but she pressed it to her as she had before.

'You'll come and see me next week?'

'Course I will,' he said. She must know what she was doing. He could feel her through the dress.

'Try and be here earlier so we can 'ave a bit of time. There's an alley down the bottom, we could 'ave a bit of chat. Go up to woods if you've a mind to, for a walk.' And then at last she let go of his hand and he was able to pick up the sack that he'd dropped and go hurrying up the street to catch the

General and the cart. He almost ran into the post-boy on his bicycle, and wondered if the lad had seen them chatting there. Pa would have him for kindling, if he ever heard.

He did the last deliveries in less time than usual, but even then he couldn't go straight home. As he turned the corner to the depot he saw Belinda in the street, so he had to go the long way round the back to put the horse away.

Stan was at the horse trough next evening, rinsing off his hands and flexing aching shoulders when his mother called. He was glad to hear her; he was ready for his tea. He'd fed the pigs and cleaned the pig house out, while Granfer did the cows and Dad unhitched the binder and brought back the weary horse. Poor creature would need a rest as much as they did, after a full day in the field. But none of them could stop until the chores were done.

He was grateful to have finished now, at last. He rubbed his wet hands on his shirt to dry them. 'Coming,' he shouted, and set off towards the house.

Mum was standing cooking at the range. Meat stew, by the smell of it, and she'd made fresh kettle bread, though it was a wonder how since she'd been helping with the others in the arrish field today. She looked up as he entered, and gestured with her ladle towards the mantelpiece. 'There's letters for you come. One from your Maudie, by the look of it, though it's addressed to all of us.'

Stan found that he was frowning, but it seemed that Mum was right. He would have recognized Maud's writing anywhere: neat and tiny, like her stitching, though when she had written once or twice before she had always addressed the note to him alone. His heart gave a horrid little lurch. Perhaps she was writing publicly like this to say it was all over between the two of them! But as he read the letter he became more and more surprised.

'What'd she say then?' Mum prompted.

Stan read the words aloud. '"I am writing to say thank you for the gift of fruit, and to wish Stanley all the very best. I hope to be able to come up and see you all before so very long, though it is hard to find a day. It would be nice if I could manage it before Stan goes away. I hope to hear more about his plans, but if I miss him I will have to wait. Madam has been kind enough to let me write this note. Hope it finds you, as it leaves me, well. Remember me to Granfer. Love to you all from Maud." Some funny little note. Using notepaper from the shop as well, by the looks of it – the address and everything is printed on the top.' He paused. 'What's that about the fruit? She can't mean those three apples that I took the other day. Trying to tell me something, do you think?' He held it out, though Mum was no great reader, as he knew quite well – unless it was words she was expecting, like on the envelope.

Mum shook her head and laughed. 'Well, course she is, but not the way you mean. Don't be so blooming daft. It's clear as daylight what's been happening. Didn't you tell me how that woman in the shop doesn't like for her girls to have admirers? Maud's asked to send a letter – and use the notepaper – but she can't hardly write you a blooming Billy Doo, if that Madam's going to read it, can she now? She's wrote to thank us for the apples, but she means the note for you. Anxious to get in touch before you leave and tell you that she will wait for you – or so it seems to me.'

Stan grinned. 'Let's have another look.' He read the note again. It seemed more hopeful this time, especially the bit about 'hearing more about his plans'. When you came to think of it, what could she mean by that, except that she was thinking over what he'd said to her? And she had promised to come and see them very soon. He took his place at the table, still grinning like a fool, as Dad and Granfer came into the room stamping their muddy boots off at the door.

'Look like you've lost sixpence and found half a crown,' Granfer said to Stan, putting his teeth in so that he could eat.

'Had a letter from his Maudie,' Mum said, doling out the stew. 'Just in time as well.' She glanced up at the mantelpiece and frowned. 'You did see your other letter, did you, Stan? Great official envelope. Looks as if your sign-up papers have arrived.'

When she heard about the blotter, and what Miss Simms had said, Belinda tried to pretend she didn't care a jot.

'Well,' she said, 'it doesn't matter anyway. I shan't be writing to that Jonah any more. I've got better fish to fry.' She managed a little enigmatic laugh, as if she had a dozen admirers waiting in the wings, but inwardly she felt a proper fool – first for not thinking about leaving ink-marks when she wrote, and secondly for bothering with Jonah Lotts at all. She was certain he had seen her in the street the other day, but he'd deliberately turned the cart away and gone off down a lane.

And when she remembered what she had written in that note! It had been rather vivid, in the hope of luring him, and the thought that Miss Simms might have deciphered some of it was an embarrassing idea. She could feel the hot flush rising up her cheeks and round her ears, and she said quickly, 'Well, we can't sit here gossiping, I've these darts to do.'

She seized the dress that she was altering and made towards her place, but she saw Maud's startled face and had the grace to add, 'Though thank you for the warning, Maudie. I might have needed it, if I hadn't started walking out with . . .' She hesitated, searching for a name, but she couldn't think of one, so she said, 'Well, never mind, perhaps I shouldn't say.'

It was more effective than she could have hoped. Maudie, who was attaching ruffles to a skirt, gave a scandalized giggle and looked up from her work. 'Ooh, Belinda Richards, whatever are you like! Break more hearts than Lily Langtry, I believe you do. Though, you might be a sport and let me know his name. You can trust me with your secret, surely, Blin, since the other girls aren't here.'

The two of them were alone together in the sewing-room for once – the apprentices had gone for a session in the 'inner room' downstairs, where ladies could try on dresses from the rack. Madam was instructing them on how to mark a hem for altering, and doubtless they were standing – as Belinda had once stood herself – silent and nervous, up against the wall, proudly clutching a piece of tailor's chalk. Next time they would do the task themselves, under Madam's eagle eye.

'Well?' Maud persisted.

'Perhaps I'll tell you later, when we go to bed.' Belinda did her best to sound mysterious. Then, to change the subject, 'You didn't get any answer to your letter, I suppose?'

'Not yet I haven't, no!' Maud said, a little mournfully. And then she added, in a more hopeful tone, 'But probably he wouldn't write me here in any case – more likely send it home, so I would get it this weekend and Madam wouldn't start wanting to read what he had said.' She turned back to her stitching. 'I hope so, any road.'

Drat the girl, she was so deft and neat the ruffle looked as if it might have been designed to run down the centre and round the hem like that, instead of being an off-cut from a bolt of tulle. Belinda picked up the purple dress she had to dart, and relieved her feelings by sticking in the pins with great ferocity.

They worked in silence for a little while, then Maud said suddenly, 'I'll find out soon enough.' She fastened off her stitching and bit off her thread. She glanced towards Belinda. 'You going home Sunday, too? Or are you off somewhere with this new beau of yours?'

'Might do,' Belinda said. 'It's not decided yet.' Sunday was generally free time for the girls and most of them went home to their family after church – if it was not too far – though otherwise Madam liked to know where they had gone. Belinda always put down that she was going home to Gran, though she didn't often go since there was not a lot of pleasure in being grumbled at. Generally, like half of the other young people in the town, she went on the Promenade – it was quite a fashion, whenever it was fine, to walk up and down a bit, dressed in your Sunday best and making eyes at what Madam called 'the other sex', while pretending not to notice when they looked at you. There would be a band in the bandstand, and the 'stop-me-and-buy-one' man pedalling up and down and selling ice-cream from his bike. Jonah had bought a penny cornet for her once . . .

Maud cut across her thoughts. 'You know, Blin, I'm some glad you persuaded me to write Stan straight away. It would have been on my mind for ever otherwise. And I managed to get it past Madam . . . Shhh! They're coming back.'

So Belinda was saved the need to say more about her beau, and when Maudie tried to press her later she pretended to be coy. She did go to the bandstand when Sunday came, but Jonah wasn't there, even though she waited for him quite a little while. Everyone else was walking in gaggles or in pairs, and she began to feel that she was making a spectacle of herself, especially when a rather poorly dressed young man came up and tipped his hat and – bold as brass – asked her if she'd take a walk with him. Of course she said she wouldn't, but he kept on eyeing her until she was so flustered that she couldn't linger on.

In the end there was nothing for it but to go and visit Gran. There she spent a cheerless afternoon, sorting out the wool-box and looking at the clock, longing for five o'clock to come around. Then, after a tea of sardine sandwiches and very heavy buns, she hurried back to Madam's with a feeling of relief.

Next week she wouldn't grumble if she had a thousand darts to do, she told herself. Even if Maudie came back properly engaged – and that was possible – she would simply count her blessings and be glad to be employed. Though Miss Simms did seem to look at her in a peculiar way these days.

# Four

When Maudie went home to Belgravia Street as usual, on Sunday after church, Aunt Jane was waiting to meet her on the step.

'Fine thing this is, I must say,' Aunt Jane said by way of greeting. 'You come already, and your Father isn't home. Gone to take Tully down to wash feet for half an hour, and give me a bit of peace to get the dinner on.'

Maudie nodded. She remembered doing the same thing herself, when she was small: going for a Sunday paddle with Father on the beach or, when it was cold, taking a jam jar to hunt for baby crabs down on the Battery Rocks.

'Well, come in if you're going to,' Aunt Jane went on. 'Don't stand there on the doorstep like an ornament.' She was bustling Maudie through the doorway as she spoke, and taking her cloak to hang it on the coat stand in the hall, just as though it was Tully that she was dealing with. You almost felt that given half a chance she'd undo your bonnet strings and wipe your nose and face with a wetted handkerchief. 'And mind you clean your boots off on the mat before you come inside.

Don't want you leaving dirty footprints on my nice clean floors.'

Aunt Jane was like that; always sharp of speech, and not at all behind hand in saying what she thought. Mind, she had been very kind, according to her lights – had sold up and come down to take over after Mother died. She'd looked after Father faithfully – he was her brother after all, she said – and she doted on little Tully and had even paid the premium for Maud's apprenticeship.

'Give you a bit of a start in life, my girl,' she'd said emphatically, when Maud once tried to thank her for her generosity. 'Always be work for someone who knows how to cut and sew – even if you marry, which I suppose you will. You clean up quite nicely, when you put your mind to it.' (She never mentioned Stanley, though she must have known.) 'So it won't be wasted on you – not like so many things you hear about these days. They're letting girls take training for all sorts of fancy jobs – typewriters and school-mistresses and I don't know what – and it all goes to ruin, as soon as they get wed. But this is a useful skill for anyone, and it will set you on your own two feet, besides.'

Get you out from under mine, was what she'd really meant, Maud knew. Aunt Jane meant well, and she did her best, but her real affection was for Father and the boy. Besides, she liked her kitchen to herself, and half-resented all attempts to help. So Maud – who missed her mother very much, and was clever with a needle – was doubly glad and grateful for this chance to learn a trade because it let her live away from home.

So she must not be unthankful. She forced a little smile and wiped her boots obediently on the mat again, though she had already cleaned them spotless on the boot-scraper outside. 'There you are, Aunt Jane,' she said with a show of cheerfulness. 'Your floors are safe from me.'

'Hmmm!' her aunt muttered, though she didn't sound displeased. 'Come into the kitchen then, your dinner's nearly made. Anyway there's something for you behind the clock. Another note from that young man of yours. Two in as many weeks. And your Father says that he was down here just the other day. You'll have people talking, the next thing you know.'

'Father see us at the station then, did he?' Maud said. She was itching to go and find the envelope, but her aunt had paused to straighten up the mat and was bending over, blocking up the hall. 'I didn't see him anywhere, though I looked out for him.'

'Saw you from the parcel office, I shouldn't be surprised. Or in that hut they go to, to brew a cup of tea. Don't know the meaning of hard work these days. Him and his precious socialists. Ungodly, I call it. Good thing that somebody saw sense about the war so they didn't all come out on strike again, like it seemed they might.'

Father belonged to a sort of mutual society at work – a 'union' they were calling it – which stood up to the company employers and was supposed to get better conditions for the engine-men, though it didn't stop at that. The railways had gone on strike, a year or two ago, in support of the dockers up in Liverpool wanting thirty bob a week, and the country had almost come to a standstill over it – no post, no trade, no passengers, even hay for the horses had been in short supply. There had been troops and riots and two people had been shot. And very little money coming in. Aunt Jane did not approve.

'Imagine!' she said now, using the banisters to hoist herself upright, still a little breathless from attending to the mat. 'Your father here in Cornwall ready to stop work, because some railway-men in Dublin have a bone to pick! And me and Tully having to make ends meet without his pay! Better to let the Irish have Home Rule, it seems to me. Most of them are Papists, anyway, I hear.'

She led the way at last along the narrow passageway and Maudie followed her, past the hall cupboard underneath the stairs and down a step into the kitchen, where a big black kettle was steaming on the hob and something was clearly burning in the top oven of the range.

'Darny!' Aunt Jane muttered, and picked up the hook, a sort of metal fork which raised the oven catch or went into a slot and lifted up the iron circles on the top. She wrapped a protective towel round her other hand and wrist, opened the top oven and flapped away the smoke. The apple tarts were scorching and she whisked them out, then opened the lower oven to reveal a dish of what she called 'shepherd's pie' – thin minced meat topped with mashed potato – which was browning rapidly. She rescued that as well. 'Darned new-fangled stove,' she muttered. 'I'll never get the hang of the confounded thing! Give me a good old baking-iron on the fire every time.'

Maudie bit back a retort. The modern Cornish range had been her mother's pride and joy and once the source of many a delicious meal. But Aunt Jane (who had never been a naturally gifted cook, even on the famous baking-iron) waged an unending, joyless war with it until even Father, who was grateful for her care, made good-natured jokes about burnt offerings.

But here was Father coming up the back steps, and stopping in the back yard to undo Tully's boots. So Maudie delayed her letter for a little while longer and went out to meet him at the door. When he saw her, he caught her in his arms and hugged her to his chest – just as if she was a little girl again – and she smelt the familiar strong tobacco of his pipe mixed with carbolic soap and brilliantine. Then it was Tully's turn to say hello, by grasping her around the knees and submitting to a kiss, before he raced into the kitchen in search of the shepherd's pie.

'Well then, Maudie! What's your Stanley got to say?' Father said, smiling at her as they followed Tully in. He sat down at the table. 'Where's your letter then? I'm sure your aunt can manage without your help, for once.'

Maudie was already putting out the knives and forks. She glanced towards Aunt Jane, who looked daggers but nodded with a sharp, 'I suppose so, if she must.'

She got it down from the mantelpiece and read it. It was fairly short, but sweet. Stan wrote to tell her that his forms had come, and he had sent them off, so he hoped she'd come and visit – like she had said she would – as soon as possible. 'I know that you will write me, and I'll write you every week, but I would like to see you properly before I go, so we can talk.'

She found that she was grinning.

'You want to do it sharpish, or he'll have upped and gone,' Father said. 'Next Sunday, maybe, on the one o'clock. Catch the eight o'clock from Truro and you could be back by nine. Or you could go up Saturday evening, when the shop shuts, I suppose.'

'Wilfred Olds! What are you thinking of? She'll do nothing of the kind. A girl of her age, staying overnight? I've never

heard of such a thing. It's just an invitation to have shenanigans.'

Father grinned and raised an eyebrow behind his sister's
back – she was fussing with the pie. 'Course there won't be;
Stan's a nice young man. And his parents and grandfather will
be there anyway.'

'All the same!' Aunt Jane said darkly, and that put an end
to it.

Maud wasn't altogether sure what 'shenanigans' might be
– she vaguely associated them with Old Rouse the chimney-
sweep, who was rumoured not to be properly married to his
wife, though what that had to do with Stan, she couldn't see.
But she was glad enough to have her father's blessing for the
trip. And she knew why he had singled out next weekend for
the trip. He worked alternate Sundays – it was an extra two
shillings in his pay-packet each time – so she would not miss
his company by failing to come home.

'I'll go up Sunday,' she said, her heart already lifting with
the thought of it. 'I'll write him after tea and let his parents
know.'

Aunt Jane sniffed. 'I should think so too. You write to them
as well. They'll be entertaining you. It's only meet and right.'

'Meat and rice!' cried Tully, thumping with his spoon, and
turned their attention to more pressing things. He would have
had a scolding if Mother had been alive, but Aunt Jane just
wiped his hands and face, and served the shepherd's pie. It
was pretty thin and watery, but it wasn't bad.

Wilfred Olds stood at the window, holding back the curtain
and watching his daughter trotting down the street. Pretty little
thing she was turning out to be, much like her mother, when
they were first courting. Same oval face, same pretty dancing
eyes, and – he heaved a little sigh – the same lithe figure and
gently bouncing walk. Funny to think of little Maudie with a
suitor for her hand, but perhaps it was no wonder. Her mother
at that age had a queue of admirers that would have stretched
halfway down the street – some of them with better prospects
than a humble engine-cleaner, as he had been then, cleaning
out the engines for ten hours a day and glad to bring home
twelve and six a week. That was all that he had been at that
stage of his life, but she'd believed his dream of working his

way up, first on the tickets, and then the parcel office, till he'd come to be in charge of it in the end, even when no one else supposed he'd rise so far. He was lucky to have won her – and he'd lost her far too soon.

He felt the old lump rising to his throat and he let the curtain fall back sharply into place. No good dwelling on what might have been. He was fortunate to have a sister to look after him – what he would do without her he did not dare to think. Cooking, laundry and cleaning were mystic arts to him: his one attempt to make a meal, when Myrtle was so ill, had resulted in the total waste of good ingredients – even next door's dog turned up its nose at it – and one of his work vests still bore the scars of his attempt to iron the dampness out of it. He gave thanks for his sister every morning, without fail. But, all the same . . .

He walked across and unhooked the picture from the nail in the wall. It was taken in a proper studio, the pair of them in happier times, with Maud a babe in arms. It had been a big extravagance, but he was glad to have it now. It was like having a little bit of Myrtle here again.

'Wilfred, are you coming to have this cup of tea I made, or have I to put the kettle on and start again?' Jane's voice, from the kitchen, roused him from his dreams.

He hung the picture on the hook again. 'Coming!' he answered, but he wasn't fast enough. Jane bustled into the parlour to chivvy him some more.

'Whatever are you doing in here in the half-dark? Mooning over that old photo again, I s'pose? I don't know what good you think that's going to do. It isn't going to bring her back, you know.' It was no good looking for sympathy from Jane.

'I know,' he said. 'I was just thinking how like Maud she was.'

Jane made a tutting sound. 'Least she's a bit more sturdy, I will say that for her. Gets that from our side of the family, of course – strong as horses, all the lot of us. Look at you and me. Neither of us ever had a real day's sickness in our lives, and we're not afraid of a bit hard work and elbow-grease.'

Wilfred turned towards her, ready to protest. Myrtle had been a cheerful housekeeper and not the least averse to working hard herself. But one glance at his sister's pursed lips and

injured frown told him that she was not meaning to draw
comparisons. Perhaps she was remembering all the years she'd
stayed at home looking after their parents till they fell sick
and died. He hadn't thought a great deal about it at the time.
Of course it was the sort of thing that lots of women did. But
she hadn't had a lot of thanks for it, and perhaps – he thought
suddenly with some surprise – Jane would have liked to marry
and have children of her own.

'Well, we should be glad the child's got the chance to have
a bit of life,' Jane said, as if in confirmation of his unspoken
thoughts. 'Though why she should deserve it, more than others,
I don't know. Still, I don't begrudge her. She's a good girl in
her way. I'll even put that letter in the post for her myself.
Now, are you coming to have this cup of tea or not? It will
be cold as Greenland by the time you get to it. And I promised Tully that you'd read to him before he went to bed, from
that book for good attendance that he got from Sunday School.'

So Wilfred went up and read stories to his son. It was a
missionary volume and much too old for him, but they looked
at the engravings and that seemed to do.

While he was up there he brushed down his uniform and
then came down and polished all the boots, brought the coal
in for the morning and damped down the stove. Jane had
already taken the darning up to do in bed, but she'd put on
some milk to warm for him, and there was just time for some
cocoa and a pipe before he turned in for the night.

Monday afternoon came and Belinda was helping a customer
– a sulky girl whose mother was choosing her a dress. They
had stepped out of the fitting room to see it in the light.

'It suits you wonderfully, miss; the colour is just right,'
Belinda said. 'Madam will be here in a little while. Just for a
moment she's with another client, but I'm sure she would agree
with me that this looks made for you.' Her tongue ran on automatically, like a wound-up gramophone, but her mind was
thinking about something else. As she had accompanied the
customers upstairs, she had glimpsed a young man loitering
about outside the shop, and she hoped it might be Jonah, though
he'd be gone by now. So her thoughts were full of what she'd
have to say when – or if – she next ran into him, but her lips
said, 'If we were to let it out a little under here . . .'

The girl looked at her reflection in the glass. The gown that she was trying on was tight-waisted and very chic indeed and cost more than Belinda would live on for a month, but the girl just made a discontented face. 'Oh, bother it, Mamma! I wanted something really special for the supper-dance. It's in aid of the soldiers and sailors charity, you know – we are to host it and one wants to look one's best. Something with more lace and an embroidered skirt perhaps?'

'This is the very latest style, madam,' Belinda said. Maybe she could find an excuse to get out of the shop – offer to make a personal delivery perhaps – and then she could waylay him somewhere halfway through his round. 'The narrow skirt and evening coat is all the rage this year. I assure you they are wearing it in the capital.'

She glanced out of the window. Was it going to rain? That would make it much more difficult to get out in time. The sky was grey and cloudy, but it was dry enough. Jonah, she knew, would be out Newlyn way today, and if she could only get away by four o'clock, with any luck she'd find him before he turned for home. Perhaps there was a letter or a bill that she could volunteer to post . . .

'Don't you think so, miss?' she heard the woman say and realized that the question had been addressed to her.

Belinda put on her best shop-assistant's smile. 'I don't think you'll find anything in such a pretty blue.' She had no idea what had been said to her, but that answer seemed to cover most possibilities.

'I don't know, Mamma. If we bought material and had it made bespoke,' the girl said, in a childish, whining voice, 'we could have it made up exactly to my taste. And I'm not sure after all that I would not prefer a pink.'

Belinda suddenly lost patience. This girl was going to take up all her afternoon, and very likely come to no decision at the end. She'd have missed Jonah, all for nothing. She glanced around. There was no sign of Madam. She took a deep breath. 'Then I shouldn't waste another minute here, if I were you,' she said crisply. 'I'd go and find the fabric that you want as soon as possible.'

The girl looked quite affronted – not surprisingly perhaps – and the woman looked around the shop as if she was going to summon Madam, who was just emerging from another

fitting-room, accompanying a different customer. Belinda was
stricken with panic and remorse. Now I've gone and done it,
she thought despairingly. Me and my quick tongue. I'm as
bad as Gran! Whatever possessed me to say a thing like that?
If they complain to Madam I'll be turned out on the street.
How could I let myself be such an idiot? I had my mind on
something else, and that's the truth of it!

She was desperately casting about for some acceptable way
to apologize, when she realized that the woman was saying,
thoughtfully, and in an undertone, 'Otherwise it might be
difficult to match this quality, you mean? With the war and
everything? Between ourselves, of course.'

Belinda had not meant anything of the kind – she had only
spoken out of wickedness – but she recognized a life-line
when it was thrown to her. She gave a little smile, then leaned
forward and said confidentially, 'Look at these velvet over
sleeves and figured crêpe de Chine. All comes from overseas.
If the war carries on for long it might be very hard to find
material like this. Though of course, I couldn't say for certain.'

The woman nodded. 'Most discreet, my dear.' She turned
briskly to her daughter. 'You see, Caroline, I'm right and your
father's wrong. It's just as Bertie said. All the factories and
mills will be turned over to making uniforms.' She glanced
towards Belinda and added with a smile, 'A relative of mine is
high up in the army and he knows, too, you see. They're getting
so many new recruits, since that defeat at Mons, he says they
haven't got trousers and tunics for them all. He had to go
back to London suddenly to help them deal with it.'

Belinda was surprised. She had heard of Mons, of course
– there had been awful headlines in the newspapers that you
couldn't help but see, even if you never read the things
yourself. Pictures, too, of wounded soldiers with bloodied
bandages. People said there had been losses and a terrible
defeat, though the retreating soldiers had seen an angel in the
sky, and Kitchener was calling for thousands more young men
to teach those foreign blighters a thing or two. But she had
never imagined that all this might make a difference at home.
After all, the other wars – the Crimea, and the fight against
the Mahdi, or the Boers in Africa – hadn't much affected ordinary life, as far as she could tell, and some of those conflicts
had gone on for years.

The young Caroline was clearly thinking the same thing. 'I don't know why you listen to what Uncle Bertie says, Mamma. It was all supposed to be over before the year was out, that's what he said before, and I'm sure we all believed him. And now he's changed his mind. Says it might be Easter, easily, or worse!' She sounded quite aggrieved, as if the Mons defeat had been designed to inconvenience her. She looked at her reflection and heaved a little sigh. 'Well, I presume this young woman understands her trade. In that case I suppose that this will have to do. I must have something for this supper-dance. Though I insist on having those alterations made. And that is such a bore. I suppose that means I'll have to come all the way back here and try it on again.'

Belinda was spared the necessity of answering by Madam, who had come upstairs again, and was bearing down on them with her professional smile. 'Thank you, Miss Richards. I'll take over now. Good afternoon, Mrs Porter ... Miss Porter, I so am sorry that I was otherwise engaged. I hope Miss Richards has been looking after you. Can I show you something else, perhaps, if that gown is not entirely what you are looking for?'

Belinda was already making for the stairs when she heard the woman say, 'On the contrary, Miss Richards has served us splendidly. Caroline has quite determined on this gown. I understand the bodice can be taken in to fit?' She dropped her voice and Belinda could not catch the rest. She started up the top flight of stairs towards the sewing-room.

'Miss Richards!' Madam's summons brought her hurrying back. 'Mrs Porter wants those alterations made, and I have promised that you will personally do the work for her. However, she wants it as soon as possible. If you would fit and pin it, you can do it straight away, and we'll arrange a final fitting for tomorrow afternoon.'

Belinda took a breath and tried to sound as humble as she could. 'The alterations I suggested are straightforward ones ...' She caught Madam's warning eyes – 'straight-forward' alterations did not command a price – and she added hastily, 'Though quite technical, of course. Still, I believe that I could get it done this afternoon. I could bring it to the house and do the final fitting there if that would be helpful to the customer.'

It was very daring, but Madam didn't scold. Instead she

flashed her an approving look. 'That would come at a premium, of course,' Madam said smoothly.

Mrs Porter was clearly wavering over this additional expense, but her daughter tossed her head. 'Oh, pooh, Mamma. What does an extra shilling matter here or there? It will save us coming all the way down in the coach, and if I'm to have the gown as soon as possible, why not let her bring it? If it isn't right she'll have to bring it back and alter it again, or you can have the sewing-woman do it when she comes. No, I'm quite determined. I shall have the dress today, and then I can show it to Papa when he comes home.'

And so it was settled. Belinda worked like a demon for an hour, though she was careful to make the work as neat as possible. She did the long seams on the treadle, then worked the rest by hand – it would have to meet Madam's appraising eye before it left the shop. As soon as it was finished she went downstairs with it, not even pausing to exchange a word with Maudie as she went.

Madam put on her wire-rimmed glasses and inspected it. 'That's satisfactory.' She peered at Belinda over her spectacles, with what might have been a smile. 'And well done, Miss Richards. I must put you on the shop floor more often. Mrs Porter and her daughter are always difficult. You must have made a very good impression on the girl. I've never known her to make a decision on the spot like that. And her mother quite insisted that you should do the work. Seemed to feel you'd given them invaluable advice. And offering home fitting was an inspired idea. I was able to ask another shilling for the work. I'm minded to put a quarter of it in your pay-packet.'

Another whole threepence! That was generous. She and Jonah could go to the picture-house with that and still have money for a halfpenny ice-cream each. Just wait until he heard! But though she hurried out to take the dress as fast as possible, and walked the long way too – right round through Newlyn where she knew he should be – she didn't catch a glimpse of him that afternoon at all. And then she had to spend a disappointing half-hour fidgeting with Miss Caroline Porter's wretched dress.

# Five

Jonah edged the General out into the lane then trotted off across the bridge as quickly as he dared. That had been a close one! If he had not pulled into the courtyard of the inn and made some excuse about looking for a house, Belinda would have spotted him for sure. Good thing that he had seen her. What was she doing here? You'd almost think that she had come out looking for him, but of course she couldn't have. Must have been out doing some business for the shop.

Just as well he'd done his rounds so quick today for once, otherwise he would have had to go on down that street, delivering the coal. But he had been working non-stop, so as to get ahead – if he could do all the regulars as usual each day, and fit in a few more of the 'occasionals' as well, he could win an hour on Friday afternoon to meet with Lily-Anne. Course, you had to be careful who you did it to. Some people would be down the office in a brace of shakes, complaining to his father, if their coal had turned up on a Tuesday afternoon this month, instead of Wednesday as per usual. But there were bigger places that didn't care what day it came, as long as they had the certainty of coal to fuel their fires and heat their cooking-ranges. The man at the Imperial Inn had said as much this very afternoon.

Jonah grinned. That was a happy accident. He'd only gone in there to get out of the way, though of course he also knew the hotel boy. Billy Polkinghorne had gone to school with him, a big, slow, chubby lad who'd got them into scrapes – like the sunny afternoon they'd been out after birds' eggs in the woods, instead of sitting in the schoolroom doing sums, until somebody saw them and they got a walloping. Now Billy was a general hand at the Imperial Inn, fetching up barrels, sweeping the yard, cleaning silver, polishing the shoes of travellers who stayed there overnight and seeing to their horses, if there were any – though because of the railways, people didn't have them like they used to do.

Billy had come out to meet him in the yard, his plump face glistening. He'd been sweeping down the cobbles by the look of it, but he put down his broom. He was older than Jonah by a year or two – he'd been kept back in class until he learned to read – and had two married sisters who still lived at home, so he was a mine of startling information about girls and married life, just as he always used to know where the best birds' nests were. He'd understand about Belinda.

And of course he did, once Jonah had explained. 'Got the same trouble myself, old lad. That Annie down the sweet shop is mad to marry me. Though I dunno. A sweet shop – might be worse ideas. Though I'd have to give my notice, 'cause they'd want me working there, and I aren't sure I'd want to, 'cause Annie's people are a miserable lot, and the owner here is quite a decent sort of chap. Gives me an hour off every afternoon as well as alternate Sundays.' He gazed at Jonah. ''Ere, I've only thought. He might be pleased to see you, since you've brought the cart. Belongs to buy his coal from Vargo's up St Just, but they've let him down twice lately and he isn't very pleased. Grumbling about the quality of the coal they sent as well. You go and see him – might do yourself some good.' He took up his broom again.

Billy was quite right. The owner had nearly snatched his hand off when he saw the cart. Jonah had won an order for two hundredweight a week before he'd left the premises. Father would be pleased. They didn't get many big new customers like that these days – a lot of restaurants and hotels were actually reducing orders now, because they were putting modern kitchens in, and not only had gas lighting but they cooked with gas as well. Mother fretted sometimes that it would spread to houses next and that would hit them really hard, but Father only laughed.

'It's just a fashion for the snobby, Ma. Older ways are best. Course, it's all right for restaurants and that sort of thing, but who wants smelly gas pipes leaking in the house, threatening to poison them or blow them to kingdom come, when they can have a nice stove burning and warming up the place? Can't beat a Cornish range for cooking – everyone says that

– and there's nothing like a coal fire for cheering up a room. Gas light, now, that's different. I admit to that. Good as daylight, a gas mantle is, if you ever see it lit. Wouldn't be surprised if that was commonplace some day. But for ordinary cooking? Don't you fret, my handsome. Always be a market for a bucketful of coal.'

Well, Jonah thought, as the General clopped across the bridge, let's hope Father's right. The business will be mine when he turns up his toes, and we can already do with all the orders we can get. Like this one today. Father'd likely give you sixpence for coming home with that, enough to take Lily-Anne out for a penny cornet if you chose. He was still whistling as he went into the yard.

Father was glad enough – you could see it in his face – though he didn't offer the hoped-for tanner after all. All he said was, 'Well, I hope we've got the stocks this week to cope with it, that's all. And you'll have to find the time to fit it in your rounds. Now, are you going to see to that horse and put the cart away? It's almost time for you to come home for your tea and there's a concert down the chapel your mother wants to go to later on. You too, of course. Supposing you aren't out gallivanting with some serving-girl again?'

'I don't know what you mean by gallivanting,' Jonah said, his heart sinking at the thought of the evening ahead. Male-voice choirs were tuneful, no denying that, but you could have too much sitting on hard chapel forms, with Ma looking daggers if you glanced around at all. 'How do I get time to gallivant?'

'Hear you were seen Friday, out chatting in the street. And on my time, not yours. Good mind to stop it out of what you get to spend.'

Jonah gave an inward groan. So he had been seen with Lily-Anne! More eyes than a potato field, some folk must have. He'd have to be more careful this week. 'It's not a crime to stop and say hello to someone now and then, is it?' he grumbled crossly. 'Anyway, you're always saying how I should settle down. How am I to do that, if I never meet a girl?'

Father shrugged his shoulders. It was Ma who called the tune. 'Do it on your own time, like I had to do,' he said. 'Besides, what decent girl would look at you when you are on the cart, covered in coal-dust from head to foot? It's like your mother says. You want to go to chapel if you want to find a wife. Cleaned up and in your Sunday clothes you look presentable and there's several nice young women that she knows who go along. Might find someone who'd take a shine to you.'

Jonah scowled. He always resented Ma's attempts to match him up. She found the dullest women, all as plain as sheep. He was tempted to retort that there were at least two pretty girls who had taken a shine to him, but he thought better of it. Ma would not approve. They didn't go to chapel and they weren't 'respectable': Lily-Anne was only a humble parlour-maid, and even Belinda – who you think might suit, because she had a proper job in trade – had earned Ma's disapproval by calling boldly at the house. 'A red-headed hussy,' Ma had said. 'She's been here chasing you.' And he hadn't argued. He'd been frightened off himself. He wasn't aiming to be married off just yet, not to Belinda or Lily-Anne or anybody else.

'Thought you'd be pleased about the order from the inn,' he said to Father now, still hoping for that tanner. But it was not to be. Father simply snorted and went on counting sacks. No point in asking outright for an hour free on Friday after-noon; Father in this mood would just find more jobs for him to do. So Jonah said nothing more, just led the General to his stall, and took out his frustrations with a curry brush.

He couldn't avoid the chapel concert though, and had to submit to being ogled at for hours by a plain young woman with a painful lisp, who turned pink and giggled when he tried to talk to her. He consoled himself by thinking about meeting Lily-Anne, though he would have to be quite careful when Friday came, he thought. He could not afford to have gossip reach Father's ears again.

But when the time came she made it easy, because she had a plan.

''Ere, I've found a place where you can tie up that old horse of yours, and leave the cart where it'll not be seen,' she said, almost as soon as they had met. 'Part of an old farm. 'Tisn't very far. I'll walk on ahead and you can follow me. Make out we're not together, if anyone's watching.'

He nodded speechlessly.

She led the way into a ruined yard, and watched while he attached the General to a tree. 'Thought we needn't go all the way into the woods, 'cause I know you are worried about leaving him,' she said. 'There's a bit of an old building there, we could go inside.'

He was a little startled. Spending an hour in a musty barn was not remotely in his mind. He had been planning on a wander underneath the trees, and perhaps the opportunity to steal a kiss or two.

But Lily-Anne introduced him to quite a different afternoon. She dragged him over to an open water-butt nearby. 'You rinse your hands and face. And you'd better take your shirt off, or I'll be all over dust.' And she undid his buttons for him as she spoke.

It was shocking and alarming but wonderful as well – so exciting that he didn't have time to do things properly, in fact. When it was over he drove slowly home, quite certain that everyone in the street must know what he'd been up to, simply from seeing the expression on his face.

Belinda was taking up a hem when Madam summoned her. One of the juniors brought the message to the sewing-room, panting up to say, 'I'm sent to say that Madam Raymond wants a word with you. In the front office, Miss Richards, in five minutes if you please.' And off she went, clattering down the stairs again.

Belinda looked at Maudie, who was working next to her, frowning over an elaborate overskirt made of silk organza, which was the very devil to sew invisibly. 'Lord Almighty, Maudie. Whatever can this be? You think Miss Simms has dropped me in the soup, over my using a sheet or two of paper from the shop?'

Maudie looked up from her stitching. 'I shouldn't think so, no. Miss Simms didn't give me that impression when she talked to me. Anyway, if she was going to give the show away, she'd have done it days ago. Honestly, Blin, it must be something else.'

She said it so calmly that Belinda could have shaken her. Didn't Maudie realize that this could cost her her job? 'Don't you be so sure! Miss Simms has been giving me funny looks this week,' she wailed. 'I'm sure she's known all along that it was me – all she had to do was read the blotter back to front. Anyway, what else could Madam want me for?'

'Someone has told her you've got a follower, perhaps? There's been that skinny fellow hanging round the shop front every day this week. Twelve o'clock as sure as clockwork, you look out and there he is. Obviously he's smitten and looking out for you – he pays no attention to the rest of us. But you told me you don't know him – so just tell Madam that. She'll soon go out and tell him to be on his way.' She gave her friend a cheeky grin. 'Unless he really is your secret beau, of course, in which case you had better get rid of him yourself.'

Belinda felt her cheeks turn an embarrassed red. Of course she'd seen the fellow and she'd worked out who he was, though at first she genuinely hadn't recognized the face. It was the boy who had accosted her so rudely at the bandstand, when she'd been waiting for Jonah and he hadn't come. She'd seen him, this other boy, standing outside in the street, and a proper fright he looked. Quite out of place outside a store like this. He was not even wearing the battered hat and thread-bare overcoat – presumably that outfit had been his weekend best. No, now he was dressed in some kind of overalls: coarse khaki ones with pockets and tie-strings around the waist, as if he scrubbed out buildings or something of the kind.

'Him!' she said sharply. 'Of course he's not my beau.' She felt quite annoyed. How could Maudie have suspected such a thing? He wasn't even good-looking, the way that Jonah was. 'All lanky limbs and spotty neck, and dirty fingernails, and at the same time cocky as a crow. I've seen him only once, and then I've hardly spoken a dozen words to him!'

She hadn't either – not even to tell him where she worked. So it did seem that probably what Maudie said was right: he had found out where it was and had come to ogle her. On his precious lunch hour, almost certainly, but she'd not encouraged him. She hadn't even so much as glanced at him – not when he could see her doing it, in any case.

Maud raised her shoulders apologetically. 'Well, you needn't be so snappy. It could easily have been. I knew that there was someone, and you wouldn't tell me who. And it wouldn't have been hopeless: he's clearly got a wage and is very taken with you, whoever he is. Besides, I know that you were keen to get out the other day, when he'd been hanging around.'

Belinda was still sulking. 'There's other reasons apart from him, for wanting to get out of here. Posting that letter to your Stan for one thing.'

Maudie had the grace to smile. 'Yes, thanks for doing that. I had the paper and envelope from home, but I shouldn't have been able to catch the post until today. And I wanted to give his family as much time as possible, to let me know if it was all right for me to come. I said I'd go this Sunday unless I heard otherwise.'

'Which of course you haven't!' Belinda gave a short, exasperated sigh. There was Maudie with a proper fellow wanting to propose, and she with only an invented beau. Even that skinny fellow at the door would be a step ahead, perhaps . . . No, she couldn't think like that! She'd already heard one of the juniors sniggering at him, and murmuring to the others as they craned to look.

It would be such a come-down, after all her boasts, and more than likely he'd be just the same as Jonah and the others anyway. Only after one thing – and it wasn't getting wed. 'Well, I hope you're wrong and Madam isn't going to give me a row on his account. I didn't ask him here. A girl can't help it, if she's beautiful.'

Maudie picked up her scissors and began to snip. 'Anyway, Blin, you had better go. Madam will be waiting – don't keep her hanging on, or whatever the trouble, it will be ten times worse.'

But, when she got to the front office, Madam wore a smile. Oddly, that made Belinda more nervous than before.

'You asked for me, Madam?' she said warily.

Madam Raymond waved a hand at her. 'I did, Miss Richards. Won't you please sit down?'

Belinda put the corner of a buttock on the seat and perched there like a parrot, waiting for the blow.

'It concerns what happened here the other day,' her mistress said.

So it *was* the blotter then! Belinda scowled in the direction of Miss Simms, who was totting up figures with apparent unconcern.

Madam saw the direction of the glance. 'Don't worry, Miss Richards, Miss Simms is well aware of what I'm going to say. In fact, it was she who brought the matter to my notice earlier today.'

'I can give an explanation, Madam,' Belinda began, desperately searching for something she could say. 'It wasn't meant as any kind of disrespect at all . . .'

'I should think not, indeed, Miss Richards,' Madam said, but it was so good-natured that Belinda realized she was genuinely in her employer's good books for a change. 'And you did very well. But it is obvious that the mother has mentioned it to friends, because today there has been another woman in the shop asking if her daughter could have her final fit at home as well. Asking for you, in particular. I thought we might put a notice in the window for a week or two, see if the idea of home fitting catches on. I should want you to do the bulk of it, of course – I shall be wanted back here in the shop, but I daresay Miss Olds could give a hand as well.'

'Yes, Madam.' Belinda was so relieved that she could hardly speak.

Madam pulled down her spectacles and looked at her over the rims. 'Of course I shall require to know exactly how you filled your time while you were out, you understand. No stopping on street corners and cavorting with young men. You know the house rules about that sort of thing.'

'Yes, Madam,' Belinda said again. She shifted on her perch. Was that a kind of hint? Suppose Madam had noticed the young man at the door? Well, Belinda was not about to take the blame for that. 'By the way, Madam,' she murmured, 'on the subject of those things, you might have noticed someone, this last day or two. Quite a trampish-looking fellow loitering in the street?'

Madam nodded. 'Thank you, Miss Richards, I have dealt with that. Sent him off with a flea in his ear, and made it quite clear to the apprentice girl involved that I won't tolerate that kind of foolishness.'

'The apprentice girl?' Belinda found that she was talking like a parrot now.

'Jenny, is she called? The little one that I sent up to fetch you a little while ago.'

Belinda nodded. She knew Jenny well enough. A plain girl with freckles and an impish grin. The same one, now she came to think of it, who had been giggling with her friends about the fellow in the street. And she herself had thought . . . She found that she was blushing.

'Yes,' Madam said, 'disgraceful, isn't it? Though perhaps it is not entirely her fault. Seems he has known her since she was very small, and since she's come to work here he found out where she was, and since then he's been hanging round and looking out for her. Well, I told her I wouldn't stand for it, and either it would have to stop or she would have to go.' Madam gave a smile that didn't reach her eyes. 'She didn't have much trouble in making up her mind. Went out and told him, straightaway, and he has disappeared.' She put her hands together in a spire and pressed her fingertips. 'But I'm sure, Miss Richards, we'll have no such tricks with you. Mr Raymond happened to see you when you went out the other day, and he assures me that you didn't dally in the street.'

Belinda gulped. So Mr Raymond had 'happened' to see her on the street! Been sent out to keep an eye on her, more like. It was only chance that she hadn't run into Jonah on the way, and then there'd have been ructions! She said, 'Of course, Madam,' in a strangled voice, and it was all arranged. One day a week she was to go out to customers.

'Going to give them fits, then!' Maudie said that night when she was told, and they both had the giggles as they went to bed. But Belinda said nothing about Jenny and the boy – let Maudie draw her own conclusions if she liked. Nor did she mention the strangest thing of all: when she was leaving the office with Madam, she was almost certain Miss Simms had winked at her.

They made a fuss of Maudie when she got to the farm. Stan's parents hadn't seen her since she was just a child and staying with Aunt Jane, so there was much exclaiming about how much she had grown. Mum Hoskins almost brought her to the embarrassment of tears by coming out and enfolding her in an enormous hug – the kind that Mother used to give.

Maudie managed to control herself and just say, 'Lovely to see you,' in a nearly normal voice.

Then Dad Hoskins took both her hands. 'My dear Maudie, you're a feast for aged eyes. Though I'm not sure that I believe it's really you. Not without your plaits and those big grazes on your knees. I do believe our Stan's brought an imposter home.'

She coloured at his teasing, and was lost for a reply, but Stan came to her rescue. He had come to meet her from the station in the cart, and had been in the stable yard putting it away, but now he strode up grinning. 'Here, Dad, what are you like! Take no notice of his fooling, Maudie. You just come on in. I know Mum's made a cake for you – the kind you always liked.' He waved towards the windowsill where a tray of buns and the cake in question were cooling on a rack. 'Hope you still like it, after all these years.'

'Put a bit of chocolate and walnut in the mix,' his mother said anxiously, as if it was Maud who had done the favour here, by turning up to eat what she had made. 'I know that used to be your favourite when you were here before.'

Maudie felt that prickle behind her eyes again. How many years must it have been since anyone had troubled to bake a cake for her, let alone remember what kind of cake she liked. 'I haven't tasted it since I was here,' she said, a little too loudly and too cheerfully, 'but if it's anything like as good as I remember it to be . . .' And then she couldn't utter any more words, just shook her head, smiled and bit her lip.

Mum Hoskins slipped an arm around her, and gave her waist a squeeze. 'My dear child, we've kept you talking and you're fair worn out, I can see. Come in and take your cloak off and we'll have a cup of tea, and some of that there cake we're talking of. Be glad to see it on the table, that's the truth of it. Some game I've had trying to keep the cats from getting it. Had to shut them in the dairy while it was cooling off.'

'Not Mouser and Tibby?' Maudie cried, remembering suddenly.

'Lord love you, no!' Mrs Hoskins was putting the kettle on the range, and poking the fire to get the flames to rise. 'Both gone long ago. These are the kittens, you remember them? Salt, Pepper and Mustard – it was you gave them their names.'

'So it was,' said Maudie, and felt more at home at once.

She was about to take her place on the chair Stan offered her, when Granfer appeared from up the stairs. He was freshly washed and brushed, smelling of tar-soap and brilliantine, and dressed up for Sunday. 'So this is Maud?' He shook her hand, then made her blush by saying, as he looked her up and down, 'Well! I allays thought you were a skinny little thing. But I see you're filling out. Coming to be some fine-looking woman now, eh Stan?' He sat down with a clatter and gave a wicked wink.

Mum Hoskins knew exactly how to deal with that. 'Have good trip on the train, did you?' she said to Maud. 'We were only happy when we got your note, saying you were coming and could we meet the train, but I couldn't help be anxious that you were on your own.' She was putting butter icing on the cake. 'But of course, I needn't worry. Railway girl like you. And, of course, you have done the trip before.'

Maud nodded. 'Easy journey, thank you,' she said with confidence, though it had felt like quite an adventure at the time. She had been a passenger several times, of course – two Sunday School outings over to St Ives (which Father had arranged, instead of them taking a charabanc like they used to do), as well as the occasion when she'd come up to Aunt Jane, but all those times she'd been in someone else's charge. This was the first time she'd travelled on her own. 'The guard looked after me, and helped me to get off.'

'Your father will have asked him to keep an eye on you,' Stan said, and she realized that it was very likely true.

She felt quite embarrassed until Dad Hoskins said, 'And I should think so. I would have done the same. Now, little lady, can Stan pour you out some tea? And there's mother with the bread-knife hovering, all set to cut that cake. Dying to get rid of it, you can see she is. So it must be horrible. Are you brave enough to try?'

There was general laughter, and some delicious cake, and then Stan took her out to see the cats. They were still the same colours, grey and peppery and brown, so she knew without Stan saying which of them was which. Stan laughed down at her.

'You see? Already half-belong here, you do, Maudie Olds. Going to marry me, are you, when I come home again, and make it permanent?' He didn't take her in his arms, only took her hand and squeezed it very hard.

And she could only squeeze his fingers in return and say, 'Course I will, Stan, if you want me to.' She grinned. 'Have to keep it a secret from Madam Raymond though. Can't stay on in the workshop once you are engaged. Though I suppose I could find casual sewing somewhere . . .'

He shook his head at her, not laughing now. 'We'll wait

till this is over – though we can tell our folks our plans. Then when I come home again, we'll do it properly. In the meantime, we can try and put a little bit aside. Course we'll have the farm one day – there's been a Hoskins tenant here for years and years and years – and there's a spare room in the house for us till then, but it would be nice to have a stick or two of furniture ourselves, or even have a cottage like Granfer did when Granmer was alive.' He pressed her hand again. 'If you're quite sure that you've forgiven me for going away like this. Only I feel I've got to do it – you do understand?'

'You just make sure that you come back again, you hear? There are such awful stories these days. Blin was telling me . . .' She was ashamed to find her voice was quavering.

'You try and stop me, when I've got you to come back for! Besides, they say that, even now, it won't be very long.'

'Do you know yet when you have to go?'

'Told you they called me for a medical, did I? Passed with flying colours, so I'm reporting Friday and they'll try to make a soldier out of me. Sent me a warrant for the railway travel and all. But that's not for ages, and we've got all day today. Now are you coming down the arrish fields with me? There's a big rock with a pattern on I'd like for you to see – turned it up when we were planting there last spring, and I remember you were always interested in that sort of thing.'

So they strolled together through the golden afternoon and sat down on the stone, tracing the ancient carving underneath the moss and watching the women gleaning between the drying sheaves. Then they continued down to the field gate where the horse was kept. Stan gave her a lump of sugar to give the animal, and she held it out for him, bewitched at feeling the warm, soft snuffle on her palm.

Altogether, it was a magic day. She was to remember it like that, for ever afterwards.

Part Two

September – Christmas 1914

# One

Father was delighted when he heard the wedding news, which he did the moment Maud got back to Penzance. He had been working Sunday, as he did every other week, and should by rights have stopped at six, but instead he'd waited on to meet her when she came back. She was glad to find him there. The platform was shadowy and echoing at this time of night, despite the lighted lamps.

He stepped out of the smoky gloom and helped her down the step. 'Well? Don't look so startled. Your Stan wrote and asked me if he could offer for your hand – and of course I told him yes. Though I couldn't answer for what you'd say to him.'

'Well, I said yes, and all,' she blurted, and to her surprise he slipped an arm around her, like he hadn't done for years.

'Knew as much, my handsome!' he said, walking her out in the direction of the street. 'Dare say the Hoskinses were as pleased as punch?'

She grinned. 'Seemed like it, from the fuss they made of me.'

He squeezed her arm. 'Well I should think so too. Come home and have some supper; Aunt Jane's expecting you. Dying to know what's happened – though she'd go to the stake before admitting it, of course.' He grinned down at her, smart as paint in his railway uniform. 'She'll be pleased for you, my handsome, whatever she may say.'

And probably she was, though all she did was grunt, 'Well, I suppose it had to happen sometime. Might as well be now. All girls think about these days, it seems to me. Well, at least you've got a trade that won't be wasted when you're wed. Though I shouldn't say too much to Madam just yet if I were you!'

'I've got more sense than that,' Maud said, knowing she'd be given her marching orders if she did, quicker than you could say 'flat herringbone'. 'I shan't say a word until we've fixed a date.' And somehow, when she got back to the attic room that night, she didn't tell Belinda either, though she'd intended to.

Her friend seemed in an unhappy, brittle sort of mood, which did not encourage secrets, so as she prepared for bed Maud simply chattered on about the Hoskins' cats and cakes, and how the guard had been extremely kind. 'Of course the man knew Father, and he took care of me.' She climbed into bed and sat there upright, hugging her knees under the counterpane.

'Well,' said Belinda, grumpily. 'At least you had some fun.' She put her hairbrush down and slammed the window shut.

She did seem in a most peculiar, sulky frame of mind. Maud tried to tease her out of it. 'You didn't meet your beau, then?' An allusion to one of Blin's admirers often did the trick.

Not this time. Belinda didn't smile. Instead she turned a mottled shade of red. 'No, I damty didn't. He couldn't come today.' She had stripped off her skirt and petticoat by now and stood in her vest and bloomers, pouring cold water from the ewer into the wash-stand bowl. She didn't look at Maud. 'I had to spend the blessed afternoon with Gran, unravelling a sweater and steaming out the wool, so she can knit socks for sailors – if you would believe!'

She said it with such feeling that it was almost comical. Maud changed the subject on to safer things.

'One of these knitting circles that they're starting in the town, I suppose?' she asked. 'Aunt Jane was telling me. Women who want to do something for the war, getting together to make comforts for the troops. Someone came round to ask if she would like to join, apparently, but she said she'd rather join a sewing bee if there was such a thing. She does her best with socks and scarves and woollen vests and things but she is no knitter, really, when it comes to it. Not like Mother was. Good with her needles though, I expect, your gran?'

Belinda was rubbing the cold flannel over her face and arms. 'You might well think so, from all the fuss this afternoon, but honestly she's hopeless. I remember she once knitted a pair of gloves for me which were fine around the wrists, but had fingers long enough to fit the Giant of St Just. And the gloves were both left handed when she'd finished them.'

It was such a comic picture that Maud laughed aloud. 'Oh,

go on, Blin. It can't be all that bad. At least you got them on. You should have seen the balaclava Aunt Jane made for Tully once. So tight it nearly took his ears off each time he put it on. And then it used to pin them folded up against his head and make him cry – till Father took him to the rocks one day and they conveniently lost it in the sea. Mind you, Aunt Jane is threatening to make another one.'

That made Belinda giggle as she pulled her nightdress on and wiggled off her knickers underneath its folds. It was a strained little giggle, but it was a giggle all the same, as if she had resolved to wash off her sullen mood, and pour it with the dirty water from the wash-stand into the bucket underneath. She almost sounded like her normal self as she got into bed. 'Bad as each other, those two, by the sound of it. Pity the poor sailors who get socks from them.' She leaned across and blew the candle out.

Belinda thumped the bolster, but she couldn't settle down. Maud could be maddening sometimes, that was the truth of it. Off to meet that precious Stan of hers all day, and back so pink and glowing that it made you feel quite cross. It was obvious she had some special secret she was hugging to herself, but she hadn't shared her news. Pity: a bit of proper gossip might have cheered the day.

And it had needed cheering. Belinda could hardly bear to think about it now. Of course she should have learned her lesson days ago, and not gone lingering on the promenade again. If she had just gone directly home to Gran, she would not have created that humiliating scene.

Jonah had been standing by the bandstand gazing at the sea, just where she had met him once or twice before, looking as smart as sixpence in his Sunday suit. He was carrying his hat. He'd clearly taken a bit of trouble with himself: his boots were newly polished, he'd put brilliantine on his hair, and as she got closer she could swear she smelled cologne. Coming to apologize and make his peace, she thought, but she hardly had the heart to be very fierce with him. He looked like some poster of a moving-picture star, the sort you sometimes saw outside the cinema. He was still staring at the water, a slight smile on his face, and he obviously had not seen her until she greeted him.

'Jonah! I'm some glad to see you. You've been avoiding me!'

She'd made a horrible mistake, she knew that straight away. Not just from the way he coloured, right to the roots of his dark curly hair, but from the way he said, 'Belinda Richards!' in a sort of strangled hiss. The smile had vanished. He ran a finger round the inside of his collar-studs, as if he wanted to loosen them and give himself more air. 'What are you doing here?'

So he hadn't come to meet her – that was plain as flour. Well, two could play at that game. She tossed her head as if she didn't care. 'Same as you, I expect. Waiting for someone. And you needn't scowl. No laws against it, are there? This is a public place.'

'Oh.' There was a silence. 'I thought – from what you said . . .'

'Well, you thought wrong then.' She half-turned away from him, and began to scan the people on the promenade as if she was looking for someone in particular. 'There's other good fish in the sea besides you, Jonah Lotts. Lotts and Lotts in fact!' She gave a scornful little smile, delighted by her joke.

Jonah looked chagrined, as she hoped he would, but then he muttered, 'Well, I'm glad I find you happy. Here's my companion now. I hope you have a very pleasant afternoon, Miss Richards.' He put his hat on, tipped the brim to her and set off down the street.

Belinda pretended to look the other way, but she could not resist peeking to see what kind of person he was so keen to meet. There he was now, at the junction of the Newlyn Road, talking to some skinny little creature in a lumpy dress. He bent and whispered something and they hurried off, turning the corner where they could not be seen.

So that was the girl whose company Jonah Lotts preferred? No one of distinction, that was very clear – the dress looked like a hand-me-down, and so did the heavy boots and the preposterous hat perched on the scraggy hair. A bottle-washer at a factory, perhaps, enjoying her day off? Or a scullery maid or scrubbing girl or something of the kind, permitted on Sunday to snatch an hour or two to attend a church or chapel, or even Sunday School – one of the ones where they still taught you how to read and write, since there were girls her age from poorer families, as Belinda knew, who were registered at school because the law demanded it, but who never learned

to reckon or to cipher properly because they were kept home
by their parents half the time to mind the little ones. This girl
looked the type. Underfed, scrawny and awkward as a rake.
Yet Jonah had obviously dressed up for her, and had been
waiting for her with that special smile. What was the attrac-
tion? She didn't care to think.

Well, she couldn't stand here gawping, Jonah might come
back and it would be doubly humiliating to be seen still waiting
on her own. People were already looking at her, she was sure.
She was just deciding on a little plan – she would stand on
tip-toe, give a little wave and hurry off as though she had just
caught sight of someone that she knew – when she was aware
of someone standing at her side.

Drat, it was that wretched ragged boy again. The one who
had been hanging round outside the shop and had almost
caused her such embarrassment – by turning out to be the
follower of someone else. Imagine if she had said anything
to Madam, as she'd intended to! Yet here he was again.

'Excuse me, miss,' he said, cutting across her thoughts.

She was torn between decisions. Should she talk to him?
Suppose that Jonah did come back and find her doing so? At
least it would prove that she really did have other fish to fry,
and this boy was brushed and tidy, if not quite respectable.
At least the equal of that creature in the hand-me-downs.

She turned towards the young man, who was twiddling his
hat. She gave a gracious smile. 'You were addressing me?'
Cool, but not dismissive, that was the tone to take.

He nodded, with an embarrassed little grin. He was quite
good-looking really, when you came to think. Belinda found
that she was smiling, more warmly than before.

'You're Belinda Richards from Madam Raymond's shop?
I think I've seen you there.'

'That's right. How do you know that? Did you follow me?'

He looked sheepish. 'Well, I suppose I did a bit.' Belinda
was almost flattered, but then he spoiled it. 'I heard of you
from Jenny – that's my girl, you know – and she said that if
there was anything to know, Belinda Richards was the one to
ask. You remember Jenny, don't you? She's a first-year learner
– the one with golden plaits.'

Belinda nodded coolly. 'Yes, I know the one.'

'Thinks an awful lot of you, my Jenny does,' he said. 'Says

you are so clever that they send you round the town, going to people's houses, so you have the chance to get out from the shop from time to time.'

'Yes, I have been very fortunate that way. Well, that's nice of Jenny. I expect her time will come.'

'Well, that's just it, miss. That might not be for years. And I can't get to see her, now her mother's dead. She doesn't come home Sundays like she used to do – she goes up to her sister, and that's too far away. I used to try to catch her for a minute dinner-time, but she could never get away without someone seeing her – not even for a word. She did come out to speak to me, just the other day, and that was very nice, but she told me that I'd have to go or she would lose her place.'

'And quite rightly too. We are strictly forbidden to have followers.' Belinda was severe. 'Anyway, why are you telling me all this?' The effrontery of it, when she had imagined that he was lurking round for her! 'I don't know who you are, we have not been introduced, and yet, by your own admission, you have followed me about, and even had the impudence to ask me for a walk! I have a good mind to call that policeman over there!' She gestured to the burly sergeant who was cycling by.

'Oh, don't do that, miss. I've told you who I am. I'm Adam Prosser, Jenny Liskey's friend, and I only wanted to have a private word with you. Jenny thought you'd help. I didn't like to ask but she said that it was common gossip in the shop that you had lots of beaux, and you'd been writing letters, so you would understand.'

Belinda found that she was standing very still. 'Common gossip, is it?' This was terrible. Why had she been so anxious to spread that kind of talk? Suppose that any word of it should come to Madam's ears?

Adam was nodding cheerfully. 'That's why she thought that you'd be prepared to help. You know exactly what it's like to be in love. So, if I was to meet you somewhere in the street one day when you are out, and slip a note to you for Jenny, could you see it gets to her? I can't write to the shop. Madam and Miss Simms open all the mail, and that would never do – and anyway the other girls would only get to hear. And I can't write to her sister's house, because she won't approve. Keeps telling Jenny to forget me and concentrate on work. It's cost the family enough to pay the premium she says, and

Jenny shouldn't take the risk of throwing it away.' He made a little face. 'If I wrote a note to Jenny there, she wouldn't pass it on.'

Belinda was very tempted to say 'no' at once, but something made her pause. It was quite romantic, in a peculiar sort of way, and it would be nice to have a proper secret she could share with Maud. Besides, she could insist on reading all the notes – if she was prepared to take the risk, she had to know what risk it was – and that gave her a pleasant little thrill of power. And, as she had already realized, there was a kind of threat involved. If she refused the favour, what would Jenny do? Give the game away to Madam about 'the gossip' in the shop?

She gave him her most condescending smile. 'Of course,' she said. 'You can rely on me. Look out for me on Fridays when I'm in the town. But not too often, mind. No more than once a month. And I can't take things both ways, that's too much of a risk. But if you want to write her a line or two now and then, I dare say I can find a moment when I can pass it on. But you are not to sign it or address the envelope – then if Madam ever should find out, I can say I found it on the mat, and nothing can be proved.'

Adam grinned. 'Then you'll help us?'

'I suppose so.'

'Thank you very much. You don't know how much this means to me. Or perhaps you do. Jenny says you have admirers, and I can see you might. You're such a pretty girl, I'm sure that single fellows would be after you like bees. Like the one that you were talking to, before I came along. But here he comes again. I mustn't keep you; I'm sure he's looking out for you, to speak to you again. So I'll say goodbye, miss, and thank you very much.' He raised his battered hat and disappeared into the throng.

Belinda was fuming. It could not have happened worse. Leaving her alone at the very moment that Jonah reappeared! But Jonah wasn't even looking. He didn't glance in her direction. He set off the other way, looking very furtive and self-satisfied. She watched him walk down the promenade and disappear, and noticed that his hair was rather mussed – despite the brilliantine – and that there were smudges on the back of his good coat.

And then there was nothing for it but to go to Gran and help her to unravel all that wool. It had put her in a funny, angry mood all day, especially with Maudie. It seemed her fault, somehow.

So, later in the week, when she met Adam in the street, she took a kind of pleasure in delivering his note. And she didn't tell Maudie. Well, it served her right. It had taken Maudie days and days to get around to telling her that Stanley had proposed, and by the time she did so it was hardly news, because he'd already left.

Life at the training camp was quite another world – though not embarrassing like the medical had been. Of course, unlike a lot of other fellows in the group, Stan had no brothers and there were no rivers for him to swim in with his friends, so – despite a brief period of being a Boy Scout – he had never stripped off to the altogether in front of other people in his life, except perhaps his mother when he was very young. So it was quite unsettling to be required to stand naked in a line with lots of other men, while some doctor looked you over in an appraising way and wrote things on a form. It wasn't even possible to guard your modesty, they wanted you to raise your arms and then to bend your knees, while they prodded you and poked you and listened to your chest.

Nor was he prepared for the comments afterwards, among the men themselves, comparing their 'equipment' and sharing tales of what they'd done with it. There was talk about their women, which made him blush for Maud. The medical had been testing in more ways than one.

Of course he'd passed with flying colours, as he'd said to her. Accelerated training, since he'd briefly been a Scout. So now he was to share a room, to dress and undress, wash and shower – if at all – only in the company of lots of other men. It was an aspect of military life he hadn't thought about, although of course one soon got used to it.

Not that Stanley was a prude at all, and there was nothing to be ashamed of in his own physique – on the contrary, it had been the subject of half-mocking flattery – but compared to some lads from the cities, he'd led a sheltered life. Yet, as a farmer, he knew much more about these things than half the others did, in spite of what they said about their so-called exploits, and they soon realized that. It earned him a reputation as 'a terrible dark horse', and people didn't tease him as they might have done.

Besides, once they were kitted out in a kind of uniform and were barked at by the sergeant-major for a bit, they began to form into a kind of group and some became good friends. There were two other Cornishmen, both red-headed ones: a handsome lad whose proper name was Pete, but who was nicknamed Charmer from the start, who chummed up with Stan at once, and the young Tregurtha boy, the one with freckles who they'd seen signing up at that recruiting rally in Penzance. He had been in training for a month or more before Stan ever came and had tried several times to volunteer for France, but he was still not fit enough to route-march with his kit and they had held him back when the rest of his intake had all moved on elsewhere – though he was bitterly disappointed to be left behind.

There was a lot of training to be done: drilling and saluting and polishing your boots, wiggling through damp ditches and marching through ploughed fields, cleaning your rifle and shooting it at things, learning how to dig a fox-hole or latrine, then drilling and saluting and polishing again. The days seemed to pass in a kind of weary blur, and there was hardly time to sink to sleep, it seemed, before it was time to be up again at dawn, to march for miles and miles carrying your pack, or to attend a demonstration on how to throw grenades.

Stan found it easier than many of the lads. He was used to keeping early hours and heaving sacks about, and a muddy field was all in a day's work to him at home. Even Charmer found it difficult, especially at first, and he was fairly strong. Young Tregurtha struggled something terrible, though he never once complained. He simply put his carrot-head down and did the best he could. He looked quite a soldier with his tunic on, but when he was forced to take it off – for a medical inspection, as happened once or twice – you could see that his body was a skinny child's, and his voice was still breaking and occasionally squeaked. Most of the men were tolerant of him and helped him if they could, but there was one lad, called Sawyer, who couldn't hide his scorn.

'Bloody infant,' Sawyer said one day, when they were struggling through a stream and Tregurtha, as usual, was bringing up the rear. 'Couldn't lift a spoon in anger, let alone a gun. Why don't they give him a perambulator and have done with it?' He raised his voice. 'Come on, you bloody slow-coach! Put your back in it! What do you expect? The war will wait for you?'

Poor Tregurtha tried to come on faster, but he slipped and lost his footing on the slippery rocks. The water took him and, hampered by his pack, he floundered helplessly. If it wasn't for the corporal in charge, who caught him by the neck, the boy might easily have been swept away and drowned.

'Baby have a bath, then?' Sawyer mocked aloud, and found himself on a charge for insubordination and insolence', because it was not his place to be bellowing orders with the corporal there. He was put on to peeling potatoes for a week, and cleaning the latrines, and he seemed to carry a double grudge against Tregurtha after that.

Then, one day, as they were lining up to get their army stew – poor stuff, Stan thought it, but the way that some lads wolfed it down you could see that they had never eaten half so well before – Tregurtha was so anxious to get into the queue that he bumped into Sawyer and made him drop the metal plate and eating irons that he was carrying. There was nothing in the mess-tin, so there wasn't any loss, and Tregurtha said 'Sorry!' nervously at once, but Sawyer turned and gave him such a savage push that it sent him sprawling to the ground.

Stan saw it happen, since he was standing right behind. Sawyer had given someone else his coat and was standing over Tregurtha with his fists clenched, as if he was going to thump him into the middle of next week. Stan tapped him on the shoulder. 'Here, save that for the Hun!'

Sawyer wasn't thinking, or he wouldn't have whirled round and hit Stan as he did. He was a big lad, fat and heavy, but Stan was twice as strong, and a minute later Sawyer was sitting on the ground himself, looking rather stupefied and fondling his chin. Unlike Tregurtha, he showed no signs of getting up again. Stan had a sense of satisfaction, though he could feel that his own right eye was swelling nastily. He brushed his hands and turned away – right into the arms of a burly corporal.

'What's the meaning of this fracas, Private?'

Of course it was no good trying to explain, and Sawyer gave a completely different picture of events. It got Stan into trouble and he was brought up on a charge. But when he was marched up before the officer, he did take the opportunity to mention Tregurtha. 'He's such a little lad, sir, I'm sure he's under age.'

To which the major answered, with his twinkle in his eye, 'But he's got grit and gumption, that's what we like to see. And he's signed himself as eighteen. It's down here on my list. And in any case, Private, that isn't your affair. Sentenced to three days' fatigues for causing an affray.'

So that was that. But in the long run the incident didn't do Stan any harm. Sawyer, and lots of other fellows, eyed him with more respect, and young Tregurtha became a willing slave. Even the major seemed to have his eye on Private Hoskins after that, picked him out for 'leadership potential' and put him on a course, with Charmer, to be an NCO.

Stan didn't tell Maudie about the petty things – he tried to made life sound amusing and exciting in his letters home – but he did write and tell her that he'd got his stripe, and that he and Charmer were scheduled for France, some of the first of the volunteer recruits to join the regulars on service overseas.

# Two

Jonah was feeling wretched. He'd had a dreadful afternoon. First that awful woman shouting after him, 'Great strapping lad like you. You ought to be ashamed. Why aren't you with the army, like you belong to be?' And she'd waved her umbrella at him, her fat cheeks wobbling, purple as a turkeycock in her preposterous hat.

He was ready with an answer. 'And who is going to lift these heavy sacks, if all the men have gone? You want to do it? Come on and have a try!' He raised his voice and gestured, so several passers-by were turning round to look.

It gave him some satisfaction to see her startled face. 'Don't be ridiculous!'

'Nah. You couldn't do it, and I'm not surprised. Takes a man to lift these sacks. And don't you forget it, next time you criticize. Need to keep the country running if we're going to beat the Hun, and that's not going to happen if there isn't any coal!'

'The impudence of it!' It was more of a mutter than a shout this time. 'I've got a good mind to call the policeman and have you on a charge.' But of course she didn't, she just turned and stumped away. Jonah watched her out of sight, then urged the General into motion and drove off down the street. People were still staring, but he didn't look at them, just went past with his head held particularly high.

He'd had the best of that exchange, he told himself, but it was unsettling. It was not the first time, either. Once or twice he had been jeered at by women in the street, calling him a coward for not having volunteered – as if they expected everyone to go. Well, he wasn't going to, so she could stick that in her hat! But it had put a proper damper on the afternoon.

And when he got to Lily-Anne it went from bad to worse. Things hadn't been very good between them for a week or two. She'd lost her playful manner, perhaps due to her health. She'd been looking peaky lately, and it was the same this afternoon, her eyes all pink and sunken, and no colour in her cheeks.

She did look up and smile at him as he tied up the General, and led the way to what had become their Friday hiding-place. But when he tried to take her in his arms, she wasn't warm and teasing like she used to be, just seemed impatient to lie down and get it over with. She'd been like that the last few times, that was the funny thing, ever since he managed to contain himself enough to 'do it properly' as Billy would have said. He could have understood it if she'd simply changed her mind. She might not have liked it – things were obviously not the same for girls – and he would have been quite happy to have found alternatives. After all, he'd got quite used to it. But she virtually insisted, and he'd managed to oblige, although when she was in this dull and hasty sort of mood it was not the pleasure he'd expected it would be.

It was only afterwards, when she was pulling on her blouse, that she dropped the thunderbolt. He was telling her idly about the woman in the street.

'Well, people can shout after me all they like,' he said. 'I aren't going for a soldier, and that's the end of that. Only just got old enough to have a bit of fun – what with finding you and everything.' He reached out playfully and pinched her skinny arm. 'I aren't about to throw it all away to fight the Hun.' He grinned. 'See, I'm a poet, and I didn't know.'

She didn't smile. She shrugged her shoulders and pulled her collar straight. 'Perhaps what you want to do is find yourself a wife. That would shut them up. Nobody expects a married man to go.'

He gave a snort of laughter. 'Who'd want that, for heaven's sake?'

She cut across his scorn. 'Looks like you might have to marry me in any case. I believe I might be in the family way.'

If she had hit him with a sack of his own coal, he could not have been more stunned. The world seemed to tumble slowly round his ears. Now what had she led him into? What would Ma and Father say – and with a scrubbing girl? They'd throw him out, most like. What would become of them? He looked at Lily-Anne, noticing, as if for the first time, her skinny shoulders and her pale, pinched cheeks. Her body was thinner than a rake handle (or was there a faint swelling in the stomach area?) and about as beautiful. Why had he thought she was desirable? She filled him now with only pity and disgust.

To think he'd preferred her to that pretty Belinda – had even deliberately met her on the Prom, so as to show Belinda that he was spoken for. And it had not been a successful meeting even then – Lily-Anne had insisted on finding a back yard and there had been a brief, uncomfortable coupling up against a wall, with Jonah terrified that somebody would see. It had been wasted too. When he walked back a minute later, there was Belinda talking to a man – which turned the tables on him, though he'd pretended not to see.

'Well?' Lily-Anne was saying, doing up her blouse.

'Well, what?' He heard his own voice, sounding far away.

He felt aggrieved and cheated. 'Don't look at me like that. I didn't ask for this. You always knew what I thought, and we both agreed. It was a bit of fun. It's not my fault if you've got yourself into a fix.'

'Well, whose else is it? We've been walking out for weeks. Everyone has seen us. Course you've got to have me – don't look at me like that. I've got a good mind to go and tell your Ma and Pa.'

He was on his feet at once. 'Don't you go doing that! They'll throw me out and all, and then where will we be?'

'Well, I got to do something. I'll be up the workhouse else. Soon as ever my employers find out, they'll turn me out on the street.'

'You should have thought of that.'

'And so should you! I don't believe you ever cared for me at all. Just taking advantage of me, that is all it was. Always had your eyes on other girls, besides – I saw you with that baggage on the promenade the other day. I thought you said you loved me.'

'Not in that kind of way.'

They had an awful row. She screamed and shouted, threatened, wept. It only ended when he walked away and left her standing there.

He was late with the rest of his deliveries. But there must have been something in his manner when he got back to the yard, because Pa took one look at him and didn't say a word. And when he went home, it was the same with Ma.

He ate his tea and pushed his plate away. 'I'm off out for an hour,' he said.

And for the first time ever, she didn't ask him where.

What he did was trudge to Newlyn, to the Imperial Inn, but Billy was working in the cellar so there was no friendly ear. It was dark and drizzling but he climbed down on the rocks and spent a miserable hour hurling stones into the sea, until the tide and damp defeated him and he went home to bed.

They let Stan come home for a weekend before he went away. Embarkation leave, they called it. It didn't give him long, but he wired to say that he would take an hour or two to come down to Penzance and to expect him on the Sunday lunchtime train.

Maudie got the message late on Friday, just as the shop was closing for the night. Father came down to tell her, and ask her to come home, though she didn't usually do that except at the weekends. Of course there was no reason not to, now that she wasn't a mere apprentice any more, as long as her work was finished ready for opening next day. She did have a little bit to do, but it was only taking up a hem and she could do that in the morning if she got up soon enough. Stan was coming Sunday, and Aunt Jane wanted a hand for an hour or two. So the minute she and Belinda had got the shutters up, Maudie put her cloak and bonnet on and hurried up the Arcade Steps to reach Belgravia Street.

The door was already open and the step was newly scrubbed. Maud had to step carefully, and only on the mat, so as not to make footprints. She found the grown-ups in the kitchen, packing Tully off to bed. Aunt Jane was in a taking about the telegram. 'Gave me a proper turn it did. Whoever heard of sending one of these? It must have cost no end.' She thrust the flimsy paper into Maudie's hand and gestured to the rows of printing, all in capitals. 'How didn't he just write us, like he belongs to do?'

'Didn't know he was coming till last minute, I should think,' Dad said peaceably. He was sitting in his favourite chair beside the fire, stuffing his special naval blend into his pipe.

'I'd have made him something special for his tea, if I'd have known. Bit of special saffron cake or something of the kind. But I'm clean out of saffron and I haven't budgeted for more. He'll just have to put up with what I've got, that's all.'

Father reached over, took a spill-taper from the jar and lit it from the fire. 'I shouldn't worry, Janey. Doubt he'll have the time to stop and have a proper tea in any case. Twenty-four hours, it says here, before they want him back in camp – and it will take him most of that just getting home and back. Good of him to bother to come down here at all. No point in wasting your special saffron cake.'

He looked at Maudie and gave her a wink. Aunt Jane's 'special saffron cake' was a family joke. Most of the time her saffron cake was a fragrant, homely treat – not a patch on Mother's but pleasant all the same – but when it came to Christmas or some other special tea, she could never resist the temptation to 'rich it up a bit'; then, of course, it wouldn't rise the same and – though it tasted nice enough – Father joked to Maudie that it should be 'suffrin' cake', because it lay on your stomach afterwards like a lump of lead.

Aunt Jane insisted on fresh jam tarts at least. 'Bound to come here, isn't 'e, after he wrote to ask your blessing and all that sort of thing. And I 'aven't seen him since I left up there. Least we can do is make a fuss of him.'

She'd devoted the afternoon to scrubbing all the floors – which was usually a job for Wednesdays – and spent the evening polishing all the ornaments and furniture in the house, as though Stan was going to make a military inspection of the place. Maudie was put on to washing the 'best cloam' – the dainty china tea set that Mother had put by, and which was never used except for births and funerals – and polishing the knives and forks till you could see your face in them.

'Be a wonder if we can last till Sunday afternoon, without somebody breathing on something,' Father said, when they had done it all at last and were sitting round the fire for a welcome cup of tea.

'Well, I'll have to take that boy Tully out somewhere tomorrow for the day. Go out for a picnic on the moors, perhaps. Can't have him mucking up the place, when we've just got it straight. And you, Wilfred, don't you go knocking your pipe out like that against the hearth. Get an old tin-lid or something and do it properly.'

And so Father had to go outside into the yard to knock his ashes out, and while he was about it he took the opportunity to walk Maudie home. 'I'm sorry you've done nothing but work tonight, my handsome. 'Tisn't as if your Stan will even notice it. I've tried to tell our Janey that – he's only come to see you – but she will have her fuss and no one's going to talk her out of it. It's her way of showing that she's pleased for you.'

Maud made a face at him. 'I know.'

'Well, you have a nice time Sunday. Go down and meet the train, and don't be in too much hurry to come home if you don't want.' He grinned. 'But you bring Stanley, if he's got time to come. She'll be some disappointed if he don't eat her tarts. Now, you going to ring the bell?'

But in the end she had to throw pebbles up to hit the bedroom window pane before Belinda came grumpily downstairs to let her in.

*       *       *

It was blustery on Sunday, and Stan was very glad of his smart new uniform and his heavy coat. He'd promised Maudie he would wear it down and let her see, though he could have worn his ordinary clothes since he was still on leave. It made him feel rather conspicuous, of course – it was a different matter wearing it in camp, when everybody else was dressed the same, but when you were in public, it marked you out a bit.

Folk looked at you in a different way, and in the carriage on the way down to Penzance, an older man actually got up and offered him his seat. 'Got to do something for you brave boys. I was in South Africa, and I know what it is!' Stan wouldn't take it, but it made him feel respected and important all the same.

Maudie was waiting for him when the train pulled in, and he thought he had never seen her looking prettier than she did today, in her best blue going-to-chapel costume with a bonnet trimmed to match. She had pinned a sea-pink to her bodice for a bit of ornament, and it matched her glowing cheeks, and her eyes were shining with tearful pride as she looked him up and down.

'My life, Stan! I wouldn't hardly have known you in your uniform. You look some handsome – like a proper man.'

'Well, that's some backhanded compliment. Thank you very much,' he said, and made her laugh.

'Oh, go on with you. You know what I mean. Anyway, it's no wonder if I can't think what to say. Be the last time I see you for heaven knows how long. Though they still say it will be all over by this time next year, I know.'

Stan said nothing. There were some who didn't think so, he reflected ruefully, judging by some rumours that had reached him once or twice. Instead he fished into his pocket. 'See what I've brought for you. Dad found it with the plough.' He reached out a clenched fist and dropped something in her palm.

She was as amused and puzzled as he'd hoped she would be. 'What is it then? Looks like a penny, only it's too fat. And the wrong colour too.' She turned it over and examined it. '1811 and a picture of a mine.'

He grinned. 'Well, 'tis a penny, in a kind of way. It's a Cornish penny. See what it says there? "Valid in the county". Granfer knew at once. Used to be a lot of them around when he was young. Issued by a local bank, apparently, when there wasn't a lot of coinage around, but the shops stopped taking them when the bank closed down. There were all sorts of little banks at one time, for the mines – used to print their own bank notes and everything – but they've nearly all gone now.' He grinned. 'So you see, it's useless. You can't spend it anywhere. But I thought you'd like to have it. Something to remind you, while I am away.'

She twinkled up at him. 'Get off with you. As if I'd need reminding! But I'll keep it, just the same.' She slipped it carefully inside her glove, against her hand. 'I've got a pretty ribbon-box that I can keep it in. Only wish I'd thought of bringing something down for you.' She unpinned the flower from her bodice and handed it to him. 'Have this for a minute. Put it in your wallet, till I find something else. I'll think of something better and send it on to you.'

He did as she suggested, tucking it in beside his travel warrant. 'Can't be anything better, with your kiss on it. I'm going to put it in this pocket, right beside my heart.' He meant it, but it sounded sentimental, like a song, and he said it quickly to cover his embarrassment, 'Now, are we going to have a little bit of a walk, or what? I want to have you to myself for half an hour. Though I suppose I'd better call in at Belgravia Street this time to see your people and to say goodbye.'

'You won't escape without it,' Maudie answered with a laugh. 'Aunt Jane's been baking jam tarts and heavy cake as if she was expecting royalty.'

So that is what they did, though there were other ways he would have preferred to spend the afternoon. A rather stultified affair it was, as well, making conversation to Maudie's aunt (lots of reminiscences about when he was young without once mentioning that he was going away to war) and entertaining young Tully, who enjoyed the tarts but managed to create a scene by getting jammy fingerprints all over the best cloth. Stan was just wondering how much longer this would last, when Maudie's father saved them by getting to his feet.

'Time for you to get a move on, Stan my son, if you want to have a minute or two with Maudie on your own. God bless you, my handsome. You just take care of yourself, you hear? Now go on, Maudie. Don't stop to do the cups. You walk down with him and see him on the train.'

They took the detour through the woods again – though there was scarcely time – and he did manage to snatch another kiss beside the stile. Then there was nothing for it but to run and catch the train. He sat there panting in the window-seat as the carriage pulled away, while Maudie stood on the platform and waved her handkerchief, the tears running shamelessly down her cheeks.

# Three

Jonah was in the stable garret that was Billy's room. He'd rinsed his hands and face under the pump out in the yard, and he was sitting gingerly on the inner step, trying not to spread coal dust everywhere. It was another Friday, just after four o'clock, and Billy wasn't wanted till five, he said.

'But how aren't you working, Jonah?' he was saying now. 'Course, I knew that you'd be here with the coal this afternoon, but you could have knocked me over with a feather when you said you had a hour. Haven't you got other deliveries to do?'

'Generally have a bit of time to spare on Fridays,' Jonah said. 'Used to work it special so I had the extra time.'

'How didn't you come here then, as a rule? You knew I had time off.'

'I've had other things to do. But today I didn't want to.'

Billy cocked an eye at him. 'It's not that girl again? I remember you were wanting to hide away from her, the first time that you came. I don't know why you do. She's quite a looker, by the sounds of things.' He was rifling for something in a cupboard by the bed. 'You want to be like me. Made up my mind to marry that Annie after all. They don't hound a married man to go away and fight, and there's worse things than a sweet shop when all is said and done. So make the most of this.' He got out a battered shaving mug and a pewter half-pint pot. He gave the pot to Jonah. 'Here. You have the pewter one. It's got a wonky handle so be careful holding it. It's all I've got to drink from but it'll do, I'm sure.'

Jonah looked at him doubtfully. 'What are these for then?'

A big, slow grin creased Billy's chubby face. 'I thought we'd have a spot of ale – drink me and Annie's health. I get a jugful, every now and then, as part of my 'lowance from the inn. It's just come up, it's on the wash-stand, see? So you've just timed it lucky. Hold out that tankard and I'll pour you some.'

Jonah frowned. He had been brought up strictly Methodist. 'I don't know as I should.'

'Ah come on,' Billy urged him. 'A drop won't do no harm. They wouldn't give it me else. Besides, you look as if you could do with it.'

Jonah, greatly daring, held out the pewter pot and took his first ever sip of what Ma called the 'demon drink'. It was a bit disappointing, when it came to it – rather warm and sour – but he couldn't back down now.

'Good stuff, eh?' Billy smacked his lips and raised his shaving cup.

Jonah nodded, trying to look more enthusiastic than he felt. He took another mouthful. It wasn't all that bad.

'Well come on.' Billy leant back against the sloping wall. 'What's the problem, then? That girl – Belinda is it? Still chasing you about?'

Jonah swallowed another sip of ale. It seemed to give him courage. 'Well not exactly that. It's someone else that I've been seeing.'

Billy gave a mocking whistle as he refilled his mug. 'You're some dark horse, aren't you, Jonah Lotts? All the girls are after you. I wish you'd teach me tricks.'

Jonah shook his head. 'It isn't any joke. I'm in a proper pickle and I don't know what to do.' He told Billy the whole story about wretched Lily-Anne. 'Trouble is she's threatening to go and tell my ma, and Lord knows what will happen if she does a thing like that. I'll either have to marry her or I'll be out the door – or maybe both, if I don't watch my step. Honestly, Billy, I'm afraid to do my rounds today. I'm sure she will be waiting and will make a scene again.'

Billy had listened in silence to all this, and when he spoke he sounded genuinely shocked. 'Dear heaven, Jonah, I see why

you're upset. I never thought you'd get yourself in so serious.'
He gave a little whistle of astonishment. 'You've set yourself
a proper poser there and no mistake. It's not like me and Annie
– I never touched her in that kind of way till we were promised. She wouldn't have allowed it, anyway. However did you
come to let yourself get carried away like that? And it must
have been some quick. Almost the first time that you met her,
from what you're telling me.'

'I didn't really mean to,' Jonah said. 'She led me on so much.'
He realized that it sounded pathetic, and he added quickly, 'And
anyway, I didn't, the first time or two. Not properly. It was all
too hasty – if you know what I mean. Though she tried to egg
me on. Seemed quite disappointed when I . . . well . . . when
that's how it was.'

Billy stopped suddenly and stared at him, his shaving mug
halfway to his lips. 'Just a minute! Say that bit again?'

Jonah was embarrassed. 'Don't you laugh at me!' But Billy
seemed in earnest so he repeated what he'd said.

'Well, there you are, then!' Billy put the shaving mug down
on the table with a bang. 'Are you sure it's yours?'

Jonah was dumbfounded now. 'Who else's would it be?'

'Oh, my dear Jonah, don't you know anything at all? From
what you say it's only a few weeks. She couldn't be certain
that she'd fallen in that length of time.'

Jonah felt cold prickles running up his spine. He put his
drink down carefully. 'What do you mean by that?' Perhaps
the alcohol was getting to his brain.

So Billy spelled it out to him and told him, in the process,
some things about women which he really hadn't known. 'So
there hasn't hardly been the time for her to be sure of anything,'
Billy said. 'The chances are she's stringing you along. Mightn't
be a child, for anything you know. And yet you say she's
showing? Well, I wouldn't stand for that. Trying to trap you,
just to give the child a name when it very likely isn't yours
– for all your wicked ways.'

Jonah felt as if a sack of coal had lifted from his back. It
wasn't his fault after all, he told himself as he went back to his
rounds. But there was still the problem of driving down that
street. He had deliberately left it to the very last, hoping that by
that time she would be wanted back at work, but there she was
– waiting for him at the corner as she always did.

He tried to ignore her and simply drive away without even stopping to deliver any coal. He did not look towards her, but she called after him. ''Ere, Jonah. Don't you pretend I've gone invisible. You know what you've done. You want me to shout it after you, out here in the street, so all the world can hear? I'm that desperate, I would do, I am warning you.' Two women who were passing stopped and stared at them.

Drat it! If he wasn't careful this would come to Father's ears. He stopped the cart and turned to look at her, and called in a voice that was just as loud as hers. 'Who do you think you are fooling, Lily-Anne? I'm not as simple-minded as you must think I am. If you've got yourself in trouble, then that's your look out. 'Tisn't my fault, and you know it's not. You go and find the father, and make your threats to him. If you can work out which one of them it was!'

And with that parting shot he drove off down the street. He carefully did not look back even once but he could feel her staring after him. And the other two women, too.

He found that he was trembling. Perhaps it was the drink. He had to stop and wash his mouth out at the public water tap on the Prom, or Ma would very likely have smelled the ale on his breath.

War wasn't anything like Stan thought it would be. One got there so quickly, that was the strangest thing. One minute, it seemed, he was saying fond farewells to Maud, the next he was packed aboard a ship, and tossing about on the Channel on the way to France.

The voyage was unreal, like a dream, a grey and heaving dream in which a good few men were sick, crammed together like herrings in the stuffy areas below. Of course, that only made it worse for all the others, too. Some started singing comic songs, to keep their spirits up, and those who could spent the chilly night hours sleepless up on deck, wrapped up in their greatcoats and huddling for warmth.

Stan was among them. He had found, to his surprise, that he suffered less than most – perhaps because his duties kept him on the move – but 'Charmer' Peter was prostrate in the quarters down below, swearing that he would rather die than spend an hour like this, and that a German bullet would be a merciful release. There was a brief scare, too, when someone thought they saw a German ship, but it proved to be a neutral freighter from America and it steamed serenely past. Apart from that, it was a strange, suspended sort of time. A breathless pause between the busy discipline of camp – route-marches and forming fours seemed miles away by now – and the uncertainty ahead.

France, when they reached it, was grey and cold and damp. The army had commandeered a sort of warehouse block which they were using as a makeshift dispersal area, with tents, a cookhouse and a drill-square in the yard. No lack of action here. The place was a flurry of men on motorbikes (dispatch riders, they were calling them), lorries, carts, columns of soldiers forming up to march – a company who'd arrived ahead of them, it seemed – and various important-looking officers with lists.

Stan had little chance to get a clear impression of the place. There was time only for a welcome, a warm but tasteless meal of stew and a draughty night spent sleeping under canvas in the rain, and then it was their turn to be moving off. They set off marching, carrying their kit (strange to be doing it in earnest at last!) but it was not to be a damp and dreary slog along the roads after all. A little distance from the depot there was a railway and a train awaiting them, and rather to Stan's surprise the company was briskly packed aboard.

It was extraordinary to be riding towards battle in a train – rather like taking a day trip to Penzance, except that this was a strange, foreign sort of train, with wooden slatted bench seats set in back to back, and every inch of space crammed full of soldiers and their kit. Stan was squashed in to a corner, beside the grimy window, and what he saw as they went on through the rain-soaked countryside made him increasingly aware that they were being carried closer to the war with each turn of the wheels.

First he glimpsed a pair of aeroplanes – the first he'd ever seen – swooping in the distance just above a line of trees, then a cluster of ominous fresh graves beside the track. They halted for a moment at a crossing place and another dispatch rider went roaring past the train, scattering a family with a heavy-loaded cart. Stan thought of markets, till he saw the bedding and the chairs and the old woman perched sobbing on the top, and realized they were people fleeing from their home.

It was soon clear why they had fled. The next little village
had a shattered church, and houses were smouldering. Stan
turned to look for Peter, who was crammed by the aisle. The
place was too crowded to talk to him direct, and half the men
were singing a bawdy comic song, so he had to mouth the
message, 'Look! Through the window. Can you see?' He
gestured to the window, and a ruined barn outside, but suddenly
above the singing and the clatter of the wheels there was a
distant rumbling that froze him in the act.

Crump! The whole carriage heard it and there was a sudden
hush. They all knew what it was: the first sound of the guns.
Charmer stopped craning to get a better view and elbowed
through grumbling men to make his way to Stan. 'Next stop
the battlefield?' The booming came again, accompanied by
flashes from somewhere up ahead that lit up the landscape
with a peculiar glare. 'That sounds like a bombardment.'

Young Tregurtha, who was huddled in a seat not very far
from Stan, let out a little moan, then closed his eyes and pulled
himself in tight as if determined not to make another sound.

Stan shook a warning head at Peter. 'A heavy gun at any
rate. Let's hope it's one of ours.'

'Well, the train is stopping. We'll find out very soon.'

In fact it was only another minor halt, the first of several
more. By the time they did lurch to a final stop at last, the
roar and crunch of heavy artillery seemed very close by, and
had been joined by a higher, more insistent rat-tat-tat that Stan
knew must be machine-gun fire. It seemed to fill the world.
As they were marched out to billets in what had once been a
farm, the universe seemed nothing but a howling wall of
sound, while the very heavens were lit up by streaks of sudden
light, and angry orange flashes against grey sullen smoke.

The officers had quarters in the house itself, while the other
ranks and NCOs had billets in the barn. Stan, as a farmer,
couldn't help wondering what had happened to the animals,
but no one seemed to know – or care. He tried asking the
bent old man who seemed to own the place, when he came
in to give them a pile of clean-ish straw, but the fellow just
looked resentfully at him and muttered something in a
language Stan didn't understand. (It turned out later that the
old man and his wife were terrified; they had been relegated
to a single room upstairs, and obliged to turn their animals

out on the open fields, so it was not surprising that there was some sullenness.)

The barn was not uncomfortable, but it was impossible to sleep. The noise of the guns was constant and that was bad enough, but besides the racket – however hard you tried – you could not help thinking of what the crumping meant and remembering that very soon it would be aimed at you. If you did succeed in dozing off at all, Stan found, every now and then there was a louder boom which seemed to shake the very ground and startle you awake.

The next day the company was divided into groups, and sent out to dig a ditch and build enforcements round a big stone granary nearby, where the army hoped to make a food and ammunition store. Sawyer came back that evening with a barrel full of home-made apple cider-beer, which he had 'liberated' from a cellar in a ruined house nearby and brought back in a wheelbarrow underneath his coat. It was very strong, but warming, and there was some for everyone. Even Tregurtha had a glass or two. They all slept a good deal better that night, guns or not.

Just as well, because the next night they went up to the front. There was transport provided for a mile or two, but after they reached the reserve lines at the back the rest was done on foot. It was a clear night, perversely, and Stan felt like a target silhouette against the sky. To reach the forward trench they had to cross an open field with just a little hedge providing cover at the edge. They had to cross the area a few men at a time, by bending down and making a headlong dash for it.

When it was Stan's turn he look a long, deep breath and set off at a trot, though the ground was so churned and sticky from the recent rain that it was difficult to run, and he almost trod on a dark shape sprawled out in the mud, which he did not dare to stop and contemplate.

It was tricky going, and mighty dangerous since evidently the German snipers had them in their sights. Fortunately their accuracy wasn't very good. A storm of bullets fell each side of them but only one man – Sawyer – caught a bullet in the thigh. Charmer saw him falling and caught him by the arms and half-dragged, half-carried him over to the trench.

Stan had heard a lot about the trenches, back in the training camp – they'd even had to dig a practice one, and fill it again, to demonstrate the uses of the entrenching tool – but that was a neat ditch in an English field. This hardly looked much like a trench at all; it had been flooded and repaired so often that it was now a sea of mud, with pools of standing water on the bottom here and there. Not much else was visible except a bomb shelter – a tin roof with a pile of sand bags on the top – and sticky, muddy look-out stations carved out of the walls.

But already a group of mud-streaked men had appeared from somewhere down the trench and were paddling to meet them through the mire. They looked oddly cheerful, in spite of everything, and the stout young fellow who seemed to be in charge advanced towards them with a friendly grin. He was a major, from the markings on his grimy uniform, and their captain snapped to with a formal, smart salute.

'Captain Rawlings reporting with reinforcements, sir.' Rawlings had to bellow to drown the sound of bullets which still sang overhead. 'I've got one man wounded.'

The major's answering salute was quite perfunctory. 'Glad you made it, Rawlings. I'm Trumbell, by the way.' He ducked as something flew by overhead. 'Damn Hun's got the distance. Lose many on the way?'

'None, sir.' Rawlings shook his head.

Trumbell whistled. 'And only one man wounded? That's miraculous – we lost a dozen people earlier today – but there's not much that we can do for him up this end, I'm afraid. We'll have a stretcher party and get him carried through; there's a first-aid dressing station further down the line. Welcome to hell, you others; keep yourselves well down. I shouldn't stand up in this sector of the trench if I were you, or you'll find yourself in heaven sooner than you think. The Jerries are dug in over there behind that ridge, a hundred yards away. So, if you care to come this way, I'll find someone to show you where you're going. Luxury accommodation, chaps, as you can see – with free musical entertainment going on every night.'

Even as he spoke there was a mighty bang and pieces of debris showered over them, half-burying poor Sawyer who was slumped helpless by the wall. The two men with a stretcher, who had struggled up the trench, had to dig him out and clear the earth out of his nose and mouth before they took

him off – though he was groaning faintly, so he was still alive.
And that was Stan's introduction to the war.

Later, as he wrapped himself up in his army coat and tried
to find a way to lie in comfort on the muddy recess in the
wall – which was the only sleeping area that he was going to
get – Stan looked up at the unforgiving barrage in the sky
and found himself wondering what Maud was doing now.

Maud was lying in her bedroom staring sleepless at the dark.
It had been an awful day. She had done something that she'd
never done in all her life before – saved a penny from her
pay-packet and bought herself a newspaper from the seller in
the street.

She had simply wanted to read about the war. But it hadn't
helped at all. There were pictures of buildings knocked down
from the air, dreadful smoking ruins that the Kaiser's men had
left, and lots of diagrams with arrows that she didn't understand.
Nothing that reassured her about Stan at all. But you'd heard
such awful things – stories about Germans roasting children on
a fire, or cutting women's hands off just to steal their rings. And
that was the enemy that Stan had gone to fight. Suppose they
took him prisoner, what would they do to him? She'd knelt
beside her bed that night and prayed an earnest prayer that God
would keep him from their hands and bring him safely home,
and help him shoot as many of the Hun as possible.

She was comfortless and wakeful. She turned to face the
wall, and as she did so she heard Belinda's voice.

'Maudie? Are you awake?'

'Yes. Sorry if I woke you. I can't get to sleep, somehow.'

'I can't neither,' came the whisper. 'Wait, I'll light the light.'

Maud said nothing. She heard the bed-springs creak, there
was a scuffling on the table, and then a sudden flare as Belinda
struck a match and held it to the taper in the candlestick. In
the flickering shadows Maud could see her sitting on the bed,
blowing on her fingers and shaking out the match.

'Here, put a blanket round you, you'll catch your death of
cold sitting in your nightie and nothing else at all.' Maud set
an example by sitting up herself, and pulling the bedclothes
up around her shoulders as she spoke. 'I'll blame myself if
you go and catch your death of cold tonight. I'm afraid I'm
restless, thinking about Stan.'

'I wasn't sleeping,' Belinda said again. 'Couldn't help thinking about that girl who came. Came in as bold as brass and asked Miss Simms for me – though 'course I wasn't here. Out seeing to a fitting. I wonder who it was. You saw her, didn't you?'

Maud dragged her mind back to the incident in the shop this afternoon. 'Yes. I didn't know her. And I don't think she knew you. She didn't actually ask for you by name – just said she wanted "that red-headed one" and wouldn't tell Madam what it was about.'

'Not one of my customers?'

'I shouldn't think so, no. Not the sort of person who comes here as a rule. Awful working boots and a shapeless sort of blouse and skirt that was too tight for her. When Madam saw her she told me to go and ask the girl to leave. So that is what I did. Politely, mind. I told her you were out and weren't expected back till closing time. She didn't say anything, just stood and stared at me, and wouldn't go away till Miss Simms threatened to call the police to her. Created quite a scene. Madam was wild about it afterwards. I daresay she had a lot to say to you when you got back?'

Belinda made a face and shivered. She still hadn't covered up. 'Had me on the carpet for half an hour at least, wanting to know who it was and what I meant by it. Of course I told her that I had no idea. I don't think she believed me. But I really don't. Unless it was Adam Prosser's sister, or something of the kind.'

'Who is Adam Prosser? Is that your latest beau?'

Belinda twiddled her hair around its rags. 'Oh no, of course, I forgot you didn't know. It's stupid. I should never have got involved in it. But you know Jenny, in the cutting room?' She told Maud the whole story, which made her gasp aloud.

'You're taking messages between the two of them? Blin, you never are? Madam will have your ears for trimmings if she ever gets to hear.'

Belinda made a helpless gesture. 'I know. But once I started it's very hard to stop. If they told tales on me I would be in a fix. The worst thing is, I think Miss Simms suspects. But I don't know who this other girl is, Maud, I really don't. I can't see how Adam would send his sister here – supposing that he had one. It would just make trouble as far as I can see. But who else can it be? Some friend of my brother's, maybe? Or some long-lost relative?'

Maud shook her head. 'If so, and it's important, perhaps they'll come again – even if they only wait for you outside the shop this time.'

Belinda said, slowly, 'Yes, perhaps you're right. Let's hope it's only that. But we aren't going to solve it in the middle of the night. In the meantime, I suppose we'd better try and get some rest.' She got back into bed and blew the candle out.

But it was almost dawn before Maud drifted off to sleep, and whoever the girl who had been looking for Belinda was, she didn't come again.

# Four

Madam had taken to watching Belinda like a hawk. It had been the same all week, ever since that wretched girl had come to ask for her – and still Belinda didn't have the first idea who it might be. Just as well it hadn't been a chap, Belinda thought, or none of her denials would have been believed. Even as it was she couldn't do a thing without feeling that her every move was being monitored. It made life jolly awkward, especially with Jenny pestering her again to take a note to Adam next time she left the shop.

'I can't,' Belinda told her for the umpteenth time. She was up in the sewing-room, and had thought herself alone, taking a bolt of lining-material for a costume from the shelf, when Jenny had seized the moment to sidle up to her and murmur her request.

Belinda looked around. There was nobody in sight. 'I've told you,' she whispered urgently. 'They've got their eye on me. They won't even let me go and do home fittings any more; they've sent Maud out instead. Don't tell me that it's just coincidence. Madam, for some reason, has got it in for me.' Belinda was so aggrieved she raised her voice a touch. It was clear that she was suspected of something untoward and – for once – she had done nothing to occasion it.

'But . . .' Jenny began, but she was interrupted by a cough. Miss Simms was standing at the corner of the stairs.

'Miss Richards, when you have finished whispering up here, Madam would like you in the fitting-room downstairs. Miss Porter and her mother are waiting in the shop and she insists on having you advise them on her new winter coat. And you, Miss Liskey, have work to do, I think.' She stood back to let the girls go past with such an arch expression on her face that Belinda wondered how much of the conversation she had over-heard.

Drat, drat and double drat, Belinda thought, preparing a professional smile to greet Mrs Porter with. What if Miss Simms had heard what she'd said about Madam!

She turned to glance behind her. Miss Simms was following her briskly down the stairs, as if intent on catching up with her. As they reached the bottom, she halted on the step and said to Belinda in an undertone, 'Come and see me in my office when you have finished, please. I have something of some import to communicate to you.'

So she *had* been listening! Belinda felt herself turn red, and it was very hard to concentrate on Miss Porter's chattering.

'This black is so awfully draining, don't you agree, Mamma? Especially when one has fair colouring like mine. It's so very aging too. But I suppose one can scarcely wear anything more lively nowadays. Everyone's in mourning with this dreadful war – even if one isn't, one's acquaintance is. Though it is so dreary, don't you think? I shall look like a shop-girl in a uniform.'

Her mother gave her a pained, reproachful look. 'My dear!'

'Even the Queen is wearing black this season, I believe,' Belinda said automatically, remembering something she'd seen in Maudie's newspaper. Mrs Porter flashed her an apprecia-tive smile.

Her daughter sighed. 'I suppose you're right. I would have favoured emerald or at least a deep maroon, but really one daren't order anything but black. Though one might have a fur tippet around the neck, perhaps, and just a touch more fullness in the sleeves.'

Belinda was obliged to smile and nod and get out her tailor's chalk. She marked the place to ease the seam – though frankly it fitted perfectly exactly as it was – but her mind was hardly on the coat at all. What was it Miss Simms wanted to talk to her about? She could hardly wait to show the Porters out, but when – after a long debate about a pair of matching gloves – they did depart at last, she hardly dared to go and knock on the office door.

'You wanted me?' she said.

Miss Simms looked up at her, as thin and grey and sharp as one of the knitting needles Grandma used for socks. 'I did, young lady, and I won't mince words. There's been a young man hanging around the shop again today, while you were in the room upstairs. I warn you, Miss Richards, it's just not good enough.'

Belinda was astonished. 'But I didn't . . .'

Miss Simms held up a bony, calloused hand. 'I haven't said anything to Madam as yet, of course, but this time I shall be obliged to do so if it occurs again. This is the third or fourth occasion we've had this kind of thing. Please use your influence to keep your friends away, or I can't answer for the consequence. We can't tolerate these people hanging round the shop – they put the clients off. And don't say it's not a friend of yours. I went out myself to speak to him and tell him to move on, and he asked for you by name. I told him that you weren't available and that you wouldn't be at any other time.'

Belinda's mind was racing. That blessed Adam Prosser, she thought, that's who it must be. She was tempted to burst out with the truth – that it was Jenny Liskey he was looking for – but Miss Simms was still speaking in her severest tone of voice. 'Madam is beginning to feel the pinch, you know – people aren't buying dresses like they used to, with this war – and you will be lucky if she doesn't lay you off. If it were not for your popularity with some especial customers, I think she would have done it yesterday.' She gave a little cough. 'I don't want to know, but if you are relaying messages on behalf of some young man, I advise you very strongly to desist. Is that clear, Miss Richards?'

Belinda gulped. She could not believe her luck. 'Yes, Miss Simms,' she managed. And then, as if it had been forced from her, 'How did you discover? What did Adam say?'

Miss Simms raised her eyebrows and looked down her nose. She looked like a giraffe. 'I know nothing about Adam. And there was the young woman who called here yesterday. Wanted you to take a message to some young man from her. I should by rights have told Madam at once, but I was young myself once, and if . . . well, never mind. Get back to your work. I have already been too lenient. I shall not warn you again.'

This left Belinda puzzled. It made no kind of sense. There was no point in trying to defend herself – and what was worse, she could not prevent it happening again. She couldn't even talk to Maudie, since she was out today, doing the house visits Belinda should have been doing herself.

She was so distracted she made a mess of Miss Porter's wretched sleeves and had to take the eased seams out and do them all again.

Maud was thoroughly enjoying her days out of the shop. Mrs Knighton had been so kind to her, sent the maid in with a cup of tea and everything, though the alteration took a dreadfully long time by hand, when it could have been done in the workshop in a quarter of the time. She had wanted her winter cape re-trimmed and turned – it was good worsted wool; you couldn't get material of that kind, with the war – and perhaps she wouldn't have liked to bring it in, and advertise that she wasn't having new for Christmas, like she might have done, but only having the same cloth made up inside out. Of course it didn't need cutting, or anything like that, and it was a simple shape that rather lent itself, but it had been a fidget making sure the earlier wear and stitching didn't show, and hiding the fluff from what had been the seams. It would have been much quicker to have done it by machine. Perhaps she'd speak to Madam and see if it was possible to take a hand-one with her, if she went another time. They weren't all treadle machines in the sewing-room.

She was so intent upon her thoughts she hardly saw the cart until it drew up close to her, and she looked up to see the driver grinning down at her. She was on the point of speeding up her step and hastening away – she didn't care to be spoken to by strangers in the street – but the cart-driver forestalled her by sweeping off his grimy cap, revealing a mop of tousled curly hair, and saying most politely, ''Scuse me, miss. Pardon me for speaking and delaying you like this, but are you Maud, by any chance? I see you come from Madam Raymond's dress shop in the town.' He gestured towards the box of trimmings that she was carrying, which said 'Madam Raymond – Ladies' Modes' discreetly on the top.

He was strikingly good-looking, in a film-star sort of way – like the photographs you sometimes saw outside the cinema. Not that Maud had ever been inside to see a moving-picture show, but she'd looked at the posters many times. This boy had a sort of Valentino look – slim, dark-haired and tall, with bold brown eyes that looked you up and down – and he had a cheeky confidence, as if he were really a sheik of Araby, in spite of his grimy work clothes and the coal dust on his face.

Maud felt quite uncomfortable in his company. She said, 'Well, what about it?' in a tone of voice so sharp it would have done credit to Aunt Jane.

He jumped down from the coal cart and hitched the reins around a gas lamp that was conveniently nearby. 'Thing is,' he said, and then paused, as if embarrassed. 'I wonder if a girl came, hanging round the shop? Asking for Belinda Richards?'

'And suppose there was?'

His face had clouded suddenly. 'I was afraid of that. It's about Belinda. You know her, I expect?'

Maudie looked at him. This must be one of Blin's admirers, then. Well, you had to hand it to her; he was a handsome chap – though Blin hadn't mentioned anything about a coalman in her list of beaux. It was almost a pity that he was spoken for, she thought, though she wouldn't really have swapped anyone for Stan. Still, it made her a bit uncomfortable, his standing close to her like that. She said, 'I know Miss Richards. Yes of course I do.' She took a step away.

His voice was just a murmur. 'The thing is, I haven't seen her for a little while. I want to get a message . . .' He tailed off again. 'I don't know what's been said.'

Maud was struck by inspiration. 'You're never Adam Prosser? Well, you ought to be ashamed.' But it wasn't Adam. She could tell by the perplexed and worried look that spread across his face.

'Who is Adam Prosser?'

She shook her head and smiled apologetically. 'Not you, it would appear. I'm sorry I spoke sharply. Who are you then, and what is it you want?'

'Name's Jonah, miss. Jonah Lotts – like it's written on the cart. I used to walk out with Belin— Miss Richards for a time. But I hear there was a girl down at the shop the other day, might have been spreading rumours about me that weren't true at all. Blackening my name because she was after me herself. I didn't want . . .' He stopped.

'You didn't want Belinda to think badly of you?' she supplied.

'That's it exactly, miss. I did come down the other day and try to put it right, but it didn't do no good. Not dressed like this, of course – I had come from a funeral and I looked something like. Looked almost like a customer, or so you would have thought. But some rake-handle of a woman came out and chased me off.'

Maud tried not to smile at the description of Miss Simms. 'If you hoped to make things better, I'm afraid you made it worse. I heard all about it – though of course I wasn't there. Belinda got an awful wigging over it, I know. Madam doesn't like us having followers, even after hours, and especially not people coming to the shop. Lucky she didn't send Belinda packing there and then.'

'Well, tell her I'm sorry,' the young coalman said. 'Tell her I'll look for her on Sunday afternoon as usual, and not to take any notice of what that creature said.'

'If you mean that skinny girl that came into the shop, she didn't say anything, as far as I'm aware. Wanted to talk to Belinda, I believe, and when she couldn't she just went away.' It wasn't quite the way of it, of course, but Maud didn't want to mention the threat to call the police – it didn't do the shop's reputation any good – and her version seemed to satisfy the boy. He looked quite relieved.

'You will take the message to Belinda, all the same? I'll see her by the bandstand, the way I used to do.'

But when he mentioned the word 'message', Maudie was alarmed. She shook her head. 'I'll say that I saw you, I'd do that anyway, and I'll tell her what you said, but I don't want to be a messenger between the two of you. There's quite enough of that going on at present as it is. Now, if you'll excuse me, I have things to do. I was hoping to go home and see my people after work; there might be a letter from my intended – he's serving overseas.' It gave her a sudden pleasure to have said the words, and she was pleased to see him go a little pink around the ears as he unhitched his animal and climbed up on the cart.

'Sorry to have held you up, miss, but thank you very much.' And off he went, clopping quickly down the street.

There was indeed a note from Stanley when she finally got home. It didn't really say much, except that he was now in France, in some sort of warehouse waiting to move on. It was days ago by this time, so it was old news, but it was comforting to see his writing, nonetheless. He couldn't tell her any more, he said, because it was not allowed, but he was safe and he would write again as soon as possible. Even then one sentence had a big black line through it, as if it had been censored – which it most likely had.

Of course she was expected to read it out aloud, but the family was sympathetic in their different ways. Father said, 'God bless him. You send him our love,' and Tully went upstairs and said a prayer for him.

Aunt Jane's contribution was mixing up some ink and fixing a new steel nib on to the family pen. She said, rather gruffly, 'There's a new blotter too. Got it special for you when the letter came. Thought you could do with it. Do him good and cheer him up to have some news from home. Now here's a cup of tea, and I've saved a bit of heavy cake for you to have as well. So you go in the front room and get on with it. I've made the fire up in there. Write him a nice long letter. Nothing soppy, mind. You never know who else'll read it. He'll know what you mean.'

And it was to be hoped he did, she thought, just as she'd done herself. She wrote him several pages, all about her news, and addressed it neatly in her most careful hand. Then she went back to the kitchen with the envelope.

'You put it up there behind the clock.' Aunt Jane was struggling with needles and thin grey knitting wool making shapeless socks that made your feet hurt just to look at them. She nodded at the mantelpiece. 'I'll take it down and post it at the same time I take these. It's the knitting bee tomorrow. I'll have this finished then.'

But Father put the letter in the pocket of his coat. I'll drop it in the post box on my way to work. Some nice neat hand-writing you've got there, Maudie. It's a credit to your school. You should see the awful scrawls that some people seem to think will get them a post in the railway office now. We've had to turn them down though we're short of applicants – but we'll have to do something because so many men have gone. They are talking about taking women after Christmas, if this goes on much longer – so there you are, Maudie, there's a chance for you.'

He was only fooling, but Aunt Jane scowled at him. 'Don't be so stupid, Wilfred. You'll give the girl ideas. What kind of job is that for a nice, well-brought-up girl? Down the station all hours with a lot of men. Don't you take no notice, Maudie.'

Maudie smiled. 'I won't do. I like it where I am. But if I don't get back sharpish they'll have locked me out, and then I shall be looking for a position somewhere else.'

And it was a near thing too, although she hurried all the way.

Jonah was cursing himself for six kinds of a fool. He could not get the meeting in the street off his mind. That girl for one thing. She was remarkable – different from any other girl he'd ever met. Clever as a kitten and cool as strawber-ries. Not exactly pretty, like Belinda was, but there was something most alluring in the set of her small head, the unselfconscious figure and the bouncing curls. And the way she looked at you, with those cool appraising eyes, and held her chin up proudly – it made you feel that it would be very nice to . . .

But there was no chance of that. She'd made it very plain. She'd talked of her 'intended' with that special tone of voice, and Jonah could take a hint if it was broad enough. It was the same tone of voice she'd used to tell him off for causing trouble down the shop. Perhaps, after all, it wasn't very wise to go, not even in the best suit he saved for funerals.

It had been rather fortunate, the way that it had turned out. The plain girl at the chapel had died, quite suddenly – ate a nut or something, and choked herself to death, and by the time they found her it was much too late. They gave the notice out at chapel about the funeral and he'd seized the chance to go – it gave him the opportunity to get out of the rounds, which had been a proper ordeal lately, because of Lily-Anne.

She had started haunting him. It was unnerving. She ought to be at work, but almost every afternoon these last few days he would turn a corner and she'd be waiting for him. Sometimes she shouted after him and sometimes she just stared. In the end he had to stop and have it out with her. People would be talking and it would get back to Ma.

'What you doing, following me around? Won't do you any good. I told you, I don't want any part of it. Nothing to do with me.' He had stopped the General, but he didn't get down from the cart.

'You don't know that. Might have been!' she said, coming over to gaze up at him. 'You were pleased enough to have me, when you had the chance. Well, now you can, for always. Wouldn't you like that? I won't ask a lot. I'm not afraid of working, and I'd look after you. Scrub and clean and cook and wash your shirts for you. Just give me the chance.' She put her hand up on the cart.

'I'll give you the chance to get off down the street,' he said, making as if to strike her fingers with the whip. 'Trying to trap me into marriage, when it isn't mine at all. There's laws against that sort of thing, I shouldn't be surprised. Go on – get off with you before I call the police.'

'It's a free country,' she retorted. 'I can stand here if I want.' But she took her hand away, and said in a different tone of voice, 'Anyway, where else am I supposed to go? They'll put me up the workhouse, like my Auntie Nell. Terrible it is. You've got nothing but a bedstead in a great big row, with a whole lot of other women – most of them are old. Not a scrap of comfort and not much to eat, but they wake you up at daybreak and you have to work all day . . .'

'That's how it's called the workhouse,' he said cleverly, but she just flung a withering glance at him.

'You wouldn't joke about it, if you'd ever been. Great stone baths like horse-troughs they put you in, and make you scrub all over with carbolic every month. Like a blooming prison, except in some ways worse, cause at least in a prison there's hope of getting out. Most people up the workhouse are there until they die.' She sounded awfully bitter, but at least she didn't cry or shout and carry on like she had done before. 'They would have to drag me to make me go up there.'

'Well, what am I to do about it?' he said sullenly. 'It isn't my affair. Now, I've told you, I got work to do. Go away and leave me be, or I will call the law.'

She did start shouting then. 'Is that all you can say? I know what it is. It's that red-head, isn't it? The one I saw you with. Well, I've found out where she works. I'll go and tell her what kind of man you are, you see if I don't.'

So, when the opportunity arose to go down to Madam's shop next day, looking half decent, he had taken it. It just meant attending the funeral service first. He had wondered if he would get away with doing that at all, but Ma was actually quite sympathetic, when it came to it.

'There you are then! I was right. I told your father so. What an awful shame. Just when you had found yourself a nice young woman, too. Don't look at me so startled; I can read you like a book. You've been preening in the mirror ever since you two were introduced, and you're always off out somewhere on your own these days. And wanting a hot kettle every Friday lunchtime for a wash, not to speak of brushing down your working clothes, like Lord Muck himself. Doesn't take a mind-reader to know it was a girl.'

Jonah didn't know he'd been so obvious. He felt himself turn pink. 'Can I take time off for the funeral, though?'

His mother patted him – a thing she never did. 'You've been looking stricken all the week, ever since she died. I feel for you, my son. I only wish you'd had a chance to bring her home to tea. Course you must go and send her off, if you've a mind to go. Your Pa and I will manage for the afternoon.'

So he had attended the funeral. Her family were surprised, but flattered, though he wouldn't stay afterwards for sandwiches and cake. He'd gone straight to Madam Raymond's, but, as he'd said to Maud, he couldn't find Belinda. But perhaps it was all right. Lily-Anne had not said anything about him, it seemed – perhaps he'd frightened her into shutting up and leaving him alone after all. In any case, he hadn't seen her since, not even on his rounds.

Of course he'd promised to meet Belinda now, which hadn't been his plan, but somehow she didn't seem to be the threat she used to be. And there was the question of this Adam

Prosser, too, the one Maud had talked about. Another admirer, by the sound of it. Perhaps it was that skinny fellow he'd glimpsed her with that day. But what had they been up to, that he 'ought to be ashamed'?

Jonah could imagine. He whistled. Surely not? A pretty girl like that! And she was not the type – wouldn't even let him put a hand on her. She was far too good for that threadbare bag of bones.

If anyone was going to win Belinda, it would be Jonah Lotts.

# Five

It was cold in the trenches. Funny thing, when there was so much fire and smoke around. But it had been getting colder ever since they first arrived, and by this time it was perishing.

Cold that got inside your skin and seemed to freeze your bones, no matter how much you tried to wrap yourself against it in your coat. When you returned from the front line to the trenches further back – as you did, if you were lucky, every twelve or thirteen days before they turned you round and sent you back again – your feet had gone all white and funny with the damp. You couldn't get them dry: out here your socks and boots were always full of mud.

There was to be a box at Christmas, it was rumoured, and that cheered them quite a lot. Oxo cubes were promised, as well as cocoa and all sorts of useful things. There had already been some presents – a box of knitted comforts, sent from the Red Cross, had reached them in the rearward lines when they were in respite. It was a bit assorted, but very welcome: socks and gloves and balaclavas. Stan had been lucky and got a pair of socks, and for days he'd had the double luxury of having warm, dry feet, and two letters from Maudie that had finally caught up with him. But yesterday they had come up to the front line again, and already everything was just as wet as it had been before. Back to the endless roaring of the guns and the pervasive smell of death. There were so many unburied corpses now that they were used to it.

It was the cold, as much as anything, that was keeping him awake, though he could not deny that he was anxious, too. They were due to make a new all-out assault at dawn to try to take the ridge. They had lost an awful lot of men the last time they'd attacked. You couldn't help be anxious when you knew what was to come.

It was relatively quiet – the calm before the storm – though there were still odd bullets and shells whizzing overhead, shaking the ground around the position where they were currently dug in. This trench was more dangerous than usual, in fact. It had been built by Jerry to face the other way, and taken over just a day or two before, by the company which Stan and his group had so recently relieved. But reinforcing it from their side it had been a major job.

Other men were stirring, too strung up to sleep. He could hear them down the trench. Somebody coughing, and someone muttering. Saying prayers, most likely, though the greatest blessing would have been a good night's sleep. Stan would have been glad of oblivion himself. He was so exhausted, after all these weeks of war, that he would have slept through a bombardment if he were only warm enough. Or so he told himself. It didn't help one's judgement to be awake all night.

As if in answer to his thoughts another shell burst nearby, showering bits of debris over everything. It was a close thing. You never knew which one would have your name on it, but that one wasn't his. There were bits of people who hadn't been so lucky buried in the mounds of mud outside. But he was still alive.

He leaned out of his dug-out and peered up at the sky. It was clear and crisp and moonlight, grotesquely beautiful, and he could see the sentry standing on the platform of the look-out post nearby. It was Sawyer, who had recently come back to them again. Only a flesh-wound in the thigh, apparently, but it had altered Sawyer – at least as far as bullying other people was concerned. Or rather, his injury had given him a personal grudge against the Hun and all his aggression was now directed towards them. He stood at the ready and – though he had a periscope – poked his head up above the sandbags now and then.

Even now, as Stan watched him, Sawyer raised his gun, took careful aim and fired off a round towards the German lines. Stan swung his feet out of his cubby hole and squelched along to him.

'Something moving, Private?'

'Somebody crawling, over there against the ridge. It wasn't one of ours. I think I saw him off though.' There was frost on Sawyer's shoulders but he flashed a smile.

'Hope so,' Stan said grimly. 'You might give them the range. Don't want them attacking as we go across. Won't be long either, by the look of it.' He nodded to the east, where the sky was already faintly lightening.

It seemed that the top brass had the same idea. A moment later came the order for the company to rouse. Men tumbled from their dug-outs, stiff and bleary-eyed. Cold fingers clamped around welcome mugs of tea, but few men had the appetite for any bread and jam. Nobody was talking. You could smell the fear. The trench was full of anxious faces.

Then the signal came.

Captain Rawlings was the first to move. 'Come on, chaps. Follow me!' And he was up and over and making for the ridge. The others followed, slithering and scrambling up the ladders with their guns. Stan's duty was to help them, tick them off the list.

'Good luck, sir!' That was Tregurtha, panting, and then he too was gone. Then went Sawyer – though he might have been excused, having been on sentry duty half the night. Stan and Charmer were among the last to go, scrabbling to the surface up rungs slippery with mud. All along the trench the same thing was happening, hundreds of misty figures emerging in the half-light. There was a moment's silence, and then all hell broke loose.

Whether it was Sawyer's firing earlier, or whether it was because Fritz himself had built the trench, the Jerries seemed to know exactly where it was and their range was immediately accurate. B Company was surrounded by a storm of deadly fire. Men began falling, all along the line – some stopped in an instant, dying in mid-stride, others less fortunate lay writhing on the ground.

'Keep moving!' Captain Rawlings gestured forward with his gun, and immediately crumpled, his stomach shot away. Stan rushed towards him and a shell flew overhead. It buried itself in the landscape not very far away, blowing several people into fragments as it went and showering mud and shrapnel over everything. Stan cowered by the captain, who was clearly dead, and realized there was no possibility of advancing into this.

He crawled into a shell-hole, There were others there: Charmer, with his hand clapped to a shoulder wound, and Sawyer lying with a twisted leg. On the rim of the crater there was a lump of bleeding flesh, hard to recognize as a human form. But it was screaming with an unearthly screech. Stan looked towards it.

'Tregurtha!' Charmer managed. He was gasping with the pain. 'Poor little blighter's had both his legs shot off. I was right beside him and I tried to pull him safe, but I could see that the movement only made it worse. Then I got hit myself. I had to leave him. He isn't going to last. Wonder it didn't kill him outright. Better if it had.'

'For God's sake, someone shoot him then, and shut up that awful noise,' Sawyer growled through gritted teeth. 'He'll show the snipers where we are and kill the lot of us.'

That was possible, Stan realized. He crawled up to the rim and looked at what was left of his fellow Cornishman. Tregurtha was half-conscious, and he seemed to look at Stan. 'Sir, please, please!' he whimpered, then let out another scream.

Stan raised his rifle and shot him through the head. Tregurtha twitched once, and was silent. Stan crawled back to the hole feeling sick and shaken.

'You had to do it,' Charmer said, but Stan made no reply. He was almost grateful when there was an explosion close by and something caught him hard, high up between the shoulder blades. 'My turn,' he thought dimly, and that was all he knew.

Belinda had been meeting Jonah again for several weeks, but he seemed very different, somehow, from how he used to be. She was not complaining, but it was not the same. He didn't make advances, for one thing, which made life easier – though rather less exciting and not quite a compliment. She had always quite liked it when she had to fend him off. Now, when she put her hand in his, he seemed to edge away.

'What is it, Jonah?' she said to him at last. It was a cold, damp, December Sunday afternoon, and they were sheltering in the bandstand looking at the sea. 'Don't you like me any more?'

He tried to rally. 'Course I do!' He gave her arm a squeeze. 'Who wouldn't like you, pretty girl like you?'

She made a face at him. 'Well, it doesn't look like it sometimes. I waited for you weeks and weeks, and you never came – and then when I did see you, you went off with someone else.'

'Well, so did you,' he muttered sulkily. 'I saw you talking to a man. That skinny fellow. Adam Prosser – isn't that the name?'

She stared. 'You're never jealous, Jonah! I do believe you are! Silly thing!' She gave his arm a thump. 'There wasn't anything in that. He is just a friend of Jenny's down the shop.' She squirmed a little closer to him on the seat. 'There hasn't been anyone else since I met you.'

'Well, it's just the same with me,' he said. 'That girl was just a friend. Someone I met when I was on my rounds. Not my type at all.' He got to his feet. 'Now are we going to walk or what? I promised Billy that I'd call and see him later on.'

So they went walking, though it was coming on to rain and Belinda's hair was always hopeless when it got damp like that. They didn't have an ice-cream; it was too cold for that. Altogether a disappointing sort of day.

She said as much to Maudie when she came home that night – though of course she had to listen to a lot of chatter first. She didn't really mind. She liked to hear the gossip and her news would wait. Maud had received another note from Stan, all about how the fellows had got some socks and gloves, and how they had comfortable billets on a farm.

Belinda settled herself on the bed and listened patiently as Maudie read it twice. 'At least you know he's safe,' she said. 'When was that written then?'

Maud shook her head. 'Oh, days and days ago. Lord knows what's happened since.' She slipped the precious letter in her pillow slip. 'Sometimes, Blin, I have to envy you. At least with Jonah you know where he is.'

'Know where he is?' Belinda gave a deliberate, hollow little laugh. 'Down the Imperial Hotel with Billy Polkinghorne, most like. He'd be down there every minute if you let him, seems to me, if he isn't actually working or meeting up with me. I aren't sure I like it. He seems to follow Billy in every-thing he does. I know he was down there Friday, and I met him in the street – he was all peculiar and I'd swear he smelled of ale, though he'd tried to disguise it by eating peppermint. Though I suppose it can't be. He is a Methodist.'

Maud turned round from the wash stand, looking scandal-ized. 'You don't really think so?'

Belinda felt she had already said too much. It was the first time she'd admitted her suspicions, even to herself. She shrugged. 'I expect I'm wrong. Anyway, he won't be going there, after the new year. Billy's getting wed. To that girl whose parents keep the sweet shop at the top of North Parade.' Another laugh. 'Only a pity Jonah doesn't follow him in that.'

Maud went over to her own bed and stretched out on it, her hands behind her head. 'You haven't managed to bring him round? I thought you would do, since he was so keen to meet up with you again.'

'No, I haven't!' Belinda turned her back and flounced impa-tiently. Everyone else was decently engaged, and here she was – the oldest of them all – obliged to admit that Jonah hadn't asked. But there was no response, and after a moment she turned around again and burst out crossly, 'He's been proper funny with me, if you want to know. All hot and cold like an April afternoon. Not a bit the way it was. He used to be a devil, and make me laugh aloud, but now he's less lively than a funeral. Really, I don't know what's got into him. I've even thought I might be better off without him, nowadays.'

There, she had said it, and Maud could laugh at her. But her friend just said, in an altered tone of voice. 'He had been to a funeral, you know, when he called here. I told you, didn't I? Dressed up in his best suit and everything. I know what funeral it was, as well. I saw it in a paper. Some girl from the chapel who got something in her throat and choked to death before they got to her. He was in the list of mourners "Mr Jonah Lotts" I thought it was his father, when I read it first, but of course when you think of it, it must have been your friend.'

Belinda turned over and stared up at the wall. There was a crack in the plaster, which you could turn into a snail if you had imagination and looked at it long enough. She said in a strangled little voice, 'You think that's what it was? He had another girl that he was walking out with, and she died?' It would explain his coolness, this last month or two, and why he was so suddenly available again. And if it was true, what was she to do? Take him back and pretend she didn't know? Say no more about it? That was possible. It wasn't like having a living rival, after all. He could hardly change his mind.

Maud seemed to read her mind. 'Needn't have been a special friend of his, I shouldn't think. Might have known her through the chapel. But it must have been a shock. She wasn't more than seventeen, and just to die like that! It makes you realize that there's nothing safe, not even over here. And there was another one in the paper, just the other day. Some kitchen maid from Newlyn, washed up on the rocks. Seems as if she drowned herself – and only just sixteen. Awful, isn't it? I wonder what drives a person do a thing like that? Lost her fellow overseas, perhaps.'

Maud was going to start worrying about her Stan again. Belinda said shortly, 'Even if she did, I don't see how it helps – her being dead as well.' She knew it was unkind and she added hastily, 'Though, I suppose, I would be terribly upset if anything happened to Jonah and I was left behind.'

'Well, it isn't likely, is it, with him being in Penzance?' Maud sounded rather bitter, though she said it with a laugh. 'So just count your blessings. Now, I don't know about you, Belinda Richards, but I need to get some sleep. We'll be busy in the morning, with the Christmas things in.'

It didn't seem like Christmas, somehow, with the war. It wasn't so much that there were minor shortages – though some things, like dried fruit, were difficult to get and treats like tinned peaches had vanished from the shelf – but nobody was really in a festive frame of mind.

People did their best, of course. Shops dressed their windows and put coloured lanterns up. Fir trees were dragged to the larger houses in the town for use as Christmas trees, and in the poorer homes the children wove greenery into Christmas hoops and hung them from the ceiling to deck with Christmas fruits.

Aunt Jane had stuck a branch of a pine tree in a pot, and Father had made some wooden ornaments, so Tully would have the pleasure of hanging them all up, and seeing it lit with candles late on Christmas Eve.

Maud had already sewn and wrapped the household gifts: a handkerchief for Father, another for Aunt Jane, and a cloth bag for Tully to take to school with him when, in a month or two, he was old enough to go. She had made a present for Stan too – a warm scarf, neatly finished, and tucked up inside of it, a single sea-pink, pressed and dried and mounted on a card on which she had written 'From Penvarris, with Love'. The other one she'd given him would have decayed by now, but she knew he would remember – so long as it arrived. She had sent it weeks ago, but there had been no word.

Madam let the girls go early after lunch on Christmas Eve. She always closed the shop at midday on the twenty-fourth, and didn't open up again till after Boxing Day, so for many of the girls it was a rare chance to go home. This year was no exception. There were very few customers that day in any case – a gentleman looking for kid gloves for his wife, and one woman seeking last-minute underwear – but most people had bought their Christmas outfits long ago, and the garments in the window weren't festive ones this year, but sober articles in heliotrope and brown. As Belinda said, people weren't wearing bright colours any more.

Madam had put up a box for all the girls: a large length of ticking, another length of cloth, a little pack of trimmings and a reel of thread. The gift was generous, though Madam always selected materials that she'd had in stock and couldn't sell. Maudie found herself with figured muslin in a striking mauve, though shirting or plain cotton would have been more use.

Still, she was humming happily as she left the store, carrying her bundle tied up with a string. There was time, for once, to walk down Causewayhead, looking in the windows, and enjoying the displays – pigs' heads in the butcher's, plums and apples at the fruiterers, and in the chemist's window, between the usual coloured jars, was a festive range of soaps and talc and threehalfpenny bottles of Cornish Violet scent.

There were mince pies at the bakers for a penny each, so she stopped to buy a few, and some carol-singers were singing at the top of Causewayhead. But it didn't feel like Christmas, not even when she got home and found Tully up to his ears in paste and paper chains, and Aunt Jane trying to supervise and put the pudding on.

'There's something for you, up behind the clock, since you've come at last,' Aunt Jane said frostily, seizing a tray of jam tarts from the oven just before they burned. 'And when you've read it, you can come and give a hand.'

Maud took the letter. It was from Mrs Hoskins and it was very short. Stan had been picked up, wounded but alive, and taken to a hospital back behind the lines. 'They are hoping that he'll make a full recovery, but he needs more operations and it will take some time. If he makes good progress, they will send him home on leave to rest and recuperate before he goes back to the front. We thought you'd like to know. Tell your father we've got some pork for you. We'll put it on the guard's van on Boxing Day, if he can pick it up. Love to all at Christmas, from the Hoskinses.'

For a moment Maud didn't know whether to laugh aloud or cry. Stan was safe, but wounded. Then she turned to Tully. 'Stanley's coming home,' she said, and went to help him with his paper-chains.

# Part Three
## Easter 1915 – May 1916

# One

It was after Easter before Stan came home again. Maud had been ready to brave Madam and actually ask for time off to go up to London and see him in the army hospital, but Mrs Hoskins wrote to tell her that she had better not.

They had gone up to visit, she said, and he wasn't up to it. He was making a good recovery from his wound, but he was very weak, and after ten minutes he had had enough. It would be better for Maud to come and see him at the farm as soon as he got home. Clearly he wasn't going to be well enough to catch the train to her.

Once he started writing letters again, Maud could tell for herself that he had changed. The handwriting was different, for one thing, all peculiar like a child's. It was his left shoulder that had been so badly hurt, but for a long time he wasn't well enough to write, and even when he did get round to it the notes were very short and didn't really tell her anything at all. A far cry from the long, amusing letters that she used to receive.

Of course, she realized he'd had a narrow squeak. Mrs Hoskins had let her know the details, as soon as they had found out. A piece of metal had gone right through him from the back – grazed a rib and shoulder blade and smashed his collar bone – but he had been lucky; it had missed the vital bits. All the same, it had made a nasty mess and he had lost enormous quantities of blood, so naturally it was going to take him time to be himself again, the letter said. When she saw him, Maud would understand.

So here she was now, getting off the train in a bonnet that she had newly trimmed especially for him, with silk ribbon roses that she'd made herself, though luxuries like that ribbon were hard to come by these days, and had become so expensive she'd had to save for weeks. Stan wasn't outside waiting with the cart, as she had half-expected he would be. Only Mr Hoskins was there, but he was welcoming. He got down to help her up, gave her a warm hug, told her how pretty she was looking in her hat and promised pasties when they got back to the farm. But he didn't mention Stan until she asked outright.

'How is he getting on, then? Doing better now he's home?'

Mr Hoskins nodded slowly. 'I believe he is. But it's hit him, Maudie. Hit him very hard. More than I expected, though he doesn't say a lot. And he's gone that pale and thin. I'm afraid you'll see a sorry change in him.'

She would hardly have recognized him as the man she'd known, sitting so listlessly by the fire with a blanket round his knees. He did look up as she came in, and for a moment there was a ghost of the old smile, but then his face went back to being like a mask again.

She went to him, family and all, and kissed him on the head. He took her hand and squeezed it in his undamaged one. 'Hello, Maudie.' It was still his voice.

'How are you, Stanley?'

'Doing well, they say.'

'You don't look very perky. Was it very bad?'

He looked up at her, and there was nothing in his eyes. He said, with an effort, 'Bad enough. But don't let's dwell on that. I'm getting over it. Tell me about you. How's that little Tully liking it at school?'

So she made conversation about other things. It was an awkward meal. Stanley hardly spoke, while the rest of the family tried to make up for it. He ate his food as if he couldn't taste a crumb – though no one made pasties like Mrs Hoskins did – and Maud could see his hand was trembling as he drank his cup of tea.

After they had finished, Maud helped to clear the plates, and Mrs Hoskins sent her outside for some water from the pump. It was clearly done on purpose, because she came out, after her and took the opportunity to murmur in her ear. 'I'm some sorry, Maudie, but you can see how Stanley is. Don't go running off with the idea that it's just you that makes him glum. In fact I saw him smile when you came in the room, and I haven't seen him do that hardly since he came.' She took the water bucket that Maud had filled up at the pump. 'It's like he's gone off somewhere else, and can't get back to us. I wish I could get him outside in the air, but he won't do anything but sit there by the fire – and shivering sometimes, as if he's chilled through to his bones. And he doesn't sleep at nights – you hear him tossing something awful. I'm at my wit's end with him. Still, I suppose it's early days. I think that seeing you has cheered him up a bit.'

So Maudie made a double effort after that. She told him little stories and tried to make him laugh, and was actually rewarded with a faint smile once or twice. But her greatest triumph was to take him for a walk. She asked him to take her out to see the cats, and he did go with her, just out to the barn.

He looked even thinner and weaker standing up, and she slid her arm through his as much to steady him as to show affection. But he stiffened up.

'Here are your cats then,' he said gruffly, and disengaged himself.

She turned to face him. 'What is it, Stan?' She said it gently. 'There's something troubling you. You don't want to talk about it, and I don't want to pry, but you'll have to tell me something because I won't leave it be. If you don't want me, say so, but if it isn't that, at least give me some kind of hint so I can understand.'

He looked at her then, so sadly it struck her to the heart. 'Not want you? How could anyone not want a girl like you? It's me, I'm just a ruin. I can't ask you to wait. I'll release you from your promise. You find someone else. I'm just not worth having, and that's the truth of it.'

'I don't want to be released. I want Stan Hoskins, not anybody else.'

He groaned. 'You wouldn't say that if you knew the truth.'

'What is it, Stan? You've met a girl in France?'

That roused him. 'Don't be so wet! Of course I haven't!' He almost laughed. 'Never had a chance – and wouldn't know a word that they were saying, anyway!'

It was a flash of the old Stan and she pounced on it. 'Well there's nothing else you could have done would make me change my mind.' She took his arm again. 'It's only pain that makes you talk like that. You've suffered something terrible

– no wonder you are down. But you'll get over it. And even if you don't, we two will manage if we've got each other – you see if we don't.'

He turned away and pretended to be staring at the cats. 'It's not the pain. You're right, I'm getting over that. But there are other things. Suppose I killed a man? How do you get over an awful thing like that?'

A flood of understanding and sympathy came washing over her. So that was it! There had been a lot of talk about that kind of thing – letters in the papers and all sorts, how killing was sin, and people with a conscience should refuse to volunteer. The vicar at St Evan, where she sometimes went, had been talking about it in his sermon just the other day, pointing out that in war these things were different and that David and all sorts of holy people had been soldiers too. 'A man can slay Goliath and also write the psalms,' he'd said.

She had thought it rather peculiar at the time, but now she was grateful to recall his words and offer them to Stan. 'I can understand,' she finished. 'Breaking the commandments and all that sort of thing. But these are special circumstances. God will understand. Come and talk to the vicar, if you like. He'll put your mind at rest.'

There was a strange expression on Stan's face. 'You really think he might?'

She nodded. 'I'm sure of it. You come down and see him and you can . . .' She broke off. She had been about to suggest that Stan ask about the banns, but it didn't seem appropriate with him in this frame of mind, and she just said, lamely, 'Come and see me too.'

'Well, I'll think about it,' Stan said. And after that he did perk up a bit, and a fortnight later he did come to Penzance, though it took him all his effort just to get there on the train. He didn't go to see the vicar, not that time nor the next, and she didn't feel able to mention it again – so nothing was done about the wedding banns.

It was the Whitsun holiday and the day was warm, but Jonah was dressed up in his best suit again. Father was upstairs getting changed, and all – done up like a turkey-cock in his Sunday waistcoat, with high old-fashioned collars, and his hunter watch and chain. Foolish, Jonah thought, all this for a girl.

But Ma had insisted, and what Ma said went. 'If you are bringing that young woman here for tea, we'll dress up proper. I've made a bit of fuss. I've got out the lace tablecloth and the china tea set that I had when I was wed. There's ham and bread and pickle, and cake for afterwards. A tin of peaches too. Show her that the Lotts know how to do things right.'

Jonah made a face. Ma's bread and cake weren't what they were these days. She said it was the flour, and perhaps it was – there were rumours that the government were putting chalk in it, to make it stretch out further – but whatever it was, her baking didn't seem to taste the way it used to do. Though Belinda wouldn't care. From what she said about her grandmother, you were lucky to get anything home-baked from there at all.

Finally he was taking Belinda home to meet his family. He'd put it off as long as possible – she'd been dropping hints since Christmas – but it had come to it at last, and to his astonishment his Ma had welcomed it.

'Well, I'm glad you've found someone, Jonah, after all. When that poor girl you were so keen on had that awful accident, poor thing, you were that pale and shocked I was worried for your health.'

Jonah said nothing. No wonder he'd been pale. He had been really worried when they found Lily-Anne's body washed up on the shore. He had been seen with her, he must have been, a dozen times or more, and everyone was talking about the suicide – how she'd been turned out from her job, and might have been with child. But no one had connected it with him at all, it seemed.

Except for Billy Polkinghorne. He had been a bit suspicious when the tale had first come out. 'Here, there's been some little kitchen maid from Newlyn has gone and drowned herself. They didn't give her name. Never your one, is it?'

They were drinking Billy's 'llowance in his room again, and they had been talking about Billy's wedding, which, at that time, was still weeks away, so the unexpected question took Jonah by surprise. It almost made him splutter into his pewter pot, but he recovered well enough to shake his head and say, 'Not as far as I've heard. Why ever should it be?' It wasn't actually an outright lie, he told himself.

Billy looked rather doubtful. 'Well, I suppose you'd know.'

'Anyway, wasn't she involved with some lad who signed up and went away?' Jonah took refuge in quoting what the rumours said. It was very likely true, he told himself: – Lily-Anne had got herself in trouble somehow, and it wasn't on account of Jonah Lotts. 'That's what I heard, anyway.'

Drat Billy. He wasn't easily put off. 'Bit of a coincidence though, isn't it, two kitchen girls from Newlyn in the family way?'

Jonah tried to appear cool and unconcerned. 'Must be scores of kitchen maids in Newlyn, I should think. Now, you want me to come down and see you tie the knot? Father'll give me an hour to do it, I expect. And it will be worth having if your in-laws do the spread.' He gulped down the last few mouthfuls and handed back the pewter mug for Billy to refill. 'Nice drop of ale, this. I'll miss our little chats.'

It was an attempt to change the subject, but Billy wouldn't let it rest. He hesitated with the beer jug in his hand. 'Seen her lately, have you?'

So Jonah was cornered into a reply. Why had he told Billy anything at all? He wished he'd never mentioned being in a fix – except it was Billy's information that had got him out of it.

'Seen her once or twice,' he muttered gloomily. 'She was all right last time I set eyes on her. Mind, she wasn't pleased. After what you told me, I let her know that I was wise to all her tricks. But she wasn't suicidal. She was hopping mad.' That much was true, but even to his own ears it didn't seem enough. 'Going to go up country to her family, so she said,' he improvised. That bit about her family was an outright fib and he was aware that his cheeks were flaming red.

But Billy merely nodded and poured out the ale. He had found his own explanation for that telltale blush, it seemed. 'And you've got other fish to fry, these days. Don't go all pink and coy. I saw you the other Sunday with that red-headed girl. Good-looker isn't she? Though I thought you were trying to get away from her?'

Jonah took the mug and took a careful sip. 'Well, perhaps I did. But now I've changed me mind. There aren't so many women who'll look at me nowadays. They all seem to have someone who's gone off to the war.'

Billy nodded sagely. 'I've said to you before – you want

to do like me. There's worse things than marriage to a decent girl. Besides, the government is planning to set up that list of theirs – every man-jack in the country will have to register, say what job he's in and where he lives and all that sort of thing. Send them to essential jobs – that's what they say it's for – but before you know it they'll be marking out the single men and sending them to France. Won't be waiting for them to volunteer. Much better getting wedded; they won't send married men.'

'It's very well for you. You've got a sweet shop at the end of it. I don't want to make a rod for my own back,' Jonah had snorted, wiping his frothy lips across his sleeve and stomping off across the yard.

Of course, all that was months ago by now. But he was coming round to Billy's point of view. Billy was married now, and it seemed to be all right. Annie cooked a decent tea – he'd been there once or twice – and Billy still managed to slip out now and then to join him for a pint of ale at the Imperial Inn, though very often Jonah had to go alone and even when they both went it cost them nowadays. He did miss those old carefree Friday afternoons.

It was getting to be a proper trial these days, going round with the coal. Women coming out and shaking their umbrellas in his face, and giving him white feathers because he hadn't volunteered. Marriage to Belinda would save him from all that, and be a bit of pleasure in bed for him besides – if he could stop feeling guilty over Lily-Anne. Goodness knows that Belinda was keen enough to wed. She'd been thrilled to little pieces when he'd asked her here tonight. Nearly as thrilled as Ma herself.

He looked at his mother now, still fetching things down from the shelf: the gauze cover for the sugar bowl with beads around the end, and the matching one for the jam pot and the milk jug too – a sure sign that there was company expected. Meant to keep the flies off, but they were seldom used.

'Of course this one's not chapel, and she's a forward thing – I remember her coming here to ask for you one time,' Ma said, rubbing the best teapot with her sleeve to polish it. 'I thought she was a shameless hussy at the time, but I won't hold it against her if she's really fond of you. Might be a blessing, really. Won't break her heart so much to know she's

second best. Now, that looks something like. Do we want a
bit of cheese as well, or have we got enough?'

It had been a funny sort of evening at the Lotts, Belinda
reflected later. Jonah's mother, plump and tightly buttoned
like a chair, trying to be welcoming in a special put-on voice,
while her husband – uncomfortable in his collar studs – earned
disapproving scowls for pouring his tea into his saucer ('give
it chance to cool') and folding his bread and butter before
consuming it.

'Manners, Jonah! We've got company!' And Jonah senior
wriggled in his chair, while his son attempted to find neutral
things to say and ended up talking about the price of coal.

Belinda had narrowly avoided disapproval herself earlier.
She would have started eating without waiting to say grace,
if Jonah hadn't mercifully caught her eye and warned her with
a quick shake of the head. Belinda was still looking at him,
rather mystified, when Mrs Lotts came to the table with the
teapot and its stand, and said in a tone of satisfaction, 'Perhaps
our guest would like to bless our food and our humble table?'

Belinda was astonished, but she managed to oblige – though
'Dear Lord, bless our humble food and table to our needs,
Amen,' might not have been entirely what Ma Lotts had in
mind. It made her too embarrassed to say anything much else,
which turned out to be rather fortunate, since she heard Ma
hiss to Jonah a little later on, when he went to get more butter
from the bussa by the door, 'Isn't as forward as I thought she
was. And nice manners too. Look how she crooks her finger
when she holds her cup. Puts your Pa to shame – blowing on
his saucerful of tea like that, and my best china too! Don't
know what on earth the girl will think of us.'

And 'the girl', who had been worried about what they would
think of her, felt so much better that she allowed herself another
piece of cake and even volunteered to help clear away, before
she said goodnight.

'Well, Jonah, don't just stand there like a lummox – even
if you are.' This from Jonah's father, who had come suddenly
to life, as if the prospect of taking off his collars had roused
him into speech. 'Fetch the poor maid 'er hat and coat and
walk down the street with her.'

So there they were, walking down the very lane where they

used to meet to be out of sight of Madam and any watching eyes. They stopped beside the solitary lamp post halfway down. The gas had just been lit and it made a little pool of brightness. He pulled her out of it, into the darker shadows up beside the wall, and put an arm around her, the way he used to do. She raised her face towards him, and he murmured in her ear, 'I think they liked you. Mother did, at least. Wanted me to ask you if you'd come with us, next time there's a slide show down the chapel hall.'

She stepped away from him. It was not what she'd expected. Not at all. Yet he clearly meant it as a compliment. She summoned up a smile. 'Would you like me to?'

'Only if you want to,' he said hastily. 'Of course, I realize it might not appeal. Missionary slides and all that sort of thing. But my Ma would take it very kindly if you came, I know. And it would give us chance to meet. I could always see you home.'

'Like you are doing now, you mean?' She side-stepped his embrace.

'Oh, Belinda! Don't be such a tease.' He reached out to hold her but she eluded him again. She was half-joking, but there was something else that made her draw away.

It was clear that this evening was an important step – taking her home to meet the family. She'd dreamed of a husband and a place that was her own, free from grandmothers and Madam and everybody else – but she could see a different future, suddenly: sharing a house with Jonah's Ma and Pa, tight lips and studs and bodices and disapproving stares, with endless evenings of missionary slides and chapel teas. To say nothing of stories about the price of coal. It didn't seem all that attractive, when it came to it.

Though it was hard to know what else to do, she thought despairingly. You wouldn't want to end up an old maid like poor Miss Simms.

Jonah had caught her by the shoulders and was holding her. 'Oh, come on, Blinnie. Just a little kiss.' He was bending over her to press his lips to hers, when they were interrupted by footsteps coming down the lane. They were in the shadows, but Belinda wriggled free and Jonah made no effort to capture her again. He understood as well as anyone that a girl – especially one of Madam's – must not be found in someone's arms when there were eyes to see.

She seized the moment. 'Goodnight, Jonah. I can walk from here. Thank your mother for the tea.' She seized his hand and shook it, then began to walk away, trying to look completely nonchalant.

'Miss Richards? Belinda? It is you, isn't it?' A figure detached itself from the shadows and stood in the lamplight, fiddling with a hat. A tall thin figure in a battered coat. 'I saw you turn down here. I followed you along.' It was that wretched Adam Prosser. She'd not seen him for months.

'What is it you want?' she called over her shoulder, walking on.

But his next words stopped her in her tracks as a signal halts a train. 'If you have finished . . . talking . . . to your friend, I need to speak to you.' There was no mistaking what those pauses meant. He had seen her with Jonah, and could tell them at the shop.

She turned back to face him. 'Well?' she demanded. 'I hope you don't want me to take a note again. I'll get myself dismissed, and Jenny too. Madame's suspicious; she's still got her eye on me. It's far too dangerous, for the both of us.'

Adam nodded. 'Jenny told me.' She must have looked startled, because he added quickly, 'I've managed to see her for a minute once or twice. Found another way of passing notes to her – put them in a special crevice in the wall. Only she doesn't always get them – children I suppose. And this one is important. I was on my way to post it in our letter-box, but then I saw you come here and I changed my mind. I can't afford to miss her. Say you'll do it, please.'

'I told you. It's too risky.' But she was havering.

He sensed it. 'Doesn't even have to be a note. Just tell her the message. Say . . .' He hesitated. 'Say the funeral is next Saturday. Four o'clock. There'll be a carriage for her.'

Belinda looked at him. 'Well if there's a death, I suppose that's different. You could have come and told her at the shop. Even Madam would have understood. Whose funeral?'

He gave an awkward smile. 'Distant relation, I suppose you might say. Very distant, from her point of view.'

'So distant her parents won't expect her to attend? I see. But you'll be there?'

'Of course. You don't have to tell her that – she'll understand. But that's the problem, see. I don't want to be the one that brings the news. Someone will put two and two together if I do, and stop her going. Better if she tells Madam for herself.'

Belinda nodded slowly. She was still a little bit reluctant to agree, but suddenly another form came looming up at them and a hand fell on her shoulder. 'What's all this, then, Blin?' It was Jonah, looking furious.

She gave him her best smile. 'Someone wanting me to take a message to another girl, that's all.'

'Well, you aren't to do it. I'm not having it. Whispering in the shadows with another man like this.' He turned to Adam. 'Go on, get off with you, before I knock you down.'

He could have done it too – he was big and strong and used to handling heavy weights about – but Adam stood his ground. 'This once, Miss Richards, and I promise you, you'll never see or hear from me again.'

She gave him a quick nod, and then he turned away. She rounded on Jonah. 'Who d'you think you are, Jonah Lotts, telling me what I'm allowed to do and not to do? I'm not married to you yet – nor likely to be if you go on like that! It's only a message about a funeral. I'll pass it on if I've a mind to, thank you very much!'

And she did so, the first chance she got.

# Two

S tan was getting stronger. He could feel it in his bones. He still woke sweating in the night, and found himself scrubbing at his face and hands as if pieces of Tregurtha might be spattered over him, but he was getting stronger – and fairly quickly too.

His parents had a lot to do with it, he knew. His mother's cooking had always been first-rate and now that he was slowly regaining his appetite she tempted him with all his favourite things. After the army kitchens it was paradise. Dad had taken him out into the fields again, as soon as he was fit enough to try, and the fresh air and exercise put colour in his cheeks, though it had taken him weeks to be any use at all. Even Granfer had tried to do his best – went up to his 'secret' hiding-place (under the mattress on the bed, as the whole household knew) and brought down ten shillings, with instructions that Stan was to spend it on tickets to Penzance – 'First class if you've a mind to!'

Stan hadn't done that, of course, but he had taken the opportunity to go down more than once on half-closing day. Maudie's pleasure at seeing him was ointment to his soul. And it needed ointment, he was aware of that. Because, although his body was recovering, he was not the same inside. Apart from Maudie's comfort, nothing seemed to make him feel.

He had become hollow, somehow, as if a part of him had died and he could not be part of the ordinary world of love and hope and happiness and grief. He was doing familiar tasks around the farm, but he was like the mechanical man in the shoe-mender's window – going through the actions automatically, without connecting with the task. Even his smile was like that, painted on his face, when there was nothing but woodenness underneath. He knew it, and was powerless to shake the feeling off. Perhaps, as the doctors told him, things would improve with time.

There were a lot of doctors – more, as time went on. He had to go for check-ups and there were always questions about his state of mind. He tried to answer honestly, but, after lots of scribbling and whispering afterwards, one man would pass him to another and it would start again. They sent him to a medical tribunal in the end, where, Stan knew, they had the power to sign him off for good. The board's examination of his case was scheduled for Whit Monday. There were no holidays from war.

They were very pleasant, all three of them. Sympathetic, too. They took his temperature and made him touch his toes and looked at what they called the 'wound', though it was healed now, and there wasn't much he couldn't do. So perhaps it should not have come as a surprise when the doctor who seemed to be in charge – a round-faced fellow with a twinkle and a big moustache – looked up and said, quite breezily,

'You're doing very well. Good lad. Have to think about getting you back on active service very soon.'

He found himself muttering, 'But . . .'

The doctor looked at him. The twinkling manner had completely disappeared. 'Come now, Hoskins. Where's your self-respect? There's no "buts" about it. You are a serving soldier on convalescent leave. You volunteered for duty, and to duty you shall go, now that you are fit for posting. No sign of shellshock – shakes, paralysis or loss of speech – like some poor fellows have. Your country needs you, and that sort of thing. The army has no patience with malingerers.'

For a moment Stan thought of all the soldiers' tricks he'd heard about – eating a bit of cordite to make your heartbeat skip, swallowing something that got into your skin and turned it yellow like jaundice, or simply rubbing raw onions in your eyes so they looked red and watery – so that you would be passed unfit to go. But he knew it was too late. These doctors had all the notes about him for the last few months and any symptoms would have shown before, so there was no resorting to such coward's acts. He wished he could be certain that he would not have done so anyway, even if he thought he could get away with it, but secretly he feared that he might well have tried.

He squared his shoulders. 'Yes, sir,' he replied. 'I'm ready to go back.' He was an awful liar, he thought grimly to himself, but at least he would not be branded a malingerer. What a way to spend a Whitsun holiday!

Maudie was shattered when she heard the news. She stood, crumpling the letter up into a ball. 'I don't believe it, Blin. Stan's coming down on Sunday, and then he's off again. Only to Reserve Battalion for a training course, for now, but they'll be sending him back to the trenches in a week or two. With his arm and everything.'

Belinda looked up from the dress that she was trimming with black beads and lace. 'Aren't hardly going to send him back without it, I don't s'pose.' She saw Maud's face and coloured, putting down her work. 'Here, I'm sorry, Maud. It isn't a joking matter. It's a shock, that's all. Truth of the matter is, I don't know what to say. Your Stan doesn't seem well enough to go, from what I've seen of him. Though I'm no doctor, mind.'

She was so earnest that Maud didn't snap at her, though the attempts to comfort were no better than the jest. Instead she put the letter into the pocket of her skirt and sat down at the table opposite her friend. She was too upset to speak. She picked up a tricky buttonhole that she was working on, glad to have something to concentrate her mind.

But Belinda was determined to make amends for being flippant, it appeared. She said, in a tone of voice that showed she was concerned, 'I knew it must be something when your Aunt Jane brought it here.'

Maud nodded but did not raise her head, using her tailor's chalk to mark the line with care. Trust Belinda to be curious about a thing like that! 'It said "Most Urgent" on the envelope, so she came down with it,' she said with an effort to keep her voice under control. 'I shouldn't have got it until Sunday, else. Good thing that Madam didn't make a fuss. She doesn't like us having letters sent here as a rule. But I suppose it was difficult to argue with Aunt Jane – she paid my indenture, when all is said and done.'

Belinda said nothing. That was unusual for her. So unusual that Maudie raised her eyes. Belinda had stopped sewing and was frowning at the wall. There was a little silence and then Belinda said in a peculiar sort of voice, 'You wouldn't think she'd mind a letter about a funeral, though.'

Maud stared at her. 'Whatever do you mean? You haven't had bad news about your grandmother?'

Belinda shook her head. 'No – course I haven't. I'd have told you, else. No, it's nothing really. Something someone said. Just there's a funeral this coming Saturday and one of our girls is wanted to go along to it. I was asked to pass on the message – which I did, of course – but I still think they could have written, and arranged it properly. If Madam let you have a letter from Stanley like she did, surely she wouldn't have stood in the way of anything like that.' She picked up another shiny bead and stitched it into place. 'Course, I know that it was only an excuse to meet a man . . .'

Maud found that she was smiling, though she'd thought it was impossible she'd ever smile again. 'So that's why you're so guilty? Well, I shouldn't worry. It isn't your affair. You were asked to pass a message and you did it in good faith. Next Saturday, you say? Funny day to have a funeral. Where is it anyway?'

'I didn't . . .' Belinda began, but she got no further. There was a clattering of footsteps on the stairs and Miss Simms came into the workroom with the two apprentices.

'Miss Richards, Madam wants to know if you are ready with that dress. Mrs Knight has called into the shop and wants to try it on.'

'Three more beads to finish,' Belinda said, and under Miss Simms' gimlet eye she fixed them into place. 'There. It's done!' She picked up the garment and hurried off downstairs. She must have had second thoughts about confiding any more about the funeral, though, because when Maudie tried to ask her later that evening in their room, Belinda refused to give any more details at all.

She just said vaguely, 'Oh, it seems to be all right. I heard the girl asking Madam for permission to attend, and to go home to her folks on Sunday afterwards – seeing it would be after closing time before she got back here, and the shop wouldn't be open till Monday anyway. Madam was a little bit put out – you know how she can be – but she gave permission just this once.' She went over to the wash stand and sat down at the mirror with her back to Maud. 'Getting soft in her old age. First your letter and then this funeral. I wish I had something exciting to look forward to. My only treat this weekend is a Sunday afternoon in that dreary chapel listening to a talk about a leper colony.'

Maud made a face at her friend's reflection in the glass. 'I'd hardly call a funeral any kind of treat.'

Belinda stuck her tongue out in childish reply. ''Tis if you're really going to meet a sweetheart there.'

'But didn't Jonah ask you to the chapel tea?'

'It wasn't Jonah asked me, it was his wretched ma – and I'll have to keep in her good books if I'm walking out with him.' Belinda turned to face her, still brushing out her curls.

'Don't if you don't want to.'

'Don't be silly, Maudie, I shall have to go. She's asked me back for supper afterwards, so that's a hopeful sign. But if there's one thing I hate it's listening to those missionaries droning on and on. Give me a good short funeral any day at all.' She put the brush down and ran her fingers through her hair. 'Not that I expect any sympathy from you. You've got your Stanley coming – and I'm sure that will be nice.'

It was, too. Stan seemed more like himself. He took her for a walk, and clasped her fingers as they wandered through the trees, although he didn't talk much. He came back to Belgravia Street, and stayed to have a meal. He'd brought some duck eggs with him, which Aunt Jane cooked for tea – an unexpected treat for all of them these days – and afterwards Stan permitted Tully to climb up on his knees and ask him lots of questions about his uniform and what the various bits of it were for. Maud was alarmed – she had learned to avoid any mention of the war – but Stan gave silly answers, like 'This 'ere's a special pocket for putting sherbet fountains in,' and made her brother grin. Father had been on duty, but by and by he came, and kept them entertained with stories of his work and how the new clerk in the office had made a mistake with the ticket-bookings, and how a hoity-toity woman had bent over to complain and got the head of her fox fur stole caught up in the grille. His impressions were so funny that even Stan had laughed. Altogether it was the happiest day that they had spent since he came home again – though of course there was the pain of separation at the end.

He clasped her to him at the station. She was trying not to cry.

'Don't forget me, Maudie.'

'Don't be silly, Stan.' She tried to make a joke. 'I got that penny to remind me, how could I forget?'

'And I've still got that flower that you picked for me. Look after yourself, Maudie. The train's about to go.' He brushed her forehead with his lips – right there, in public. Anyone might see. And she didn't care a jot – not even when customers from the shop walked by.

Wilfred Olds was walking down the platform to the parcel van, thinking of his household and the price of bread. Getting stupid, it was. Prices were going up like a steam-whistle. And it wasn't only bread. A man could hardly make ends meet. 'Here, Wilf! Isn't that your maid Maudie over there?' George, the chief porter, was jiggling his arm. 'Better than the pictures down the cinema.' He gave a wicked leer.

Wilfred looked up to see a couple locked in an embrace. He coughed. He seemed to have something in his throat. 'Yes, that's our Maudie, by the look of it. And that's her intended.

He's off back to the war. Aren't going to blame her, if she wants to say goodbye.'

George gave a chuckle. 'Nice-looking fellow, too.'

'Been home with a war-wound, but he's better now. Well, more or less. He tends to get depressed. Bit of a worry, to tell you the truth, but she's that wrapped up in him, I wouldn't say a word. I hope it works out happy, that is all I know.'

He hadn't meant to say so much, but George had changed his tone. 'Spit of her mother, that one, isn't she? You must be proud of her. Going over to have a word with her, are you?'

Wilf shook his head. Stan had clambered up into the carriage by this time, opened the window and was leaning out of it 'Short enough time they've got together as it is. Don't want Father barging in on them. Be embarrassed if she knew I'd seen them too. She'll come and try and find me after, very like.'

'See her often, do you?'

'Often as I can. Don't really like to have her living down the shop, but Jane would never give her any peace if she was home. And Maudie's got a friend there, which is just as well. Looks like she'll need somebody to comfort her tonight.' Dammit! Now he had a cinder in his eye as well. He brushed it off fiercely. 'Any road, can't stand here gossiping. Here's the train and I've got work to do. And so have you, old lad.' He walked away briskly, but not so briskly that he didn't over-hear George muttering to another member of the platform staff.

'Do anything for that girl, I believe he would. Jump through circus hoops if she requested it.'

And Wilf was not offended, because he knew that it was true.

# Three

The first sign that there was anything amiss came on Monday, shortly after the shop had opened for the day. Belinda was in the work-room shining up her pins with a piece of emery

paper to take off the rust. It was a tedious job, but it was neces-
sary now and then – especially as new pins, like everything
else, were becoming increasingly difficult to get. It was quiet
in the room. One of the apprentices was there as well, but she
was cutting out a blouse, following one of the brown paper
patterns that Madam herself had made, and all her concentra-
tion was focused on the task. Maud was downstairs doing
something with a customer, so Belinda was thinking about
nothing very much except Jonah and whether she still wished
to marry him, when Miss Simms came pounding up the stairs
in a ruffled hurry, which was not usually her way.

'Miss Richards! Come downstairs at once.' She was breathless from the climb. 'And Lucy, you as well. Madam wants to
see you in the office right away. No, don't stop to finish anything.
Drop what you are doing and come down straight away.
Something serious has occurred and your presence is required.'
It was no good asking questions and there was no chance anyway,
since Miss Simms was already trotting down the stairs again.

Belinda and the apprentice girl exchanged a startled look,
then, without a word, got to their feet and hurried after her.

Madam was waiting in the office, her lips folded into a thin
disapproving line and her hands pressed together firmly at her
waist, pulling herself up to her full five feet of height, so that,
in the dark dress she always wore when serving in the shop,
she reminded Belinda of an illustration in a book she'd had
when she was very young, depicting a severe governess who
was very much displeased.

The impression was made stronger by Madam's tone of
voice. 'Come in, Miss Richards, and stand over there. Lucy,
there is room for you beside the windowsill.'

The two girls shuffled into place as they were told. There
was not a lot of room in the little office since all the other
girls were there as well, it seemed – though Belinda didn't
dare to look around too much.

Madam tapped the desk top with Miss Simms' wooden
ruler. 'Now, since we are all assembled, I have grave news
for you. It has come to my attention in the last few hours that
one of our number appears to have behaved herself in an
appalling way, bringing discredit on herself and on the good
name of this establishment. I take this very seriously indeed.
I'll ask for your assistance in arriving at the truth. I warn you

this is not the time for misguided loyalty. Miss Olds, Miss Richards, you're the eldest here. Do you know anything about this regrettable affair?'

There was a little stir. Belinda glanced around the room. Maudie, standing on the other side, was looking fidgety and burst out suddenly, 'If this is about my behaviour at the station yesterday . . .'

Madam waved her silent. 'If you have something on your conscience in that regard, Miss Olds, I'll see you afterwards. But that is not the matter of immediate concern. This concerns a young improver whom I had taken under my care, and who has taken advantage of my good nature, it appears. Jennifer Liskey has not come to work.'

Maudie cleared her throat and seemed about to speak, but Belinda found her voice. She said, almost before she thought about the implication of her words, 'But she went to a funeral on Saturday, didn't she, for some distant relative, and then went home for the rest of the weekend? I know they live a mile or two out Marazion way. Perhaps she was simply delayed in getting back.

Madam turned towards her with a face like ice. 'Miss Richards, you seem remarkably informed about Miss Liskey's plans.'

It was a question, Belinda realized. 'Well, I thought that everybody knew. About the funeral, I mean. And Maudie – I mean, Miss Olds – told me that she heard Jenny ask permission to go home afterwards.'

Maudie had turned scarlet. 'Yes, that's true. I did.'

Madam's expression froze a little more. 'I don't approve of gossip, as you are well aware, and eavesdropping is not an occupation I applaud. Miss Olds, I have already said, I'll see you afterwards. But it is Miss Richards' testimony that I'm anxious to pursue. I don't recall the details being mentioned at the time when Miss Liskey requested additional permission to go home. Yet you'd heard of it, you said? From whom, may I enquire? Miss Liskey told you, did she?'

Belinda didn't answer. She had an awful premonition suddenly. She found herself fidgeting and staring at the floor.

'Miss Richards, we are waiting. I am interested to know where you got the information about this funeral. You say it was a distant relative. That's interesting to hear. Particularly as no such funeral took place at all, it seems.'

'But it must have done – there was a time, and everything.'

'I ask again, where did you hear this from? Can you oblige us with an answer please? I warn you, Miss Richards, the police may be involved. Miss Liskey is missing. She has not been at her home. I supposed – as you did – that she had been delayed and I sent a message with the post-boy to enquire if she was unwell. Her father works in an office not very far from here, and I'm afraid I took the tone that it was discourteous of him not to have brought me word if she was taken ill. He came to see me, half an hour ago, distraught and furious. There was no funeral, as far as he's aware – no relative, distant or otherwise, is recently deceased – and Jennifer has not been home. He fears she has absconded with a young man she knew, a must unsuitable young person, of whom he disapproved. The question is, how did they lay their plans? There has been no exchange of letters through the post, and – as far as I'm aware – the young man in question has not been here again since – following her father's instructions on the point – I ordered him away. Yet they have clearly been in touch. I will be frank, Miss Richards, I believe it was through you. Several of the girls have spoken of the fact that you were once seen handing Jenny some secret envelope, and once before I had suspicions of something of the kind, when somebody was careless with the blotting paper here.'

The world was crashing around Belinda's ears. 'But that was months ago. And this was different. Honestly, I thought there was a funeral. He said there was a carriage laid on and everything. Four o'clock on Saturday it was supposed to be.'

Madam was as cold and unblinking as a stone. 'So, you admit it, Miss Richards? You see what you have done. I'm sure if we make enquiries we shall find that at four o'clock on Saturday there will have been a train. Up country somewhere, it doesn't matter where. Perhaps they were hoping to make for Gretna Green. I hope so, for her sake. She can't escape disgrace, but at least she might be married, which is something I suppose.'

'You mean . . .'

'Yes, Miss Richards, I see you understand. The carriage in question was on a railway train. I accept that you acted without understanding this, but you were still an accomplice in this horrible affair. I'm ashamed of you. It was not only foolish, it was disobedient. You know my policy on having followers.'

'I'm very sorry, Madam,' Belinda managed through her tears. 'It won't occur again.'

'You are quite right, Miss Richards. Not on these premises. You cannot expect that I'll continue to employ you after this. Please pack your things and go.'

Belinda felt herself go cold. 'But, Madam, where am I to go? What's to become of me?' She'd not only be without a job, she'd be out on the street. Gran, she knew, would never take her back if she went home in disgrace.

'You should have thought of that, Miss Richards, before you acted as you did. I will do this for you. If you should seek employment, I will give you a short note vouching for the quality of your sewing work. That is all that I can do. You can't expect a character from me when you behave like this. Now, the rest of you may go, with the exception of Miss Olds. I believe she has something she wishes to confess.'

The next few minutes were among the most uncomfortable Maud had ever spent. She was intelligent and honest and her work was good, so she had rarely felt the lash of Madam's tongue – except perhaps a sharp rebuke for chattering to Belinda now and then. Today, though, she had a dressing-down that would have shamed Aunt Jane.

'I am disappointed in you, I regret to say, Miss Olds,' Madam began, delivering this in an unforgiving tone. 'I trusted you to be a good example to the younger girls, but you have not only let me down, you have let yourself and your family down as well. Perhaps it was the unfortunate bad influence of your friend, but I expected you to have more character. You have always been honest and open in your own affairs, asking for leave to write a farewell to your friend instead of attempting to do so secretly, and I've rewarded that. So I am doubly disappointed to find you indulging in thoughtless gossiping, and gloating over other people's secrets as it appears you did.'

'There wasn't any gloating. It was not like that at all.' She was attempting to defend herself, but it earned her another stern rebuke.

'Don't interrupt, young lady, and don't answer back, or I shall be forced to take the steps with you that I have already taken with Miss Richards. As for keeping gleeful secrets – you deny you knew about the notes and messages?'

Maud hung her head. 'No, Madam. Belinda did mention something of the kind – though I counselled her against it more than once.'

'But you did not see fit to tell me or Miss Simms about these misdemeanours?'

Maudie raised her head, and for the first time looked her employer in the eye. 'No, Madam. Belinda is my friend. I wouldn't get her into trouble by telling tales on her – though of course I didn't realize how serious it was. I'm sorry, Madam, but that's the truth of it. I'm sure you would have felt the same yourself.'

Madam curled her lip. 'A pity that your loyalty was so foolishly misplaced – and that it did not extend to me and to the reputation of the shop. And what is all this about your conduct at the station, may I ask? Inappropriate behaviour in a public place?'

And so it went on, for half an hour without a pause. When it was over and Maud emerged again, red-eyed and shaken, it was to meet Belinda coming down the stairs. She was carrying a bundle containing her belongings and though she was pale she held her head up high and there was a defiant swagger in her step.

'Hello, Maudie!' she called in a voice that seemed to Maud to be unnecessarily loud. 'You out on your ear as well?'

Maud shook her head. 'It didn't come to that. But you, Blin! I'm some sorry. What are you going to do?' She asked the question automatically, but what else was there for poor old Belinda but to go back with her tail between her legs and beg Gran to have her? Without the money in her pocket to put down on a room, it would likely be the workhouse otherwise.

Belinda tossed her head, but spoke more softly now. 'Won't be crawling home to ask for charity, at least, though I thought at one time it would come to that.'

'Where will you go then?' Maudie said, trying to picture Belinda in a workhouse uniform.

Belinda gave a giggle. 'You will never guess. Miss Simms, of all people, came to look for me when I was packing up. She says there is a box room in the place she rents – it's the top floor of a little house over Newlyn way – and I could have it if I wanted it. No cooking, but I could use the tap and

privy in the yard. One and three a week and no deposit down
– at least until I've found myself a job.'

'Miss Simms?' Maudie blurted.

'Ssshh!' Belinda warned her. 'Don't shout it out like that.
It's quite a risk for her – Madam won't be happy if she gets
to hear of it.'

Maud could only stand and shake her head, amazed. 'Who
would have believed it? I'm sure I shouldn't have. Miss Simms,
having a soft spot for you like that!'

Belinda coloured. 'Don't know that she has. She said a
funny thing. "I had a young man once of whom my family
disapproved, and I've always regretted that I let them interfere." Then she wouldn't say any more. So I suppose she's
sympathetic. Whatever her reasons, I'm jolly glad of them,
though I won't impose on her any more than I'm obliged to.
I'll sort something out. Soon as I find someone who wants a
sewing-girl. Though Madam's determined to make that difficult. Not many will have you without a written character –
no matter how good she says your sewing is.'

'You could always take work in and do it at home, I suppose,'
Maud said.

Belinda looked doubtful. 'That's not so easy these days,
either. Folk are making do. But I'll find something, you see
if I don't. Might not be sewing, even. People are taking girls
on for all sorts of things these days.'

Maud had an inspiration. 'Here, why don't you go down
to the station then, and tell them you have come about a clerk's
position there? I know they're looking for one. You've got
neat writing, very nice and clear – you could write out tickets
and all that sort of thing. And you're good at sums. You could
make the bookings and read the timetables.'

Belinda snorted. 'Me, as a clerk? Oh, come on, Maudie,
how could I do that? Don't have the first idea of what's
involved.'

'Well, neither do the boys when they first come from school.'
Maudie was keen on the idea, now she'd thought of it. 'And
they haven't all got shorthand or book-keeping, you know.
Especially not the candidates they've had recently – Father
says they're simply hopeless, one or two of them. Can't add
up or spell, or write a decent hand. Wouldn't be considered,
if it wasn't for the war, and when they do come half of them

don't last. I mean it, Blin. Why don't you go and see? Can't hurt to ask them; they can only turn you down.'

Belinda made a face. 'Without a character?'

'Father would speak for you, I'm quite sure he would,' Maud said impulsively. 'And—'

Madam's voice interrupted from the bottom of the stairs. 'Are you still here, Miss Richards? Please leave the premises. And you, Miss Olds, I am surprised at you again. I thought I'd made it clear I did not care for gossiping. I shall deduct sixpence from your wage-packet for wasting working time.'

Belinda turned crimson and seemed ready to protest, but Maud prevented her. 'I am sorry, Madam. We were saying our farewells.' And before Belinda could protest she kissed her on the cheek. 'I wish you every happiness, wherever you may be.' And with that she turned swiftly on her heel and clattered up the stairs, back to the dress that she was working on.

By the time Madam came upstairs a moment later, Maud was busy with a buttonhole, though her mind was not wholly on the task in hand. She was wondering about Belinda and Jenny and Miss Simms, and whether Father would be angry when he learned that his daughter had cheerfully volunteered him to give a character to Belinda Richards, a girl he scarcely knew. A girl who had just been dismissed for bad behaviour too!

Never mind, she told herself, it wouldn't come to that. It had been a mad idea of hers to suggest the railway job at all. Belinda wouldn't dare to try, and even if she did, she wouldn't be considered, so Father would not be asked to put in a word for her. It was just as well. Probably he wouldn't have done it, anyway – he was very conscientious about that sort of thing, and he really didn't know enough to recommend the girl. And then they would both be embarrassed and cross with silly Maud. Meantime, no doubt, Madam would have her on the mat again, wanting her to answer for that defiant kiss.

As it turned out, she was wrong on all counts. But she was so distracted by her thoughts that she pricked her finger twice.

'You never did, Belinda?' Jonah was amazed. 'Walked right in as bold as brass and asked them for a job? Down the station office, where they've always had just men?' He was genuinely shocked, though truth to tell he was secretly admiring of her daring, too, and he couldn't help grinning at the thought of it.

'I did, then!' Belinda was sitting on the sea-wall next to him and as she turned her head to grin triumphantly her bonnet fell askew, caught by a gust of salty breeze, and her hair, escaping from its pins, tumbled in appealing red waves down her back. He wished she wouldn't pin it up again, but of course it was the first thing that she began to do.

'Course, they didn't take me straight away – made me do a writing test and all that sort of thing,' she said, twisting the loose tresses into a neat coil, then wiggling the hairpins to skewer it in place. 'But I think Maud's dad said something, cause they told me to come back, and when I went this morning, they said they'd have me for a trial and I could start next week. It's only writing tickets and entering them up, but the boy they had before had made a proper mess of it. He lasted just a week, but I'll do better, you see if I don't.'

Jonah muttered something like, 'I'm sure you will.' He was wondering what his Ma would make of all of this. Disapprove, most likely, but there was one good thing: since Belinda had already found another post, there would not be too many questions about why she'd left the shop.

Belinda was still laughing. 'And that's not the best of it. If I suit they'll give me nineteen bob a week – more like a man's wages than a girl's – and there won't be stoppages for board and everything. Be better off than ever I was down at Madam's shop.'

Jonah nodded. That would answer Ma. She always had a keen eye for the money side. A decent wage was halfway to respectability in her books. And Belinda was boarding with this lady from the shop, so there was no hint of impropriety in that. Ma might even think that paying your own rent was a sign that you could manage money, which was her highest praise – especially if Belinda could put a bit aside. Indeed, if she was able to do that, he thought, perhaps they could think of having somewhere of their own, and he could get away from Ma and her eternal strictures about how he should behave. It had never occurred to him as a possibility before. He said, with more warmth than usual, 'Sounds very good to me.'

'Anyway, I'm only doing what the government is urging us

to do. There have been adverts in the papers, this last week or two, saying how women should take on all sorts of jobs and free the men for war. Mostly thinking of coalmen and that sort of thing, but it could apply to me.' She twinkled at him.

She was teasing, but it was an uncomfortable thought. All the more reason to make a set at her. He snuck an arm around her. 'At least we won't have to skulk around, the way we used to do, making sure you're in by eight o'clock and keeping well away from Madam's shop.'

She nodded. 'Of course, I can't be too late – I can't upset Miss Simms – but if we are not working, and the weather's fine, we can come down to a place like this and sit here in public any time we like. Especially these light evenings. So what do you think of that?' She was undoing the ribbons of her hat from round her neck, as if she wanted to put it on again, but a playful gust of wind came by and whisked it from her grasp. He had to lean across and snatch it so it didn't blow away to sea. 'Oh, well done, Jonah. I nearly lost the dratted thing!' She took it from him, giving his fingers a quick affectionate squeeze.

Jonah felt a tide of something warm rise up inside of him – it might have been desire, except it was nothing like the feeling he'd had with Lily-Anne. More a mixture of admiration for what he called her 'cheek' (only Belinda would have the nerve to go for such a job) and a sudden recognition of what she might offer him: a dab hand with a needle, companionship in bed, and – if she could go on earning something like a proper wage – possible freedom from his parents in the end. Above all, no one expected married men to go and volunteer, though there might not be freedom on the subject very long, with this new National Register that they'd been setting up for all men over fourteen and under sixty-five. Of course, the government denied that there were conscription plans afoot, but why else would they have the ruddy register at all? No, it was clear that what he needed was a wife.

And, of course, she was a smashing looker, too. Why had he run a mile, all those months ago, when she was dropping hints that she was looking to be wed?

Well, he knew better now. It was time to take the plunge. Billy Polkinghorne was right. She was clearly not unwilling

– his arm was still around her waist and she had not complained. He leaned a little further forward on the wall and bent across to kiss her on the cheek. It was chilly, and tasted a little bit of salt. He caught her by the hand. 'Belinda, there is something I want to say to you. Something I want to ask you. You must know what it is.'

She smiled at him, but took her hand away and used it to hold her bonnet in place, while she tried to tie the ribbons with the other one. One-handed it did not look a very easy task.

He pulled her to face him, and did the bonnet up. 'Well?' he urged, as gently as he could. He found his heart was pounding, unexpectedly.

She gave that smile again. 'I haven't heard the question.'

Was she teasing him? 'Whether you will marry me, of course. You will do, won't you?' he insisted. She did not reply so he stumbled on. 'I mean, you've hinted . . . that is, you've let me know . . .' She was looking at him oddly, and he was floundering. 'I mean, drat it, Blin, you have led me to believe that you were very keen.'

She put her hands down on the wall and swung her legs around, giving him a tantalizing glimpse of petticoats, and ended up sitting with her back towards the sea. 'I don't know, Jonah,' she said thoughtfully. 'It's rather different now, what with this new job and everything. Can't hardly start on Monday and then say I've got to leave directly because I'm getting wed. They may be taking women, but they won't have married ones. And now I've got my lodgings sorted out and everything . . .' She tailed off into silence.

For a moment he could scarcely believe what she had said. 'You're saying you won't have me? After all you've said? When I've taken you home to meet my mother and everything?' He swivelled round and got abruptly to his feet. 'It comes of sharing lodgings with that old maid, I suppose. You want to end up like her? Well, I'm only glad you've told me now, before it's too late.'

She reached up and tugged his coat sleeve. 'Jonah, don't be silly. It's not like that at all. I'll marry you, of course I will – just not now, that's all. Much better if we waited for a little while – perhaps until this war is over and the men come back. That would be next Easter, by what they're saying now.'

She sounded almost pleading. 'Wouldn't you want me to put some money by?'

It was so exactly what he had been thinking a moment earlier, that for an instant he could think of no reply. It had not really occurred to him that she would have to leave her job – because Pa owned the business, his Ma had always worked, doing the books and ordering as well as keeping house. Yet what Jonah wanted was a wife as soon as possible. 'I can see the two things don't quite go together,' he said, more in answer to his own thoughts than to her.

It must have been exactly the right thing to reply, because she stood up quickly and looked into his face. 'Oh, Jonah, I might have known that you would understand. And of course I promise that I will marry you someday. Next summer, perhaps, if you will wait for me?'

It was not the sort of answer you expected from a girl. He said crossly, 'I s'pose I'll have to. But don't blame me if they go calling people up, and I never get a chance to marry you at all.' He didn't try to kiss her or take her in his arms.

She didn't seem to mind. 'Well, if that happens – which I doubt – I will marry you at once.' She grinned at him. 'So it's agreed then? Shall we go and tell your Ma? And this evening I'll write and tell Gran.' She turned away and led the way along the street back to the house, where Ma was waiting with tea and National Flour buns.

His mother showed her pleasure – if there was any – in an unlikely way, by pecking Belinda on the cheek and then showering her with sharp advice on how to keep a house, and promises of linen for their 'bottom drawer', while Pa took Jonah to one side and spoke darkly of having a little talk sometime about the facts of life.

It was a strange sort of proposal, looking back on it, though it wasn't quite the way he told the story later on to Billy Polkinghorne, over several pints of ale, during a stolen evening in the Imperial Inn.

# Four

It was peculiar without Belinda in the attic room, at first. Maudie wondered if Madam would move one of the junior apprentices in from the dormitory next door – or worse, suggest that Maud move back and sleep in Jenny Liskey's bed, but nothing happened, except that the rules were even stricter than before, and Madam kept a closer watch on everyone.

Maud was quite relieved that Stan had gone the week before: it would have been very difficult, the way things were, to ask for leave to go and see him off. Some of the junior girls were grumbling that Madam was checking up on them, even when they wanted to go home on Sunday after church. Maud herself kept running into Mr Raymond on the street when she went out to do the private fittings for the shop – too often for it to have been a mere coincidence.

Of course, Madam was worried about trade as well. People weren't buying like they used to do, and even if they did, pretty dresses and material were becoming hard to find. Madam and Mr Raymond spent hours with Miss Simms, in the office after the shop was shut at night, poring over the ledgers and coming out grim-faced. Altogether, the atmosphere was not a pleasant one, and Maud found she missed the cheerful company and idle gossip of her friend.

She was both delighted and amazed therefore, on the Sunday a fortnight after Belinda had gone, to go home as usual to Belgravia Street and find Belinda waiting on the step.

'My dear Blin, how are you?' Maud hurried up to her and held out both her hands.

Belinda scorned the timid gesture and took her in a hug. 'I'm very well. Your father told you that I went for that position down at the station office? And got it, thanks to him.'

Maud nodded, grinning. 'No, he didn't tell me that. Said

you were a darn sight better than the lad they'd had before, and they were glad to have you – even though you were a girl.'

Belinda made a face. 'Not all of them are glad! You'd be surprised the way some of the men go on – as though I was going to bring ruin on the place by simply being there. Distract them from their duties, if you ever heard the like.'

Maud found that she was giggling aloud, so much so that the woman at Number Seven opposite – who had come out to tip the tealeaves down the drain and see what was going on – looked quite askance at them and slammed the door. 'And do you?' Maud enquired.

Belinda rolled her eyes expressively. 'Not as much as some of them would like me to, I think.' She leaned closer and murmured confidentially, 'I went into the cupboard yesterday to get some envelopes, and one of the older men came in there after me. Said he was wanting some stationery too, but there weren't any envelopes where he tried to put his hands! I had to slap his face and threaten that I'd call for help – though I don't suppose I would have, if it came to it. Might have lost my position if I had, before I'd really begun. Fortunately, it was enough to do the trick. He hasn't even looked in my direction since.'

'My lor!' Maudie was genuinely horrified by this. 'Well, who'd have thought that one of them would carry on like that? They're supposed to be respectable in the office there – proper clerks and all. Father always said that they were very nice.'

Belinda laughed. 'So they are, too, most of them. Some even try to help – tell you what to do, and all that sort of thing, instead of leaving you to flounder. Though they tend to talk to you as if you are a bit soft in the head, just because you are a girl. Not used to having them, I suppose – as you can tell. Got to go all the way down the station to the Ladies if you want to wash your hands – there's only a men's cloak-room on the office side.'

Maud found that she was blushing. 'At least we don't have that kind of problem down the shop. Now, you coming in or what? Aunt Jane will be wondering what's become of me, standing here gossiping instead of going in straightaway.'

'Oh, she knows where you are. She told me I could wait. She would have asked me in, I think, but I told her that I would stop out here and watch for you for you to come. Wanted to have a quiet word with you alone. Thing is, Maudie, I've got a bit of news.'

'What's that, then?' Maud knew her voice was sharp. 'Haven't come to tell me that fellow's put you off and you are going to quit the job?' Pa would be disappointed, she thought, when he'd supported the idea.

To her relief, Belinda shook her head. 'No, nothing of the kind. I'm really loving it. You meet all kinds of people, and there's such a lot to learn. And folk are so grateful when you get it right. You really feel you're helping. Beats sewing for a living. And it's better pay. You want to try it, too. There's another lad down there who's going to volunteer, and they'll be wanting someone directly to take his place, as well.' She looked at Maudie with a little smile. 'Though I don't suppose you would. Too careful, aren't you, Maudie? You wouldn't take a risk. Afraid you might upset the boat.'

Maud was stung but she just laughed and shook her head. 'It's not the same for me. I'm doing what I wanted and I enjoy the work, especially now I'm out of training and get to do things on my own. That may seem dull to you, but then you never liked it much – though you were pretty good at it.'

Belinda shrugged her shoulders. 'We are in the twentieth century. Girls don't *have* to sew. Don't you sometimes feel you'd like to strike out a bit?'

'I don't *have* to sew, but I'd rather do that than push a pen and risk getting pawed in cupboards like you seem to do. I really love to cut a pattern and make a thing from scratch, and know that I've accomplished every bit of it.' She was speaking rather sharply, though she didn't quite know why. 'And I won't have to stop when I am married, like I'd have to in your place. If you're a seamstress you can work from home.'

Blin giggled suddenly. 'Well, perhaps it's something I'll have to think about, 'cause that's the very thing I've come to tell you, Maud. Jonah Lotts has asked me to be his wife, at last.'

'Oh, Blin!' Maud quite forgot her pique. 'How simply wonderful. I know you wanted it. I wish you every happiness. When's it going to be?'

Her friend gave her an uneasy look. 'That's just it, Maud.

We haven't set a date. Jonah wants to do it as soon as possible, yet now that it has come to it, I'm not so sure myself. I've told him that I'll have him, but he'll have to wait.'

Maud had to smother a chuckle. 'You are a funny one! A week or two ago, you couldn't wait, you said.'

'I know. But things were different when I was down the shop. Now, it's like – I don't know – like a door that's opened suddenly. And it is lovely having a place to call your own – even if it is a little cramped and there is no fire. I can buy a penny pie, or a bit of bread and cheese, and I manage splendidly, especially if I can get a cup of something hot at work – cocoa or beef tea or something off the platform stalls. And Miss Simms asked me in to have a cup of tea with her the other day. She is almost human when you get to know her.'

'But you're going to marry Jonah?'

'Well, naturally I will. A girl's got to think about her future, hasn't she? But the thing is, Maudie, I haven't told my Gran. You wouldn't come down with me, I suppose, and help me talk to her?'

'Me?' Maud said with vigour. 'I don't even know her! How's that going to help?'

'She won't make such a scene if there is someone else about.' Belinda sounded sheepish. 'Truth is, Maudie, I haven't even told her I've been turned off from the shop. There won't half be a row – she'll go on and on and on about how she gave me money so I could have my chance, and how I'm throwing it straight back in her face, and what an ungrateful disappointment I've turned out to be. I can just imagine it. Won't be half as bad if you're there. Please say that you'll come.'

Maud was just deciding what to say to this – as an invitation, it was not an appealing one – when the front door was thrust open and Aunt Jane appeared.

'My dear life! You still out here, gossiping on the step like a pair of fishwives? I never heard the like. Maud Olds, your tea is on the table getting cold and Tully's getting fretful waiting for 'ee too. So if you've quite finished chattering, perhaps you'll come inside, instead of catching cold out here, and making an exhibition of yourselves besides.'

'But Belinda wanted—' Maud began.

Aunt Jane cut her off. 'Belinda can come on in as well if

she's a mind to, I suppose. Your Pa will soon be here, and she works at the station office as I understand, so they won't be strangers. I haven't got fried shrimps to go around us all, but she can have some bread and butter and a drop of tea.' Aunt Jane addressed all this to Maud directly, as if Blin wasn't there, but Belinda said politely, 'That would be very kind.'

So they went in, and had their tea. Maud even offered to share her sprats with Belinda, but her friend seemed quite content with bread and homemade marrow jam (not the promised butter – you did not have both at once). It was a tactful choice, and she set out to charm in other ways as well, chatting to Aunt Jane about the knitting bees, and telling Tully funny things to make him laugh. By the time that Father came in later on, Belinda had made herself so much at home she even offered to go out to the tap and fetch the water to wash up.

'Nice girl she seems to be, your friend,' Aunt Jane said approvingly, while Belinda was in the yard. 'I'll bet your Madam was some sorry to have to let her go.'

Maud was about to mutter something, but Father winked at her. 'We'll have to have her here for proper tea sometime,' he said.

Maud sighed. She wasn't sorry that Blin would come again, but it was going to be hard to wriggle out of going with her to her Gran's.

Stan had been put on a course about Mills bombs and grenades, which hadn't been so bad. He felt quite proud to have his wound stripe up, and had shown a fair proficiency at lobbing bombs at things. They even gave him a gun again – '1 rifle: high-velocity, bolt-action, repeating' according to the book – and he learned to shoot again, though he was not as good as he had been before. The recoil still made his shoulder ache, but he didn't want to seem a coward, so he made light of it. So, for a fortnight, he was content enough. Then there was a new offensive and they packed him off to it.

It was like a nightmare, going back to the war. The crossing was even worse than he'd remembered it, and by the time Stan got to the dispersal centre his nerves were taut as wire. This time, however, he was sent somewhere different.

Eat Apples, they were calling it – spelt Etaples if you saw it written down – and it was quite a place, full of warehouses and dormitories and hospitals and things, with its own railway siding and huge barrack yards. They called the yard the Bull Ring and it was easy to see why: hundreds of men in uniform charging everywhere.

It made him feel a very little cog in the machine. The more so since, unlike most of the other new arrivals, he was not a new recruit fresh from initial training camp, so they all knew each other and he knew nobody, although he was temporarily attached to their platoon. But he need not have worried – he wasn't there for long.

He was called before the duty officer next day. A weedy fellow with an apologetic air, he shuffled his notes a moment without looking up. When he did so, he flapped a hand at Stan. 'Hoskins, is it? I have good news for you. A brace of shakes and we'll have you back with your old company again. We've got a consignment of supplies to send to the rear trenches there. Transport will be leaving for that sector at first light from the yard outside of here. Report there in full kit, and hand this chitty to the officer in charge.' He scribbled something on a form and handed it to Stan.

'Yes, sir.' Stan hovered, not sure what to do. He had saluted, but he hadn't been dismissed. He looked uncomfortably at the officer, who was busying himself with documents again. After a minute he looked up, and snapped, 'You've got your orders, soldier, what are you waiting for?'

And that was that. Stan shuffled from the room. The orderly, who was waiting at a little desk outside, gave him a cheerful grin. 'Wrong-foot you, did he? That's what he always does. Apt to ignore you when you first walk in, but woe betide you if you don't salute. You'd think that he was running the whole damn war behind that ruddy desk. I see you've got a chitty. Let's have a look at it. Ah yes, going up with the ammunition convoy to the front. B Company at Doumiens. That where you were before?'

Stan nodded. 'Though it was months ago. Before I got wounded. Christmas time, it was.'

The fellow grinned again. 'You won't see much difference there though, I shouldn't think. Been a proper stalemate in that area. There have been a few offensives, but they haven't come to much. I shouldn't think we've pushed Fritz back more than a mile or two.'

'Soon find out,' Stan said mechanically. 'Permission to dismiss?' The conversation brought back things he wanted to forget. Even here, in this safe and dusty corridor, he found his hands were shaking. He pressed them to his sides, and only moved them stiffly to get his chitty back. The orderly switched off the grin and got all businesslike, no doubt thinking Stan was choosing to be formally correct. A pity: Stan had relished the moment's friendliness.

The orderly was right about one thing at any rate: the trenches, when he got there, were depressingly the same. B Company was back behind the lines for respite – in the very same farmhouse they had occupied before – but they were due to go back up again within a day or two.

'Same trench we were holding when you got your wound.' That was Saywer – Sergeant Sawyer now. He'd come out to meet the convoy when it first arrived, and bustled round it barking orders. Then, when he had a detail unloading the supplies – 'Come on you lazy blighters, put your backs in it!' – he led Stan to the Commanding Officer himself, talking all the while as though they had been friends.

'Not many men left that you would recognize. We've taken a fair few losses since you went away. Your friend Charmer is still with us – though he isn't here right now. In the hospital for a day or two – got some wretched infection in his foot – but we're expecting him back before we go back up the line. Who else would you remember? Rawlinson was killed, you knew that of course. Been a couple of officers come and gone since then. Present one's called Bennett. Hasn't got a clue. Don't tell him I said that. Here you are!' He pushed open a door. 'Sergeant Hoskins for you, Major. He is reporting back.'

Major Bennett, a fair-haired boy – he looked no more than that – glanced up at Stanley. 'Evening, Corporal. Welcome back. Be with you in a jiffy.' His voice was clipped and rather upper-class, and he was obviously relishing the moment of command. He was nothing like Tregurtha, so why was Stan suddenly reminded of that poor lad?

Bennett put his pen down and looked at Stan again. 'Good journey?'

Stan thought back to the last ten miserable hours, jammed

in a lorry-cab between a silent, surly driver from the transport
corps and a spotty young mechanic who talked incessantly,
until he felt he would rather have travelled in the back, among
the crates of ammunition and the petrol cans. Progress had
been pretty fair at first, through a score of little villages with
shops and shuttered houses and fountains in the squares, the
cobbles rattling all the teeth inside your head. Old women in
black dresses and improbable white caps, who sat in door-
ways knitting and glowering as the convoy passed; younger
women with strained faces carrying long loaves, and bicycling
priests in long black robes, like bats. Then on through the
ruined country that he remembered from before, only this time
there seemed to be even more of it: blasted trees and buildings and sullen-faced families with their homes on carts. Then
he heard the distant booms and flashes of guns. Closer and
closer to the reality of hell until Stan had to hold on to the
seat edge with both hands and sit on them. He could detect
the sounds of the bombardment now and it dried his mouth
and made his throat constrict. Fortunately Major Bennett did
not want to know all that.

'Very good indeed, sir,' he managed to reply.

Three days later, they were at the front again.

The visit to Belinda's grandmother took place at last, one
Sunday when Belinda wasn't working shifts and had been
invited round to Belgravia Street for tea. Maudie clearly didn't
want to go with her – she made every kind of possible excuse
– but Belinda was adamant. She was desperate to have Maud's
company. After all, she hadn't been to see her gran for weeks
and she would be expected to be dropping in by now. It might
not be so easy to find another time when both of them were
free. People wanted train tickets on Sunday, same as any other
day, but it was Sunday that Gran would be looking out for her.

'Wonder you haven't been before then,' Maud said as they
set off through the Morrab Gardens on their way. It was her
suggestion, and Belinda had agreed, although it wasn't the
shortest route by any means. 'To tell her about Jonah, at the
very least.' She stopped beside the fish pond and began to
watch the fish, as though their bubbles were the most important things in life.

'Well, I did.' Belinda tugged her arm. 'Wrote her a letter

soon as he proposed, but I haven't heard a word. Not to wish
me well, or even to say that I'm a fool. And don't say she
might have sent an answer to the shop – I know she might
have done, but Miss Simms says that's she's not been near
the place and she ought to know. There has been no letter
either, though I'm not surprised at that. Gran's not much hand
at writing, though she can read all right, provided it is set out
nice and clear –like print, that is, without the curly bits.'

'Perhaps she had trouble reading yours then,' Maudie said,
still gazing at the fish.

'She's managed to read my writing scores of times before.'
Belinda was impatient. 'Didn't approve of what it said, more
like. Or she was in a sulk. Will be again, if we don't hurry up.'

Maud looked unconvinced, but she did move down the path.
'You haven't let her know that we're coming then?'

'Hardly liked to, what with this and that.' Belinda walked
faster, to hurry her along. 'Thing is, there was a bit of an
argument the last time I went,' she confessed, reluctantly. 'You
know that rainy Sunday we had a month ago? Gran was
complaining that I hadn't wiped my shoes – that was all she
could find to say to me, after I'd traipsed all the way down
there in the pouring rain, that I was making puddles on her
precious mat. I was that soaked and furious I walked out and
slammed the door. One reason why I wanted you to come
down there with me today.'

The horrified expression on Maud's face was almost
comical.

'Course – she still thinks it's my free day, you realize.
Doesn't know that Madam's turned me off. That's another
reason why I want you there. Might stop her throwing things.'
She meant it to be funny, but it was a mistake.

'She wouldn't do that, surely?' Maudie sounded shocked.
She had stopped again, this time at the bandstand, and was
looking as if she'd stay and listen to the concert for two pins.

'Not if you're there, Maudie.' She was almost pleading
now. 'She minds what people think. Be nice as pie to you.
Probably even offer you a cup of tea. You've got to come
down with me. She'll pay some heed to you. She won't listen
to anything I say, as usual, just tell me what a disappointment I've turned out to be. You're the one can tell her all
about the job: say you told me it was coming up and how

your father recommended me. Don't have to tell her how I came to leave the shop. I want to make it out as good as possible.'

Maudie, being Maudie, had conscientious doubts. 'That's all very well, Blin, but I can't go telling lies.'

Of course, that's what she would say. Belinda should have guessed. She said crossly, 'What's "telling lies" about it? It's all completely true. I'm only asking you to miss bits out, that's all. Unless you want to get me in more trouble than I'm already in?'

Maudie was lingering by the flower beds by now, watching some children with a hoop and stick. 'Well, if she asks me questions, I'll have to answer them.' And even when Blin nodded, she went on doubtfully, 'I'm still not sure this is a good idea. But I'll come for your sake, if you are set on it.'

'Let's go and get it over with,' Belinda said, relieved to be on the way at last. Maud plied her with questions as they walked along – what Gran's maiden name was; what her family did; where she came from and how old she was – some of which Belinda didn't know herself.

When they reached the door she knocked, but there was no reply. 'Bit deaf,' she said to Maudie. 'She doesn't always hear.' She pushed it open – Gran never kept it locked – and called out cheerfully. 'Gran? It's me. It's Blin. Brought somebody to see you.'

There was still no answer. Belinda was surprised. Gran didn't usually have a nap in the afternoon, like some old people did, though she had been known to drop off, once or twice. Perhaps that's what had happened. Belinda went into the passage, taking care this time to wipe her feet on the doormat that was lying just inside the door.

'Can't be very far. Her coat is on the hallstand,' she called back to Maud. She walked down to the kitchen and pushed back the door. There was no one there. Cup and saucer on the table, and a dirty plate. That wasn't like Gran either, and the fire was out. Belinda for the first time felt seriously alarmed. Was Gran feeling poorly, perhaps, and taken to her bed?

She went back to Maudie, who was still waiting outside on the step. 'I can't find her for the minute. Might be upstairs in bed. You come into the parlour and I'll run up and look.'

Maud looked even more reluctant than before, but at Belinda's insistence she did come inside, and sat down in the parlour in a horsehair chair, looking as stiff and awkward as the stuffed bird in the case, or the sepia photographs of great-uncles in ill-fitting suits that frowned down from the walls. They were even more forbidding than the furniture. It was not a room that made you feel very much at ease.

Belinda left her to it and ran up the stairs. Gran was not in her room, nor in the tiny spare room where Belinda used to sleep. Everything up there was neat and in its place – typical of Gran – though there was an unexpected hint of mustiness. Belinda pushed the window open, but that seemed to make it worse.

She went downstairs again and out into the yard. She was not mistaken; there was a funny smell. Could it be the privy? She pushed the door ajar, half-fearing to find Gran in there in some distress. But there was nothing in there, though the smell was worse. Was it from the wash house then, which was next door to it?

This time when she pushed the door it did not yield. Something was behind it. She leaned on it again. It budged a fraction, and the smell and the realization both hit her at once. She felt weak-kneed and sick.

She dashed back to the privy and got there just in time. She came out shaking with remorse, grief and shock. Fortunately Maud was there to fetch the neighbours in and send a passing urchin off to get the police. It was Maudie who put the kettle on and made a cup of tea, Maudie who had the wit to send for Jonah Lotts and get him to take Belinda back to Belgravia Street. It was Maudie who later found her letter too, lying unopened, underneath the mat.

# Five

J onah did his very best to try to comfort Belinda, but it was not easy.

'Never understand women, I shan't, Billy,' he said to his friend afterwards, pushing a precious shilling coin across the bar. This was a moment that called for an extra drop or two of ale. He lifted one of the brimming pint pots to his lips. 'Never did anything but complain about the old besom when she was alive, so now the old girl's dead you'd think she might be pleased. But is she?' He took a soothing sip. 'Nothing of the kind. Crying like Noah's flood, she was, and shaking like a leaf. I couldn't stop her nohow.'

'That so?' Billy was not the help he used to be these days. His Annie had got herself in the family way and was sickly with it, so he didn't like to be away from her for long.

'Still snivelling the last time I saw her,' Jonah said. 'And she'd found out by that time that there was money left to her. Not the house and furniture, that's all gone to the boy – supposing he ever comes back from the war – but all the clothes, her wedding ring and brooches and all that. And there was twelve pounds underneath the mattress in the bedroom. Took a bit of sorting, but it seems that's hers as well.'

Billy did look interested then. 'Enough to get married on, that is. What you going to do?'

Jonah shrugged. 'What is there? I've already asked her if she'll have me, but she says we have to wait. Be worse than ever if she's got that money, I suppose.'

'Well then!' Billy made a suggestive face at him. 'Only one thing for it, far as I can see. Have to see if you can charm her into you-know-what. Shouldn't be impossible; you've managed it before. Get her in trouble and she'll have to marry you. And it wouldn't be a hardship, with a girl like that.'

'Belinda'd never let me!' Jonah said at once. 'And Ma'd have fits, besides.'

Billy shrugged his shoulders. 'Well, it's up to you. Worth a try, in any case, I would have thought. I always said they'd use that list to bring in conscription. And now they're starting, by the sound of it. You could find yourself in front of the tribunal any time, without you try and find another girl to marry you.'

'I've thought about it,' Jonah admitted. 'But I've rather taken to Belinda, in the last few months. She's got her wits about her and Ma's accepted her. Where would I find another one in time? Besides, I asked her so I'm promised, you might say. Especially if she's got that money coming to her now.'

Billy downed his ale. 'Well, I'll have to go. Annie will have my guts for garters if I don't. But think on what I've said. All this thought of being a father makes you feel quite proud. Pity you didn't take that little kitchen maid while you had the chance, perhaps.'

'Here!' Jonah protested. 'What d'you mean by that? She had some fellow in the forces. It was never me.'

'I never said it was. But you were afraid it had been – which comes to the same. And she would have had you. You told me so yourself. Anyway, like I said, I'm expected home. See you Friday fortnight?'

'If I can get away,' Jonah said resentfully. He had to drink the next two pints alone. He didn't like what Billy had said about them calling people up. He would begin a serious campaign to charm Belinda into you-know-what.

Maud did not ask for time off to attend the old lady's funeral. One of Belinda's stern great-uncles, from the photograph, came down to organize it, which was just as well, since Blin went to pieces when it came to choosing hymns, and didn't have the first idea of what was to be done.

'He's seen to everything, thank the Lord,' Belinda said to her friend. 'Even arranged some sandwiches down at the chapel hall in case the neighbours come – though Gran had fallen out with most of them and hadn't spoken to them for years. That's how she wasn't missed for days and days, I suppose. But there's another cousin and his wife I've never met – he's been in touch with them and they are coming down from Fowey. So there's lots of family.'

'Only a pity your brother can't be there.'

Belinda nodded. 'Great-Uncle's going to write to the army and let him know, of course. And the lawyers will want to contact him about the legacy. I only hope they reach him. He was in a front-line hospital the last time he wrote – got a nasty bullet in his leg again – but he was expecting to be moved on to another down the line. But I haven't had a letter since – well, not a proper one. The last one I got from him was almost half crossed out. All over, in indelible pencil, so you couldn't read a thing. Just "Dear Belinda" and then his signature. Waste of time to send it. Who wants a letter that's only purple lines? Don't know why the censor had to do a thing like that – it's not as if my brother would be passing on secrets.'

'Might have told you where he was or something,' Maud said soothingly. 'They censor that, Stan says. But at least you know that when he wrote it he was safe and well.' That sounded rather odd, since the poor man was wounded, and she added hastily, 'But I'll come to the funeral with you and support you if you like – you hardly know these people, by the sound of it.'

Belinda actually smiled. 'Oh, it's all right, Maudie. Jonah will be there. He's been some good about it, though he'll have to miss his rounds. So there'll be someone to support me, as you put it, anyway. No need for you to lose your wages over it. Nice of you, and I would love to have you there, but nobody could really expect you attend. After all, you'd never actually met my grandmother alive.'

'Well if you're quite sure,' Maud murmured. Secretly, it was rather a relief. She hadn't been looking forward to asking Madam for the time: after the Jenny episode the words 'Belinda' and 'funeral' were like red rags to a bull.

But when the shop was shut that evening she called round at the house, rather expecting to find Belinda in and wanting to hear all about it and offer sympathy. When she rang the doorbell, Miss Simms answered it, and Maud explained her errand.

Miss Simms said, 'Come in. I'm afraid Miss Richards has gone out again. Her great-uncle, I believe, is entertaining her. He and some other relatives are staying at the Imperial Inn, and he has arranged for them all to have an early meal there.

But come in and wait by all means. She should not be long.'
She led the way along the passage, which was long and high
and narrow, with the top half painted green and crammed with
pictures and hand-embroidered texts. The bottom half was
cream Lincrusta like the hall at home. 'Come into the parlour.
Would you like some tea?'

This was so unlike the Miss Simms she knew at work that
for a moment Maud could not reply. Then she murmured
politely, 'That would be very nice,' and was duly ushered in.

The parlour was a dark but handsome room – not the sort
of thing that Maud would have associated with Miss Simms
at all. Large brown leather armchairs, a harmonium, book-
shelves and a gate-leg table by the fire. Tasselled red plush
runners on the surfaces, curtains of the same, and walls and
rug of a much deeper red. No ornaments to speak of, just a
vase or two, some faded photographs and one or two stuffed
sea-birds in a case. Only the embroidered antimacassars on
the chairs and a sampler on the wall gave any hint that this
was a woman's home.

Miss Simms caught her glance and gave a little smile. 'This
was my father's favourite room,' she said. 'I haven't changed
it much.' She looked around. 'I could do, I suppose, but there
doesn't seem much point. He always insisted on good quality,
and it's comfortable enough. I don't have many visitors.'
Suddenly her manner changed and she said briskly, 'Tea, I
think we said? I was just going to have some when you knocked
the door. Sit down while I fetch it. I won't be very long.'

Maud sat down dutifully while Miss Simms trotted off, and
could be heard in the kitchen rattling the cups. Maud wriggled in the chair. It was very comfortable, as Miss Simms had
said, but it somehow wasn't possible to feel very much at
ease. After a minute she stood up again.

She was gazing idly at the photographs – quite peculiar
really, all of the same man – when Miss Simms came in a
moment later with the tray. Maud whirled around, feeling
herself turn crimson. It looked extremely rude. She said, to
cover her embarrassment, 'Fine-looking man, your father. I
presume that's who it is? I couldn't help but notice – so many
photographs.'

Miss Simms put the tray down and turned slightly pink
herself. She said primly, 'Yes, these are of my father. He went

for a sitting when my mother died, and they took several
portraits. He liked to see them there.' She was setting out
some cups and saucers as she spoke: 'eggshell china with little
roses on. It was so beautiful that Maud was quite alarmed.
Supposing that she dropped it, or did something terrible?

She found herself gushing, 'So you have kept them as he
liked them – and the room as well.'

Miss Simms said nothing, just poured out the tea – through
a strainer made of proper silver, by the look of it. She cleared
her throat and handed Maud the cup.

Maud was all contrition. 'Now I have upset you. I'm some
sorry about that. Of course I shouldn't prattle on about your
poor father in that way. You must miss him something terrible
. . .' She tailed off in dismay.

'And why should I do that?' Miss Simms was offering her
the sugar bowl and tongs, but Maud was too startled to think
of sugar lumps. 'To tell the truth, Miss Olds, I think I hated
him. He ruled our lives – my mother's and my own. We were
a disappointment. I was not a son, and my mother was not
able to produce another child.' She dropped a lump of sugar
in her tea, and stirred it briskly as she spoke. 'Of course, he
provided for us very handsomely, but nobody's wishes counted
but his own. Surely, Miss Olds, you can see that from this
room. This was my mother's home and mine, but his stamp
is everywhere.' She tapped the teaspoon on the cup and put
it down. 'Since Miss Richards has been living here, I had
come around to thinking I would alter it at last – bring a
little more light and colour to the house – but now it seems
I might be losing her. You know she has come into some
money, I presume?'

'She told me there was something,' Maud replied. 'But I
don't think she has any thoughts of moving out. Going to
save the money till she gets wed and has to leave her job
down at the booking office, she says.'

'Thanks to your father.' Miss Simms sipped her tea.

'Thanks to you as well. She would never have got it without
a respectable address. It was good of you to have her. You
have been very kind – especially when Belinda was turned
off in disgrace.'

'For carrying letters between Jenny Liskey and her unsuitable young man?' The older woman gave a bitter laugh and

put her teacup down. 'But that is just the point. She told you, I imagine, that I had a young man once?'

Maud did not know how to answer. She felt her cheeks turn pink. 'She said you allowed your family to interfere, and you now regretted . . . Oh!' She turned to look at the photographs of that handsome face that dominated the room. 'It was your father, then?' she blurted out.

'I see you understand,' Miss Simms said softly. 'It is all right, Miss Olds. I did not delude myself that she could keep it to herself. Miss Richards is always bursting with what she calls her "news", so one gives her only the broadest outline of the truth. Yes, it was my father who put a stop to it. There was a young man who came here to paint – my father did not think that he was suitable, and forbade me to see him or communicate with him. The young man wanted me to run away with him, but, unlike young Jenny, I didn't have the nerve. I didn't even dare to write and tell him so, in case my father intercepted it. If I'd had Belinda's courage I might have married him – though I would prefer that the full story didn't get about. I shouldn't care for Madam to get to hear of it.' She saw Maud's startled face. 'That's why I would not have told Belinda this. You, I imagine, are a little more discreet?'

'I . . . well . . . that is . . . I try to be . . .'

'Then we are agreed. Another cup of tea?'

Maud was still shaking her head in disbelief. 'And because he was a painter, your father disapproved?'

Miss Simms smiled sadly. 'Because he was a painter, among other things. Though his family had money – quite a lot of it. Mostly, I think, my father disapproved because the young man came from overseas.'

'He wasn't English?' Maud was so startled that she put the cup down hard. 'American, perhaps? Or from the colonies?'

Miss Simms looked long and hard at her. 'Not even from the English-speaking countries, I'm afraid, although he spoke the language very well indeed. He was a lovely man. But he was German. Isn't it absurd?'

'A German?' Maudie was appalled. She thought of Stanley, out there fighting them. 'But that would mean . . .'

'Exactly. So you see, Miss Olds, if I had married him I might have been the wife and mother of an enemy.' She got abruptly to her feet and scooped up the tea tray. 'And now,

I am afraid that I have said too much. I would be grateful if you didn't mention this tête-à-tête to anyone. Especially not Miss Richards, whom I think that we can hear coming up the path this minute. She couldn't hold her tongue – and with this war on I don't think Penzance would really understand.'

'I won't say anything to anybody,' Maudie promised her. And she didn't either, not even years later, though she was never to forget. How could anyone have imagined such a secret for Miss Simms?

Sawyer was right. There weren't many of B company that Stan recognized, and some of those had grown so worn and pale that he would hardly have known them if they hadn't greeted him. Exhaustion and war had aged them, turned them lined and pale, though they were surprisingly cheerful and outwardly stoical, and there were grisly jokes about the trench that they were moving to relieve.

The same trench. The one that had been taken from the Hun. The defences were now better, with a higher parapet, and there was nothing recognizable about it but the site, but it was the same. All that loss and effort and there was no advance. There had been, someone told him. They'd once made a hundred yards, but were driven back again. That enterprise had cost the company more than a man for every foot of ground.

Even the muddy duckboards were essentially the same. Stan had rather expected that, since it was summer now, the problem would have vanished, but Sawyer simply grinned. 'Every time it bloody rains it bloody floods in here,' he said. 'Still, we've got a few new amenities that you won't have seen. Look at this, for instance.' He unslung his rifle and hung it on something that stuck out from the wall. It looked like . . .

'Someone's foot?' Stan ventured with disgust.

Sawyer only laughed. 'Used to be. Don't think he'll be wanting to use it any more.'

'Whose?' He hardly liked to ask.

A shrug. 'Might be ours or Jerry's – it's very hard to know. Got buried sometime in the last attack – found it when we took the trench again – and it's quite impossible to move it as things are. Not even sure if it's only just a foot, or whether the owner is in there somewhere too. But it has its uses. Keeps your rifle dry.' His voice was casual. He slapped Stan on the back. 'Don't look so shattered, Hoskins. These things happen here. You won't even notice it in a day or two.'

And the worse thing was that he was right. You didn't notice it. There was too much else to think about. Shells that whined and screamed and landed frighteningly close, with that familiar crump. Men, beyond hope of rescue, who whined and screamed as loudly as the shells, sometimes for hours before they faded out. Others whose agony softened into moans. Snipers that filled the night with deadly bursts of fire, and threatened to blow your head off if you raised it for a second above the parapet. There were three skulls, like mushrooms sprouting from the mud, in an enormous crater just in front of them. Not the same crater where he'd got his wound: there were new ones every day, blowing the previous landscape into oblivion.

And yet the weary soldiers, on their dug-out sleeping shelves, made jokes about the war and sang songs about 'whizz-bangs', even though their hands were trembling as they lit their fags. Stan tried to join the singing, to keep his courage up.

There were rumours of another offensive to be made soon, but for the moment it was just a waiting game, sitting in your dugout wondering when the Germans would mount a raid on you. From time to time a party was sent out to mend a wire or glean intelligence, or, once, to storm a German look-out and machine-gun post. (It failed. Another party was sent out afterwards to bring survivors back.) Stan, with his new-found expertise with bombs, was rather in demand. He went on three such parties, lobbed a grenade or two, and each time crawled back into the trench again, relieved and trembling. He wondered if Sawyer could smell the fear on him.

Sawyer, though, still talked about his 'old comrade, Stan', and seemed to have forgotten that Tregurtha had ever existed. There was a gangling youth from Sussex who was now the target of his bullying. 'Beanpole' Smith was naturally clumsy, but Sawyer made it worse: every time the poor lad did something maladroit – let something fall or tripped over his own enormous feet – Sawyer swore and sneered and ranted and made him look a fool.

Perhaps, then, it was a particularly unhappy stroke of fate

which meant that when Stan went out with a grenade party
again, Smith and Sawyer should both be of the company:
Sawyer commanding a diversionary group, and Smith chosen
as lookout for his extra height.

The day had been a fine one, and the sky was clear, and
though the sortie was intended to be carried out at night, under
cover of darkness, there was a brilliant moon that lit the ruined
landscape with an eerie light. The ground was full of traps
and obstacles – pits and ruts and craters which loomed at
every step, and piles of soft debris which gave way under you.
There were other hazards too: bits of jagged wood and metal
and fragments of other, softer things one didn't care to look
at very much. In daylight this area was the playground of the
guns; in total darkness it would have been well-nigh impossible. But the moonlight could make them targets every time
they moved.

Their objective was a ruined building over to the left. It
was said to be abandoned – a small force had abandoned it
a day or two ago, according to intelligence that Bennett had
received – but the idea was to lob a grenade or two inside
and ensure that this was accurate, and Jerry wasn't in there
waiting to attack. If it was deserted their unit would move in.
A Company had tried to storm it a month or two before, when
more of it was standing, from what Sawyer said, but the
Germans had defended it. It had been so knocked about in all
the fighting since that it was hard to see how it could be
defended now, or what advantage it was supposed to offer in
its present state – just half a wall and piles of debris all around
– but those were the orders.

They were halfway by now. The shell craters looked like
ghastly sand dunes in the ghostly light, an innocence that
made them doubly treacherous. Ahead of them the ruin stood
out in ghastly silhouette. There was no sound to speak of. The
big guns were silent now. Only the occasional sputter of a
sniper to the left, or the slow creak from a broken panel
swaying in the wind. At the order Smith crawled on ahead.

They saw him dimly creeping to the ruin, and saw his
gesture beckoning them on. 'Now!' Sawyer whispered. Stan
got to his feet.

The first blast sent him backwards, showering him with
dirt. For a moment he just lay there, trying to work out if he

was dead or not. He decided that he wasn't. He wasn't even hit. His limbs all seemed to function when he asked them to, but he was too shocked to move them very far. He winced as something else went whizzing overhead. There was another thud. He pulled himself together, and sat up, spitting earth. Very cautiously, he looked around, slightly surprised to find himself unhurt.

Between himself and Smith there was now another crater. Sawyer and the others were a yard or two ahead, all of them half-crawling up to it. By some miracle, they seemed to be all right. Sawyer looked back, and saw Stan. 'Hoskins!' He crawled back a pace or two. 'Thought you were a goner. Come on then! Good man!'

Stan stared at him a little stupidly.

There was another explosion to the right of them. There seemed to be a barrage starting right along the line.

'It's not us they're after. Come on! On your feet. Or are you wounded somewhere?'

Stan couldn't answer. He just shook his head.

'Come on then! That's an order. We've got to clear that barn. There isn't time to dally. They're softening up the line – probably planning to attack when it gets light. Pick up your gun, man, and start running now!'

Stan, still in a kind of dream, picked up his gun and ran.

# Part Four
## July 1916 – June 1919

# One

Maud was getting worried. Here it was, midsummer, and no word from Stan since May. What with him being so down and everything, she couldn't help but worry.

His last letter had been a much more cheerful one, too – all about how he was settling into the life again, and full of wry jokes about the awful food. 'Bully beef and biscuits – that's the feast today. No one can open a tin quite like our army cook, and scorch it so the outside tastes of burning and the middle is still cold. Some of the men call this particular offering "burf-a-la-reetz" – that's French for "beef in the Ritz fashion", apparently, though I don't believe the Ritz could do it that way if they tried – but I think cook lost his taste buds in the last attack.'

More bitter than the old Stan, but it still made her laugh out loud. She had written an excited letter in reply – and then there had been silence. Weeks and weeks of it.

It was the first thing she asked as soon as ever she got home. 'Anything from Stan?' The question had become mechanical by now, like one of those blessed new-fangled gramophones. And Dad would answer, just as certainly, ''Fraid we haven't had a letter this week either, love.'

'Beginning to think there never will be,' she said bitterly one day, when they'd had the conversation for the umpteenth time. 'Can't sleep for thinking about him, worrying what's wrong. If something's happened, I would sooner know, whether he's hurt or ill, or has gone raving mad – he looked as if he might do, last time he was home – or blown himself to pieces with his wretched bombs. Least I could stop imagining all the other things.' She found her voice was trembling as she spoke.

Tully reached out a friendly hand to her, but she shook him

off. She went into the scullery and took off her coat and busied herself helping Aunt Jane with the tea.

Dad came up behind her, and said gently in her ear, 'I know how you are feeling – I'd be the same myself. But don't you fret, my handsome. Anything serious and you would have heard. You ask me, it's likely just a hold-up with the mail. The post is something chronic from overseas these days, what with Jerry attacking railway lines and roads and ships and that – we're always having people come down the station now with tales about how such and such a thing has been delayed.'

She didn't turn around. She bit her lip and went on fetching cups and saucers from the shelf. 'That's supposing that he wrote a letter at all, and hasn't fallen for some saucy girl in France. You hear such stories about what they're like.'

Dad gave a little laugh. 'I shouldn't waste a minute's worry on that score. Stan's got eyes for nobody but you.' He squeezed her shoulders gently in a gesture of support. Dad didn't generally belong to do that sort of thing, and the unexpected moment brought her close to tears.

He was embarrassed, too. She could tell by the way he coughed and muttered gruffly, 'Well, I'm off upstairs, so I can take me studs out before I have me tea. This collar's killing me.' And off he went.

Aunt Jane, bustling about with bread and potted ham, had been listening in, and she tried to be sympathetic, in her way. 'Couldn't help overhearing what your father said. And I'm sure he's right. There's some good reason for it, if Stan hasn't wrote. He's a nice boy, is your Stanley, and he wouldn't simply stop – not if he could help it, any road.'

'That's what I'm afraid of,' Maud replied. Her voice was very small. 'Like I said, he could be ill, or hurt. I should be glad if it was only that.' She went through to the kitchen with the pile of cups, but she put them down and dashed back into the scullery again. No good letting Tully see her bursting into tears – it would only upset him, and that would make things worse. She splashed her face with water from the jug beside the sink, but it didn't help.

There was a handkerchief of Father's, rolled up to be ironed, and Aunt Jane took it from the basket and held it out to her. 'Here, stop your snivelling and wipe your face with this. You're worried about Stanley – can't say that I'm surprised. But like your Father said, we would have heard if anything like that had happened.' Aunt Jane was severe. 'Stan's got his stripes and that. You know what happens in a case like that – they notify the parents straight away. So don't start getting notions that you're going to find his name stuck up in a list of dead and missing on a lamp post anywhere, like some folks have to do.'

Maud flushed. She had been looking on the public lists, but Stanley's name hadn't featured. 'It did occur to me.'

Aunt Jane tutted. 'Upset yourself for nothing. Stan wouldn't have been there. They only do it local and he isn't from Penzance. And he's a proper nincio, I've heard your father say.'

Maud was puzzled for a moment, then she realized. 'NCO, you mean?'

'Well, however you pronounce it.' Aunt Jane sounded sharp. 'I know he's quite important with his bombs and that. Look at that family across the road – three boys they've lost, in this last month or two – only had one stripe up, not corporals like your Stan – and each time there was a proper letter from a senior officer, saying how they had the army's sympathy and all that sort of rot. Poor woman almost lost her mind when that last letter came – she knew what was in it before she opened it – but shows you what they do. No, your father's right. If anything like that had happened to your Stan, Mrs Hoskins would have let you know, for sure.'

Maud scrubbed at her face with the handkerchief again. 'That's what I keep trying to persuade myself,' she said.

'Well, there you are then,' said her aunt, as though that settled it. 'Come in and have your supper, before the tea gets cold.' She was trying to offer comfort in the only way she knew, but Maud had no appetite tonight for potted ham and buns – even though Tully had helped to mix the cakes himself, as he proudly told her, through a mouth full of crumbs.

'You eat mine for me, then,' Maud said. 'I've got to hurry back.'

She could not have said why she was anxious to be on her own again, and it was worse, if anything, when she did get back. The attic room had never seemed so lonely as it did that night. She tossed and turned for hours, thinking about Stan, and wishing she had Belinda to confide her troubles to.

Perhaps she'd make the time, some evening, to go and see
her friend. Nobody, surely, could object to that? It would be
nice to catch up on Belinda's news, as well. She wouldn't
even mind hearing about Jonah and his Ma.

Belinda was sitting in Miss Simms' kitchen, sipping cocoa,
listening to the rain and attempting unsuccessfully to write a
note to Maud. How could she put it? That was the awkward
thing. She wasn't at all sure that she wanted to confide. Not
just now, at any rate. Perhaps a little later, when she was safely
wed, and before the problem got too obvious, supposing that
it did. She wasn't even really certain, even now, that what
Jonah said was right, that she might have a baby from him
touching her like that. She'd always had a notion there was
more to it than that – something rather shameful that you
didn't talk about – and Jonah said there could be, but touching
was enough. Billy Polkinghorne had said so, he declared, and
Billy ought to know since Annie had given birth to a bouncing
girl a week or two ago.

In the first drafts of the letter she had poured this out to
Maud, but on second thoughts she'd screwed them up and put
them in the fire. That wasn't any good. Maud couldn't tell
her if her fears were justified, any more than Blin had any
clear ideas herself. She would just be shocked. Blin knew that
from their conversations in the attic room.

If only Grandmother was still alive, she thought, she might
have plucked up courage and asked her what was what, but
as it was there was no one she could turn to for advice.
Obviously she couldn't ask an old maid like Miss Simms –
though they had become quite friendly in the last few weeks,
and more than once Miss Simms had let her come and make
a cup of something warm, or heat up a bought pasty when
the range was hot, or even invited her to come and share a
frugal meal. It was one of the reasons that Belinda had never
moved away, though she could have afforded something, after
Grandmother had died.

It was almost as if Miss Simms quite liked to have her there.
Probably wouldn't even mind that Belinda was sitting here,
helping herself to paper and the cocoa tin, while she herself
was out at some committee do, aiming to raise money for
comforts for the Wounded Soldiers' Fund. All the same, when

a minute later there was a footstep at the door, Blin stuffed the paper in the fire and poured the cocoa down the sink. No good killing the fatted calf, as Gran would have said.

But instead of Miss Simms' latch key turning in the lock, there was a rapping on the knocker. Belinda went to answer, a little nervously, and was delighted and surprised to find Maudie on the doorstep, in a shawl and bonnet dripping with the rain.

'My life!' she said, seizing her friend's hands in both her own. 'Imagine seeing you! I've been wanting to run into you for simply days and days. Came past Madam's once or twice, to see if you were there, but I couldn't see you and I didn't dare come in. I was trying this minute to write a little note to you, thought I would seal it and send it with Miss Simms . . .' She tailed off, suddenly aware of damp from Maudie's sleeve. 'But here, what am I thinking of, standing here like this. Come on in out the wet. And you with no umbrella – you must be soaking through.' She led the way into the narrow hall.

'Didn't pay enough attention to the sky when I went out.' Maud wiped her wet boots on the doormat and took off her dripping hat. 'This shower came on sudden and it proper caught me out. Trouble is, you don't expect this kind of weather in July. But it's been odd for days. Aunt Jane thinks it's all these new-fangled aeroplanes. Stands to reason, she says, sending things up in the air. Bound to affect the climate.' She shook her skirt. 'And now look what I've done! Made a puddle on Miss Simms' tiles. Don't know what she'll think.'

'I'll see to it directly,' Belinda said. 'She's not in tonight, and what she doesn't see won't hurt. You come up with me.' Then, on a sudden impulse, she added daringly, 'I'll make you a drop of cocoa, if you've a mind to it. Miss Simms lets me use her kitchen now and then.' She tried to sound as if it happened every day.

Maud didn't seem to notice. 'I'd be some glad of something.' She glanced around the room. 'But I'd better find something to put down on the bed, or I'll damp the bedclothes when I sit on it.'

Belinda found a towel and the bit of sack she used for dirty laundry. It was one of Jonah's coal sacks but it had cleaned up nice. 'Here, you have that, and I'll go down and make this bit of drink. You look proper famished. You all right, are you?'

Maud gave a weary sort of smile. 'Tell you all about it in a minute,' she replied. 'If you're going to make that drink . . .?'

Belinda nodded. 'I got news for you, as well. Won't be a tick,' she promised, and she went downstairs. She'd have to use Miss Simms' cocoa tin again since she'd used up all her own – and she'd better look lively doing it as well, or Miss Simms would come and find her and that would never do. The kettle was beside the hob and still a little warm, and though she'd been careful to bank the range down for the night, it wasn't hard to stir it up again – just enough to heat the water for a drink. Two minutes later she was up the stairs again.

'Here you are,' she said in breathless triumph, thrusting back the door. 'There's milk and sugar in the corner, you can add your own . . . Why, Maud, whatever is it?'

Her friend was standing by the window, staring at the street, but it was clear that she'd been crying while Belinda was downstairs. Her eyes were red and swollen and there were smudges on her cheeks.

Belinda put the cup down. 'Come on, out with it. You can have your cocoa after.' A dreadful thought occurred to her. 'My lor'! It isn't Stan?'

Maud nodded wordlessly, and pulled her lips in hard. Then, as though she almost didn't trust her voice, she said, 'Well, it is and isn't, I don't know either way. That's the worst of it. I'm worried, Blin. I haven't heard from him. Not though I've written half a dozen times.'

Belinda's mind was racing. 'They haven't sent them back to you? Your ones to him I mean?'

'No, why would they?' Maudie looked surprised.

'I mean, if he was dead or anything . . .' No sooner had she spoken she wished the words unsaid. She hadn't meant it to come out like that, all bald and horrible. But Maudie had stopped crying – that was the funny thing.

Maud swallowed, sniffed a bit, and said, 'I suppose you're right. Return them, wouldn't they? If not to me, at least to Stanley's folks. That's what Dad and everyone's been telling me for days. But I don't know. I've written Mrs Hoskins, but there's no reply from there, either.' She got out a handkerchief and blew her nose in it.

Belinda tried to think of something comforting to say. 'Perhaps he's in the hospital again, and they've all gone to see him, like they did before. You said before he went back overseas that he wasn't really fit to go.'

Maud had screwed the hanky up into a ball. 'Even so, you'd think she'd write and tell me something, wouldn't you?' She dabbed her swollen cheeks. 'Dad says it might be a hold-up in the mail.'

Belinda put on a serious expression. 'Or perhaps it's the censor or something got to it. I told you what happened to that letter that I got. Or perhaps Stan's posted somewhere where it's hard to post things from. My brother was at the hospital, so it wasn't hard for him, but your Stan's up at the front. I don't suppose that getting mail sent home is a priority.'

Maudie looked doubtful. 'I suppose you're right. It's only, after a little while you start to fear the worst. Anyway, thank you, Blin, for listening to all this. I had to talk to someone, and I couldn't do it at home. Can't really say too much there, with Tully listening in.' She took the cup of cocoa and sat down on the bed. She took a grateful sip. 'I knew you'd be a help.'

'I haven't done anything,' Belinda said. But it made her feel virtuous and important all the same. She wished she could think of something else to suggest that would be helpful. But there wasn't anything. Unless . . .

'You hadn't thought of going up to Truro, to talk to Stanley's folks? Soon find out then, if there was anything.'

Maud drained the last of the cocoa from the cup, and looked at Belinda across the rim of it. 'I did wonder about that. But the farm is miles away from where the station is. How would I ever get there if they didn't meet the train?'

'Bet you'd find some wagon that was driving out that way, give you a lift for sixpence if you smiled at him. And there must be horse-buses or something that go somewhere near – even in wartime, people got to shop. Didn't you say you used to catch a bus sometimes, with your Aunt Jane, when you were up that way? I remember some story how she told the driver off, when he went fast round a corner and she slid across the seat.'

That almost made Maud smile. 'That's right. Bus stopped a mile away. There's a path across the fields. Wonder if I'd find it. Be afraid of getting lost.'

Belinda was still glowing with the pride of helpfulness. She said, before she'd stopped to think it out, 'I could come with you, if you'd like me to.' What had she said that for? She hated walking far, and it would cost the ticket. 'Have to be a weekend, mind,' she added hastily. 'And I couldn't be there hours.'

'That's good of you,' Maud said. And then, to Blin's relief, she frowned and shook her head. 'But I couldn't ask you to go to that expense. Any road, it's better if I go up on my own. It's private, between me and Mrs Hoskins, after all. And you don't know the family – it would be difficult. But thank you for the offer. Makes me feel better, just to hear you say.'

'Well if you are quite sure, then,' Belinda said, and then added quickly before Maud could change her mind, 'Make sure you come and tell me if there is any news.'

'Course I will,' Maud said. She looked much happier. 'And talking about news, wasn't there something you wanted to tell me? You said when I arrived.'

Belinda fidgeted. 'Oh yes, of course there was. But I feel a bit awkward telling you this now, what with your worries about Stan and everything.' She was amazed to realize that it had almost slipped her mind. Thinking too much about what Maud had to say, perhaps – or was it really that she didn't want to face it, now it came to it?

'Well?' Maud said. 'I'm waiting.' Then suddenly she grinned. 'You've set a date to marry Jonah? That's it, I suppose?'

Belinda made a face. 'Wasn't much news then, was it? Since you guessed at once. But yes, you're right. Next month it's going to be. At least we hope it will. Jonah has gone to see about the licence and publishing the banns. Thursday morning, we were thinking of. Don't suppose you'll be able to get the time to come?'

Maud didn't answer that directly. She said thoughtfully, 'Made up your mind to do it quickly, when you did decide? After you have kept him waiting all these months, as well.'

Belinda held her breath. Any minute Maud would ask her why she'd changed her mind

'What is it, Blin? You don't seem very cock-a-hoop. Always thought that it was what you wanted, in the end. And you can't be having doubts. You promised Jonah that you'd have him, months and months ago.'

Belinda forced a smile. 'Of course I did. I said I'd wed him in the summer, and that's what I'm going to do. Only it doesn't seem kind to tell you, when you're worrying for Stan.'

Maud stretched out a friendly hand and squeezed her on the arm. 'Oh, so that's what upsetting you. Well don't you worry, Blin. I'd rather one of us be happy, than us both be miserable. No, you marry Jonah, and I wish you joy. You let me know what day it's going to be, and I'll get some time off – even if I have to lose some pay to manage it.' She grinned. 'Though I'll have to tell Madam what I want it for, I suppose, and she mightn't let me, if she knows it's you.'

Belinda found it was her turn to grin. 'Well she's going to know about my getting wed in any case. You know that I had a little bit of money that Gran left to me? Well, know what I'm going to do? Walk into Madam's, bold as brass, and buy something to wear – not a fancy wedding gown or any fool-ishness like that, but a smart skirt and coat perhaps, or a nice two-piece and blouse. Something really nice that I can have for afterwards as well.' When I can get back into it, she added to herself.

Maud looked startled, but her eyes were sparkling. 'Blin, you couldn't. Not after everything.'

'Don't see why not!' Belinda answered airily, but the plan was strengthening, the more she talked of it. 'My money's good as anybody's. Serve Madam right, as well. She'd have to call me "madam" if I was a customer.'

Maud's shocked, delighted giggle was music to her ears. Perhaps, Belinda thought, this wedding business might be quite fun after all.

Jonah's heart sank when he heard about her plan to go down to Madam's and make an exhibition of herself. Why look for trouble, when it didn't look for you? And it would cost money that she didn't need to spend. Ma would have some-thing to say about that, if she heard.

They were sitting in their usual Sunday place on the sea-wall again, dangling their legs and watching a solitary crabber drifting home, its red-brown sails hardly filling in the wind. The afternoon was mild; the squally showers of the last few days had given way to misty sunshine now. He slipped his arm around Belinda's waist.

'What do you want new clothes for? Those look fine to me.

Bit of trimming and you'd be as smart as paint. Better to put that bit of money by – put it towards our own place, in a year or so, 'stead of having to stay living in Ma and Pa's best room.' He gave her a squeeze and his most winning smile. 'And you so handy with your needle too. Make yourself something smashing in a brace of shakes.'

But she wasn't falling for his flattery today. She pulled away from him. 'That's as may be, Jonah, but I've made up my mind. I can afford it, what with what I earn, and that bit of money I was left by Gran. And there'll still be something to put by.'

'But . . .' he began, but she interrupted him.

'It's my money, Jonah, so it's up to me.' She meant it, too, he could tell that from her tone.

Jonah felt like arguing, but he didn't dare. When they were married it might be different, but first he had to get her safely up the aisle. Have to look jolly sharp about it too – already they had started calling people up, from that confounded register of theirs. And now they were talking about taking married men too – they had voted for it in Parliament last month. Thank heaven he'd put his occupation down as 'coal'. That was an 'essential industry' or something of the kind, and he'd heard that miners didn't have to go. Of course it didn't really stretch to coalmen like himself, but he'd put it down in any case – it wasn't actually a lie – and they hadn't yet caught up with him. But it might come to it, and if he wasn't married they would have him over there, quicker than you could say 'best Pembroke, guaranteed to burn'. But if there was a family, well, that was a different thing.

That's why he'd been forced to play that little trick on Belinda. He hadn't meant to lie. But although he had pressed her every week, she wouldn't set a date. She seemed to like working down the station and living on her own – not a bit like she had been when she was down at Madam's shop. He'd done his damnedest to persuade her to a bit of you-know-what, as well. As Billy had once said, if she was in the family way, she'd have to stop this shilly-shallying and marry him at once. But she wouldn't have it, no how. She allowed him a little bit of groping here and there, and then she put her foot down. 'That's enough of that. Not until we're married.' She'd been very firm on that and he hadn't liked to force it, in case she changed her mind and decided that she wasn't going to marry him at all.

Luckily she'd let it slip that she had no idea – otherwise he could not have fooled her like he did. He'd played it fairly cleverly – or so he thought – drawing back his hand one day as if he was alarmed, and saying he was sorry if he had gone too far. Then came a week or two of pretending to be worried, and asking how she was. 'But don't you worry, Blinnie. It will be all right. It's not what we intended but I will stand by you if there's a child. And Billy says that it could happen, after what we've done. Of course it isn't certain; we'll have to wait and see. It's just what folks will say that I'm concerned about. Mind you, if we get a licence now we could be safely married before anyone finds out.'

Yes, it was quite clever. And in the end it worked – though it was a pity that he'd had to bring Billy into it. Funny to think she'd once been so keen to marry that she'd almost put him off. The tables were turned on that score now and no mistake. He daren't even cross her on the question of this dress. She was still going on about it.

'When a girl is getting married she wants a bit of a treat. I've never had a shop-bought dress in my life, and if there's a baby coming, I might never do again. It isn't easy finding time to sew things properly, when you're out working all the daylight hours. I don't even have a machine these days, to do the seams, and you can't leave snippings all over someone else's house. But I could do with something new.' She never looked at him. She was watching the crabber as if her life depended on the catch. 'You want to be proud of me, don't you, on the day?'

She had him there. What could he say to that?

'I'd be proud of you if you were wearing a coal sack,' he declared, and earned a flattered glance. 'But I suppose you're right. You go to Madam's, if you've a mind to it.' There! He'd given in.

She turned to face him fully, smiling and looking up under her lashes in that way she had. 'You're very good to me.'

And so he was, he thought. Too damty soft by half. Though things would have to be a bit different after they were wed.

# Two

For over a week after her little chat with Belinda, Maud could not decide whether or not she should go to Truro. She had talked herself out of the idea a dozen times. But on Friday evening, after the shop was shut, she came to the decision she should have made at first. It was getting late; the lamp-lighter was already on his rounds and the first glowing gas lights were casting little pools of light as she hurried up the Arcade Steps and to Belgravia Street.

The outer door was open, and she didn't stop to knock. She went straight into the kitchen, where her aunt was sitting by the range, and blurted out the little speech that she had inwardly rehearsed. 'Shan't be here to tea on Sunday after all, Aunt Jane. Going to go up Truro, see the Hoskinses. I wanted to have a word with Mrs Hoskins about Stan. She's always said I'm welcome, any time I like, and last time I saw her I promised I would come. I've been meaning to go up there ever since he left.'

Her aunt looked up from darning socks, and gave a doubtful sniff. 'Bit of a sudden thing, though. I hope you let her know, so that you're expected. You can't go dropping in. People want a bit of notice, if they've got to give you tea.' That was meant as a rebuke. Aunt Jane was put out, as Maud had known she would be – she'd probably made a bit of extra stew for Sunday tea, and now Maud wouldn't be there. Aunt Jane sniffed again. 'Specially with the war on. Things are hard to get.'

'Oh, they know I'm coming. I wrote them in the week.' Maud tried to sound as confident and casual as she could. She didn't mention that she'd written days and days ago, in plenty of time to get an answer – but there had been none. She just said, 'Thought I'd go up on the early train and get home before dark.'

'I should think so too. At your age! Bad enough you traipsing round the streets here at this hour. Don't know what your father would say if he was home!' Aunt Jane wove the needle through the darn again, but she pulled it so tight that she cobbled it. Poor old Tully, that sock would rub his heel. Maud was fairly itching to get her hands on it, but Aunt Jane hated interference in that way.

She sat down on the settle. 'Well, he'll be here very soon. I'll stay and talk to him, since I won't see him Sunday, by the look of it.' Aunt Jane was struggling to rethread the needle now. Maudie took a risk. 'I'll finish off that darning while I'm waiting if you like – give you a chance to get his supper hot.' She saw her aunt's expression and she added hastily, 'After all, you paid for me to learn to sew. Might as well have a bit of benefit yourself.'

It did the trick. Her aunt got up and gave the sock to Maud. 'Well, here you are then. Mind you do it firm. It's no good having dainty little darns that wear through in a week. Tully's too hard on his socks.' And off she went to scrub potatoes in the scullery, leaving Maud to do the rest of the mending in the pile: one of Father's socks and a pullover of Tully's that had gone though on the sleeve.

Maud was deft at darning and she quite enjoyed the task. She had soon worked down the pile, and was tactfully unpicking the sock Aunt Jane had done, when there was a scuffle at the doorstep and her Dad was home.

'Why, hello, my lover! What you doing here?' He came across and ran a friendly hand across her hair.

Aunt Jane looked round from the doorway of the scullery and said, 'Come to say she isn't coming, if you heard the like. Going up to Truro, to talk to Stanley's mum.'

Dad was taking off the jacket of his uniform. He glanced at Maudie sharply. 'That right? Heard something, have you?'

Maudie shook her head.

He hung the coat on a chair back and brushed it carefully with the curved clothes-brush from the mantelpiece. He spat on any dirty spots and rubbed them gently clean, then polished up the buttons with his handkerchief. Maudie had seen him do the same thing every night all through her childhood, and it made her smile, though it brought a secret lump into her throat as well.

Perhaps that was what made her murmur, so that Aunt Jane couldn't hear, 'I wrote to Mrs Hoskins. She didn't answer me. But I've got to go and see her. Find out what is what.'

He didn't look persuaded, but he kept his voice down too. 'Do you think that's wise?'

'Think if it was Mother, and you hadn't heard.' She chose the one argument that he could not resist.

He nodded slowly. 'I suppose you must. You sure you'll be all right? Here, wait a minute.' He searched his trouser pocket and took out half a crown. 'You take this, in case.' He held it out, a big round heavy silver coin.

She shook her head. 'Two shillings and sixpence. That's more than a day's wage. Dad, I can't take it. Anyway, Aunt Jane . . .'

Dad shook his head. 'That's my baccy money, and it's mine to spend. Nothing to do with Jane. She has the housekeeping. You don't have to spend it – if you find you don't need it, you can give it back – but if you're going to Truro on your own like that, I'd sooner you had a bit of extra money in your purse. I don't know how to say this, Maudie love, but if the Hoskinses aren't answering there may be something wrong. Mightn't be your Stanley. Might be illness in the family, or maybe Granfer's died. Could be anything. But if they can't run you to the station in the cart, you might be glad of money to get yourself back home.' He sighed. 'Only wish that I could come up there with you myself, but I'm working Sunday and I can't be spared. There aren't the men round like there used to be before. Can't even swap my shift.' It was a long speech for Father and he stopped for breath.

Maud nodded. 'I know you would. But I shall be all right.'

He pressed the coin into her palm and closed her fingers round it. 'Just you make sure you come and see me when you get back to Penzance. I'll be at the station. Just to see that you're all right.'

'Wilfred, now what nonsense are you putting into the child's head?' Aunt Jane was at the doorway. 'Sit down and eat your tea. I've made some mashed potato and a sprinkling of cheese and I found a bit of onion that I've grated in as well. I had some with Tully a little earlier.'

Father sat down at the table. 'And what about our Maud?'

'I expect she's eaten.'

Maud said, 'Yes, I have,' though it did smell and look delicious – much better than the boiled fish stew that was always
Friday dinner for the girls at Madam's shop. 'Now I've done
the darning and I've talked to Dad, it's time that I went home.
Be back a week on Sunday. I will see you then.' And before
either of them could stop her, she was through the door and
on her way to Madam's, with the half a crown clutched like
a magic talisman in her hand.

Belinda's appearance at the shop on Saturday did not cause
quite the commotion that she hoped it would, though it promised well enough.

Madam came out to meet her, her face as hard as stone.
'Miss Richards, I thought I'd made my position very clear.
There is no longer a position for you in this establishment.'
There were several customers already in the shop, and Madam
was hissing softly so they couldn't hear, then fixed an imita-
tion smile firmly on her face.

Belinda was disappointed. She had ruffled Madam's
feathers, that was very clear, but nobody looking could have
guessed what was going on. She said in deliberately ringing
tones, 'But, you misunderstand, I wish to make a purchase.
There was a nice mid-brown wool ensemble which you had
on display. Two and a half guineas, I believe it was. I'd like
to try it on.'

Madam muttered furiously, 'Is this some kind of joke?'

'On the contrary. I have the money here.' Belinda was still
speaking so the whole shop could hear. 'So I would like to
see that outfit, and any other two-piece costumes that you
have. And perhaps a blouse to tone.' That was reckless. She
hadn't really budgeted to buy a blouse as well, but it was
almost worth it to see Madam's face.

There was a stunned silence. People by now were turning
round to stare. Somebody tittered. Madam had turned red.

'Well!' She tried to usher Belinda towards the office door.
'Perhaps we could discuss this in private somewhere else . . .'

Belinda stood her ground. 'There's nothing to discuss. I'm
getting married soon and I want to buy a special outfit for
the day. Of course, I could always buy one off the peg from
somewhere cheap like White's Emporium in town, or send
off mail-order to the guinea tailors that the papers advertise,

but since I have the money I'd like something nice.' She could
not resist a horrid little jibe. 'But of course I'll go elsewhere,
if you don't have the stock. I gather you might be struggling
a little with the war?'

Madam looked as though she might explode. You could see
that she was tempted to do something vigorous – call the
police, perhaps, and have them throw Belinda out, or at least
give her a public dressing-down. But there were customers
present and Madam was clearly anxious to avoid 'unpleas-
antness'. That was what Belinda was now banking on.

'So, may I try the brown one on while I am here? I'm sure
you wouldn't like it to be thought in town that you've had to
start turning customers away?'

It was funny watching Madam struggle for control. The
fixed smile had turned into a sort of a grimace, and when she
spoke it was through gritted teeth. 'Not at all, Miss Richards,
if you'd care to step this way . . .' She waved a hand towards
a cubicle. If looks could poison, Belinda would be dead. 'I'll
find a girl to help you as soon as possible. The thrush-brown
woollen costume, I believe you said?'

So Belinda had her little triumph, but it didn't feel like one.
It was almost disappointing how easy it had been. Perhaps
those two and half guineas were too good to miss. She would
like to have insisted on Madam serving her, but there were
limits to her daring. She tried a final trick. 'I should like Miss
Olds to serve me, please, if that is possible.'

That was a mistake. Madam almost grinned and you could
see the glint of satisfaction in her eyes. 'I am afraid Miss Olds
is not available,' she said. 'She's doing private alterations all
afternoon. But our Miss Tresize will look after you, I'm sure.
She'll be pleased to bring you everything you need.' She
summoned with a gesture. 'Miss Tresize, you're wanted, if
you please. Bring that two-piece from the window for this
customer to see.'

So Belinda was obliged to make do with Miss Tresize – a
skinny girl, with mousy hair pulled back into a bun. Belinda
didn't know her, she was obviously new – a replacement for
the truant Jennifer Liskey perhaps – and she clearly had no
idea who Belinda was. So, although she was pathetically
anxious to oblige, calling Belinda 'madam' every time she
spoke, and would have fetched and carried every costume in

the shop, there was not much satisfaction to be derived from the experience.

If only Maud had been there, it would have been more fun. Imagine the secret giggles that they would have shared! As it was she could only try on the thrush-brown costume – to find it fitted perfectly almost straight away. She did try on a few other things as well, just for appearance's sake, but everything was in drab shades of grey or brown – perhaps because so many women were in mourning nowadays – so there was no pleasure in it and she soon lost interest. Not that she could have bought a colour anyway; she needed something sensible she could wear afterwards.

'I'll take the first one, thank you very much.' Then an idea struck her. 'Actually, I'll have it put aside. There is a little alteration I'd like doing to the hem. I'd like Miss Olds to do it. I've seen her work before. I'd like to book a fitting with her sometime when she's free.'

'Naturally, Madam. Though if it's just the hem wants changing, I could see to that.' The poor girl sounded chagrined. 'But if that's what you prefer.' She went over to the counter and brought back the fittings book. 'She could manage Wednesday, or Tuesday afternoon.'

That was impossible of course, so Belinda had to say, 'I can't come then, I'm working. Well, it doesn't signify. It was an excuse to see her. She's a friend of mine. I'll take the costume with me. It will be all right.'

'Of course, Madam,' said Miss Tresize, in a tone of voice which said that she didn't believe a single word of it, but felt Belinda was being difficult.

And somehow even handing over lots of money for the suit, and having it folded up in tissue in a box, and being called 'madam' as she left the shop, wasn't as satisfying as she had thought it would be.

There was no cart waiting at Truro station. Maud was not surprised. Somehow she had not really expected there would be, since there had still been no answer to her note. But she had been planning what she would do instead, and so she made her way down to the town, and the corner where she'd caught the horse-bus with her aunt.

There was no one waiting, which surprised her, and she

stood for a long time on the empty street until an old man on a bicycle stopped to speak to her. He was a strange kind of fellow, in a sort of uniform, with a great big tuba strapped on the front of the bike. Maud was anxious for a moment, and then she read the words on the badge: 'Blood and Fire'. The Salvation Army, so it was all right. She stopped being frightened, and took in what he'd said. 'Not many buses, Sunday. Where did you want to go?'

Maud told him, feeling foolish that she hadn't thought to check the timetables.

'You must have just missed one. The next one's not for hours. I'd go and find somewhere to have a sit if I was you.'

Maud shook her head. 'Might as well go back and catch the next train home again. It's not as if I'm staying. There's a long walk when I get out to the other end as well – and I got to get back to catch the six-thirty to Penzance in any case. What a waste of time and money,' she added dismally. 'Thought five hours up here would be plenty long enough.'

'Be all right once you got there,' he said thoughtfully. 'There's a bus that runs late afternoon, would get you back in time. Problem is getting you out there to start with, seems to me. Young man in the question, is there, I suppose?'

Maud blushed and nodded, but he held up his hand.

'No, don't tell me, it's none of my affair. I could see it was important – to you at any rate – or you wouldn't be making all this effort to come up on the train.' He pushed his bandsman's cap back and scratched his thinning head. 'Wait a minute though! I think I know how you might manage it – if we're still in time. You stay here a minute . . .' As if Maud had anywhere else to go! 'Won't be a jiffy!' And with that he disappeared.

He had been gone so long that she thought he wasn't coming back. After all, why should he? She was nobody to him. But twenty minutes later she saw him pedalling towards her up the hill, so fast that his face was turning quite scarlet with the strain.

'There you are, young lady. It's your lucky day. You come along with me. My friend Lionel, who's in the band with me – worked with him down the buses, you might almost say, except that I was blacksmithing and he's the workshop side – they've given him a motor-cycle just this week, to go out on call, get to any motor-buses that are broken down.' He grinned. 'Always used to tease him about that, I did. Never get horses breaking down miles from anywhere like that – though he still thinks that motos will take over in the end. Anyhow, he's been tinkering with this thing for days, he's got some petroleum and he wants to try it out. Of course it's the Sabbath, but it's the only chance he's got. Doesn't matter to him which way he goes, he says – his mother lives out that direction, so he could call on her – and he's willing to take you, if you want to come.'

'Me, on a motor-cycle?' Maud was horrified. Of course there were a few of them about before the war, but they'd always struck her as awful, noisy, smelly, dangerous, masculine sort of things. She realized she had sounded very impolite. 'However would we manage? And with a stranger, too!'

He laughed. 'Don't look so startled. I should have mentioned it. He's got a little side-car for carrying the bits, so you would be all right. Bit of a squash of course, because he'll have his wife along, but she's a skinny object and there's no size to you. But he's said he's willing, if you've a mind to it. And it's the only way you're going to get out there this afternoon, I think.'

Perhaps it was the mention of the wife that stilled her fears. Of course it was a dreadfully daring thing to do and not a bit the sort of behaviour that Madam would approve of – more the kind of escapade that Belinda would enjoy. But choice was limited. She could not afford the train fare to come another day and this was obviously a Christian offer, very kindly meant. Besides, some little demon whispered in her brain that there was nobody in Truro who knew her to tell tales.

'Well, if you say so. It's very kind of you. And your friend, of course. I'll let him have a shilling for his trouble,' she added, as if this would somehow make it more respectable. 'Don't want him out of pocket on my account, as well.'

And so, greatly daring, she went with him to the house, where the famous Lionel and his wife – both in leather helmets with driving goggles on – were already in their places and awaiting her.

Which is how she came to be riding out towards the Hoskinses' farm in a side-car, squashed to death, with a middle-aged man and woman that she did not know. She had wondered what on earth she would find to say to them, and whether they'd ask questions, but she need not have worried: it was so bumpy and noisy you could not have heard a word and in any case the wind made speech impossible. In fact, if it wasn't for her shawl – which she tied around her head – Maud felt that the draught would have blown away her hair, let alone her bonnet, although she'd pinned it tight.

So she sat in silence, gripping very hard, as they bounced and bumped and skidded down the dusty roads. Lord knows what she must look like, she thought; she must be grey with dust. From time to time the woman caught her eye and grinned encouragingly at her. Maud smiled wanly back, but her teeth were being jolted together in her head, and she was never so pleased as when the motor-cycle stopped.

'This do you then?' the driver called, and Maudie realized that they were at a bend not far from where Aunt Jane used to live. She had been so bounced about she hadn't recognized the place. 'Take you a little bit further if you like.'

'It's grand here, thank you.' Maud found her voice at last, and scrambled out with quite unseemly haste. It was difficult to do it decently at all – her skirts were quite a hindrance – but she no longer cared. 'Here!' She fumbled for her money, but he waved it away.

'Glad to be of service. Give it to the Lord, or put it in the poor-box next time you're in church. Hope your young man's pleased to see you. I know how it is. We got a boy in the services ourselves.' A wave, and they were gone, roaring down the road in an oily cloud.

Extraordinary people, Maud thought, as she dusted down her ruffled skirts. Not at all what one expected from a Salvationist. But it had been rather an adventure in its way, though heaven knows what Aunt Jane would have to say if ever she found out. And it was not impossible, she realized with dismay. There was someone standing at the bend – someone she hadn't noticed, walking with a dog – who must have witnessed her unorthodox arrival and seemed to have turned round to get a better look. The story would be round the district in a brace of shakes, which meant that Mrs Hoskins was almost sure to hear. And the fellow was still staring in her direction now.

She refused to look that way. Just as well he couldn't see her from close to, she thought, or there would be a tale. She was dust from face to elbows – everywhere the shawl had not protected her, in fact. She couldn't turn up at the Hoskinses' like that. She brushed off her shoulders as best she could, then took out a pocket handkerchief and wiped her face and hands. Thank heavens for the streamlet that ran beside the road – at least she was able to rinse off the worst of it. A few minutes later, she could face the world again.

She put her damp handkerchief away and raised her head. The figure was still watching, and as she looked again, she realized there was something familiar about the distant onlooker.

Granfer! She was almost sure of it. She put the handkerchief away and began to walk towards him, but to her astonishment he turned and hurried off. She called, 'Granfer? Mr Hoskins?' But he did not stop. In fact, he seemed to quicken his footsteps even more, and by the time she reached the corner he had disappeared.

# Three

Maud soon reached the gate opening to the farm, and for a moment she stood irresolute. Where was Mr Hoskins? Not down the farm lane; she would have seen him there. He hadn't climbed a stile: the fields on either side were empty, with not so much as a solitary cow, and there was nothing whatsoever moving in the yard.

Maud frowned. There was a pair of cottages that stood beside the road. Had he gone into one of them? She peered in that direction, but there was no sign of him. Yet he had seen her. She was quite sure of that. Was he trying to avoid her? Why should he do that? Had she managed to offend the family in some way? Was that why Mrs Hoskins had not replied to her? But for the life of her she could not think what she'd done.

She was standing stock-still in the middle of the road, still staring at the cottages in some perplexity, when a woman came out from one of the front doors. She was enormous, wearing a big pinny and an even bigger scowl, and her arms were folded like battle-armour high across her chest.

'Looking for someone, are you?' The tone was challenging.

'I wondered if Mr Hoskins had come this way,' Maud said. 'I thought I saw him in the lane just now.'

There was a faint change in the expression – a hint of softening. But the voice was still emphatic. 'No one of that name 'ere. What did you want him for, in any case?'

Maud tried a smile. 'Oh, it wasn't him especially. I caught sight of him, that's all. I've come to see the other Hoskins family, at the farm.'

A hint of curiosity flickered across the face. 'You a relation?'

'Not exactly.' Maud was flustered. 'More a family friend. Though I might be related one day, if everything works out. That's why I've come up from Penzance to see them this afternoon. Better go and do it, if I'm going to, I suppose.'

'Could have saved yourself the journey, then. There's nobody at home. Though you could have told that by looking at the place.'

Maud looked in the farm's direction and saw that it was true. She had already taken in the empty field and yard, but now she saw the other signs that she had overlooked – no sound of dogs or chickens; no sign of cats or goats; no smoke from the chimney; the doors and windows shut. The inner gate, when she looked hard at it, seemed to be chained and padlocked. The whole house was closed up.

She had a sudden feeling that the world had stopped. Nothing was quite real. She was still breathing somehow, but the wall did not seem solid when she put a hand on it as if to prevent herself from giddiness. She heard herself saying, as though another person was speaking through her lips, 'They've gone away then for a little while?' Could Belinda have been right? Was Stan ill and in hospital again?

'No "little while" about it, far as I can see!' There was a grim satisfaction in the woman's voice. 'Sold up and left, a week or more ago. Just like that, without a word to anyone – never said goodbye, or said where they were going. They didn't even tell me that they were going to leave; I had to hear it from a carter who was moving furniture. After I've been their neighbour for nigh on twenty years! So don't talk to me about the Hoskinses!'

Maud was struggling to make any sense of this at all. 'But I saw Granfer Hoskins, just a minute since. I'm sure I did.'

'Refused to go with them, from what I understand. Gone back to the cottage that he used to have. Said he was born here, and that's where he would die. Come to some arrangement with the new folk, I expect, though what he's going to live on I'm sure I don't know. Turned into a hermit and won't talk to a living soul except that dog of his. 'Spect he knows where the rest of them have gone, but he's saying nothing – though dear knows people tried. Knock on the door until my knuckles ache, I do, but he won't answer. Just sets the dog on you. Best you go back where you came from, if you know what's good for you.'

Maud was hardly listening. The words seem to come from very far away. Her legs refused to hold her. She sat down on the wall.

The woman seemed to notice that something was amiss. She left the doorstep, waddled over and looked at Maud with concern. 'Here, you all right, my maid? You've gone whiter than a sheet.' She called towards the cottage, though she didn't turn around. 'Sarah, my handsome, come out here and bring my smelling salts. They're in that little bottle on the bedroom shelf. And be quick about it. This here young lady has had a nasty turn.' She made a tutting noise. 'Never thought I'd upset you like this with what I said.'

Maud wanted to protest that she was quite all right, but her lips had turned to rubber and no sound came out of them. It was only after the smelling salts were brought – by a solemn small child in a ragged pinafore – and Maud had been forced to take a whiff or two, that she found herself able to say anything at all.

'I'm very sorry. It's a shock, that's all. You must think me an ass. Only I've come all the way up here to see them, on the train – live in Penzance, I do, and Sunday's my free day. And then I missed the bus and had to get a lift, in an awful side-car on a motor-cycle. And it's all for nothing. And I wrote to Mrs Hoskins several times, as well, though she never answered. Gone astray, I suppose, since there was no one here.

But you think she might have said. After all, she'd invited me to come.' She realized that she was wittering, and brought herself up short.

The woman was gruffly gentle in her manner now. 'I don't know, I'm sure. Not like Mrs Hoskins to do a thing like that – any more than I'd expect her to go off without a word. It's because of what happened to that boy of hers, I 'spect. I suppose I shouldn't judge her – it's an awful thing. She almost lost her reason when she first heard the news. Came in here sobbing, and I haven't seen her since.'

'Her boy? You mean Stanley? What happened? Is he . . .' She couldn't finish. The ground was giving way. It was no longer solid – or so it seemed to Maud – and if the woman hadn't waved the smelling salts again, she would almost certainly have fallen in a faint. She almost wished she could, so she didn't have to know. 'Tell me what happened. I've a right to know. After all, I was going to marry him.'

'Oh, my poor maid!' The tone was kinder now. 'You mean they never told you? Tried to spare you, perhaps, though I expect that someone would have written to tell you in the end. I'm sorry I went blurting it out to you like that, but how was I to know that you were Stanley's girl? I'm sure you never said so.'

Maud was quite impatient. 'Never mind all that. Tell me what happened.' She closed her eyes in anguish. 'Stan's dead, isn't he? Or they've shot his legs off, or something terrible.'

The woman didn't answer for a minute, then she said, 'They put it in the paper. I think I've got it here. You stay here a minute – I'll look it out for you.'

Maud nodded. She was too shocked to say anything at all. She found that she was trembling, and wondered dully how she'd ever manage to walk and catch the bus. Her legs did not feel as if they'd carry her.

But the woman was already waddling back to her again, as fast as her swollen legs would carry her. 'Here! I've got it. Thought I'd cut it out. Saw it on a bit of paper from the fishmonger. There it is, look. Hoskins, Stanley Lionel. The bottom of the page.' She pushed a stubby finger to indicate the place.

Maud forced herself to read the paragraph. It wasn't very long. 'Formerly of Pentrethick Farm. Aged nineteen years.

Died of wounds. France. May 31st.' Maud could not remember afterwards walking to the horse-bus or getting on to it, but she must have done it somehow, because she found the ticket in her pocket later on, and she must have caught the train, because her father was waiting for her at the station in Penzance.

Wilfred knew that there was something wrong as soon as Maud appeared. She got out of a carriage, looking as white as chalk, and walked along the platform like an automaton. She even barged into someone and didn't seem to notice, just kept on walking, her face pale and set, leaving the woman staring after her.

He had to touch her arm to tell her he was there. 'What is it, Maudie? Bad news about Stan?'

She didn't seem to have been crying, that was the funny thing. She looked at him blankly. 'Killed. Dead. Died a month ago. I saw it in the paper. And the Hoskinses have gone. Just gone without a word. I can't take it in.' Then suddenly she broke down, flung herself at him, buried her head against his shoulder and burst into floods of tears.

'Now then!' he said gently, but she didn't stop, just sobbed and shuddered and clung on to him. He patted her, rather awkwardly, on her back and let her have her cry. People were turning round to look. He pretended not to care. At last he took out a handkerchief and handed it to Maud. 'Here, blow your nose and wipe your eyes. You're coming home with me. Can't have you going back to that shop alone, in this state, can we now? I'll write a note and say, and we can put it through the door as we are passing by. Come while I find a bit of something I can write it with.'

He steered her to the parcel room, and sat her on a chair – she did not seem able to move of her own accord – and hunted down an envelope and a stump of indelible pencil. It was all that he could find. Well, it would have to do. 'Dear Madam Raymond,' he wrote carefully. 'Maud won't be back tonight. I'm her father and I'm taking her back home. She's had distressing news.' (He wasn't sure how many 's'es there were supposed to be in that, but he put in four to be on the safe side.) 'Someone she was fond of has been killed in France. I'll bring her back tomorrow before you open up. Your obedient servant, Wilfred Olds.'

It was a good letter. He read it out to Maud. She nodded, but she didn't really seem to take it in. He took her arm again and led her up the street, paused a minute to put the letter to Madam through the door, then round the corner up the Arcade Steps and finally got her to Belgravia Street.

Going home wasn't a great success. Jane hadn't been expecting her, and had to whisk around and make some extra tea, and even then Maud couldn't eat a crumb – just kept picking her fork up and dropping it again without even getting it to her mouth – until Wilfred went out into the scullery himself and made some bread and milk. It was something she had been very fond of as a child when she was ill, and she did manage to take a spoon or two of that.

Then Tully picked up the mood, and he began to cry, so Jane had to go upstairs and pack him off to bed. Wilfred cleared the table – not a thing he often did – then put Maud to sit beside the fire. It was a warm evening, but she was shivering so much he even fetched a blanket to put around her back. Then, very slowly, by gentle questioning, he got the whole sorry story from her bit by bit.

He had to be quite firm with Jane, when she came down and heard, just to stop her fussing and going on and on. 'Who would have thought it of the Hoskinses? You'd think they might at least have wrote and told us, wouldn't you?'

'Just leave it, Jane. Can't you see it isn't helping?' He didn't reprove her often, and it silenced her. She pursed her lips and pretended to go on with her book – it was her treat on Sundays, to have a bit of a read. But it didn't suit her to be quiet and it wasn't long before she announced that she was going on up to bed because she had a headache – which he doubted very much.

But it did give him a chance to be alone with Maud. He sat down on the settle next to her and tried to make her talk. Best thing for grief, he knew that for himself – it didn't do to bottle it all up. He could still remember what it was like when her mother died.

He could not coax anything out of Maud at first – as if she could hardly bear to think of anything – but he allowed her silence, and gradually she talked. She talked about Stanley – how they'd met and what they'd hoped to do – and after a little while the tears began again. She wept and wept as though she'd never stop, till at last, exhausted, she drifted into sleep, her head against his shoulder and his arm around her back.

He let her stay like that, without disturbing her, for hours, while the fire burned slowly out and the sky gradually lightened into another day. Next morning he was very stiff, cold and sore, but, whatever Janie said, he was glad that he had done it, for his daughter's sake.

How she got through that next day at the shop, Maud could not have explained. She was sent up to the workroom, to her great relief – she didn't think she could have coped with customers today – and she sat at the table and picked up her work, moving her fingers in a kind of trance. It was plain sewing – there was not a lot of business for the shop these days, and even the senior girls were doing simple tasks – but today she didn't mind it. The simple repetitive action was soothing, and in fact she had to stop twice and unpick what she'd done because she'd gone on stitching where she hadn't meant to. It wasn't carelessness. Her hands were going through the familiar motions, but her mind was numb and blank – not so much that she thought of Stanley all the time, more that she could not bear to think of anything at all.

Ann Tresize – the bony girl who'd come in Jenny Liskey's place – came up later in the afternoon to use the hand machine. 'You all right, Miss Olds? You don't look very well. You've gone all pale and pink round the eyes, if you don't mind me saying so. Mind you aren't took poorly. There's a lot of it about.' She fussed with the bobbin, getting it to thread, then clicked it into place. 'I heard Madam saying to Miss Simms you ought to have stayed home.'

Maud muttered something about having had a shock, then bent her head over her seam again. She wished that the other girl would go away again, or at very least keep quiet and leave her to herself. But Ann Tresize was looking at her sideways as she worked and seemed determined to start up a conversation.

'There was someone here looking for you, Saturday,' she said, as she got the needle threaded and whirred along the seam. She lifted up the pressure foot and turned the work around, ready to oversew it back the other way. 'Meant to have told you when you got in, but with one thing and another it completely slipped my mind.'

Maud did not answer, but it made no difference.

'Wanted you in particular. She made a point of it. Wanted a skirt shortened, and it was you or nobody. I offered to do it, but she wasn't having that – decided that she'd take it exactly as it was. Mind, it did look nice on her. Can't see that it needed altering at all. Shouldn't do at that price. Two pounds twelve and six. Didn't look the sort of girl who generally bought things new, if you know what I mean – though perhaps I shouldn't say that if she's a friend of yours. Though she did say she wanted it to be married in.' She was pinning in the sleeve. 'Madam seemed to know her. Miss Roberts, was she called? Roberts, Richards, something of the kind.'

Maud wasn't really listening, but she heard Belinda's name and it penetrated even her numb and deadened world. 'Belinda came here? She told me that she might.' She said this without interest, but Ann Tresize whirled round.

'So that was Belinda. Oh, I wish I'd known. I could have told that poor young man that was downstairs just now. Mind, he seemed to think she worked here.'

'So she used to do. Left at the same time as the girl that you replaced; only Madam never took on another senior when she was gone.' Maud stressed the word 'senior'. She meant it as a hint. 'Not the trade to warrant the extra cost these days.'

The Tresize girl had pins between her teeth by now, but it didn't stop her talking in a rather muffled way. 'Well, I'd never heard of this Belinda – so I went and asked, and Madam went over and ordered him away and sent me packing up here to get on with this. Seemed mad as hops that I'd been talking to him in the shop at all. But I ask you, what are you supposed to do when someone comes in asking?'

Maud was struggling dimly to make sense of this. A caller for Belinda. Whoever could it be? Perhaps the famous Adam, who'd sent the fatal note? But what was he doing coming to the shop, asking for Belinda in that open way? And it would not be Jonah, surely. He knew she wasn't here.

'I just thought he'd got the wrong address. Still, I couldn't have helped him very much I don't suppose.' Ann Tresize was like a river, burbling on and on. 'I don't know where she lives, or anything like that. But obviously she's local. I could have told him that at least.' She put the last pin into place and began to tack the work. 'Came all the way down from the Wounded

Soldiers' Home up at Trevarnon House. It can't have been easy for him – it's at least a mile – and him on crutches and having lost a foot. Nice-looking fellow, he must once have been, even looks good in that convalescents' uniform. If I was this Belinda, I'd want him to call. Her sweetheart, was he?' And then, without a pause, 'No of course, she's getting married. What a fool I am.' She waved the scissors. 'Oh, dear! I hope he isn't someone from her past. Won't half be disappointed, won't he, when he finds out?'

Maud still said nothing.

Then, at last, Ann scrambled to her feet and gathered up the garment she was working on. 'Well, I'd better take this down and let Madam look at it before I sew the sleeve. She'll have my guts for garters if I get it wrong. Nice to have a chance to talk to you, Miss Olds.' And with a clatter of toe plates on the staircase she was gone, leaving Maud to merciful silence and her own melancholy thoughts.

But the one-sided conversation had one effect at least. She would go and see Belinda after work tonight – if she was in, of course. She might be out with Jonah, but she'd be there otherwise. The news about the unknown visitor gave an excuse to call, and it would be nice to have a bit of company besides. And it was an opportunity to tell her about Stan.

She desperately hoped Belinda would be in. The thought of the empty attic room was very bleak. In the meantime, life went dragging on. It seemed like hours before the shop was shut.

# Four

Belinda was trying on the wedding costume in her room, admiring her reflection in the wash-stand glass. It wasn't a big mirror, and it had spots on here and there, but if she leaned over to the right, just so, and bent her knees a bit, she could get a fair picture of the whole effect.

Yes, it was very fetching. And so it ought to be. It would have to last a long time after she was wed. She pulled in her tummy and tugged down the skirt. It didn't need shortening, really, in the least. She only hoped that she would still get in it, on the day. Fortunately there was no sign of any swelling yet. In fact, something had happened just the other day – a personal sort of something – which had made her wonder if Jonah's fears were wrong. Another of those moments where a mother would have helped.

But altogether, this was a success. She was wondering whether she ought to get her best boots re-heeled when there was a knocking at the outside door.

She paid no attention. It was for Miss Simms, no doubt. She heard the front door open, and somebody came in, but the footsteps came on up the stairs and stopped outside her door. She flung it open, and there was Maud, with her blouse all sideways and her bonnet all askew, looking as if the sky had fallen in on her.

'My dear Maud, you gave me such a fright. However didn't you let me know that you were going to call? Anyway, come in. What do you think of this? I'm glad to have someone I can show it to.'

She was expecting thrilled compliments, but Maud said, 'Very nice,' in the dreariest of tones, and scarcely glanced at the ensemble. You'd think she didn't care.

'Think I should have it shortened? I thought I would, at first.' Belinda pirouetted to show off the skirt, though there was not a lot of space to do so in the room.

Maud said stiffly, 'It looks all right to me. Lucky that you and Jonah . . .' She broke off with a gulp, unable to go on.

Belinda whirled round to look at her. 'Maud! Whatever is it? You haven't heard from Stan?'

Maud shook her head. 'I haven't. And I'm not likely to. He's dead, Belinda. Died of wounds at least a month ago. I saw it in the paper. And don't tell me there must be a mistake.' She sat down on the bed, heavily and abruptly, as if the words had taken all the stuffing from her legs. 'There isn't. It's all over and that's an end to it.'

Belinda sat down beside her, at a loss for words. 'Dear Lord! I'm sorry. Did you go up there? What did his mother say?'

Maud looked at her with eyes that had lost all their glow. 'That's just it, Blin. She didn't say a word. Not to me, and not to anyone. They simply disappeared. Yes, I mean it. They've given up the farm, and gone off somewhere, and nobody knows where.'

Belinda shook her head. 'It's . . . unbelievable. They must have been terribly upset at losing Stan.'

But Maud was shaking her own head in reply. 'No, I don't believe it. It's something more than that. If Stan had been killed like anybody else, they'd have been sad, of course. But not this – not this running. And they'd have written me. I know it. There is something wrong.'

This was uncomfortable. Not the sort of thing that you expected anyone to say. And Maud's face was unnatural – so closed and white and set. Had grief affected her so much that it had turned her mind? Blin put out a hand. 'Maud, it's bad enough he's dead. You mustn't start imagining other things as well.'

Maud shook the hand off. 'I'm not imagining. Stan was ill, you know. There was a fellow, in the same company with him, was always bullying the weaker boys. I'm starting to wonder if that was part of it. Stan told me that he could have killed him, once or twice. Supposing that he did it – if he was pushed too far? He asked once if I thought it was ever forgivable to kill a man. I thought he was talking about Germans, and of course I told him yes. But I'm starting to wonder . . .'

Belinda was also beginning to wonder – about sending for Miss Simms. 'Maudie, don't be silly. You said he died of wounds. He was in the trenches. Isn't that enough?'

Maud shook her head. 'But that's the point. The wording. Don't you see? It doesn't say the other things it generally says, like how he was a hero or what the battle was, or how he fought bravely defending so and so. It just says "died of wounds".'

'But supposing he didn't die in battle, the way we think of it? They do have accidents. I read the other day about some fellow who was killed – blown up by his own Mills bomb. That's "died of wounds" all right.' She was being brutal, but she couldn't help it now. Anything was better than these imaginings.

Maud's eyes had become as expressionless as fish. 'Then the Hoskinses would have told me. Just like they did last time when they knew that he was hurt. No, there's something else. I've even wondered if he . . .' She swallowed. 'I don't know – committed suicide or something of the kind. The woman I spoke to, who lived next door to them, said Stan was a nice boy, "whatever people said". What do you suppose she could have meant by that? Must have been something, to make her choose the words.'

'You didn't ask her?' Belinda would have done.

'I was too upset. I didn't think of it. I only really thought about it after I got home.' Maud closed her eyes, as though she wished she could cut out the world. 'But I've made up for it. I've thought about it every waking moment since. Mum Hoskins went there crying and told her everything, that's what the neighbour said. Then she went all peculiar and wouldn't say no more. I'm sure there was something that she wasn't telling me.'

Oh, dear Heaven. Maud was going to cry again. Belinda wanted to put her arms around her friend but she couldn't, with this new costume on; she had already creased it up with sitting on the bed. She did her best. 'You are making mountains out of molehills, Maudie, that's all it is. You're that shocked to hear the news that you can't let it go, and you're reading meanings into things that weren't intended in the least. Look, I think you should go home and try to rest. I've got a bit of laudanum, somewhere, that Gran used to take. You have a bit of that, and it will help you sleep. Tomorrow you will see things more clearly, you see if you don't.'

Maud shook her head. She could be stubborn if she tried. 'I don't want a sleeping draught. I just want the truth.'

'Well, why don't you write to the army and ask them?' It was a simple answer, once she'd thought of it. 'I'll talk to Peter when I see him next, and ask where you should write to.'

Maud was staring at her. 'Peter?'

'Oh, lor. I didn't tell you, what with Stan and everything! Yes, it's true. My brother has come home – or at least, he's come back to Penzance. He's up the convalescent home and might be for a while – that bullet in his leg went septic somehow and they had to take it off just above the ankle. But there's one thing good come of it. He's home for good.' She could not help but smile. It wasn't very kind, when Maud was in this state, but Peter was now safely out of danger's way and nobody could grudge her this bit of happiness. 'I didn't know that he was here. He came and found me at the station – went to Jonah's coal yard and they told him I was there. Apparently he called in at Madam's earlier – he hadn't had my letters, so he didn't know I'd left – and Madam sent him off in no uncertain terms, and wouldn't tell him anything.'

Maud nodded wearily. 'That's what I came to tell you, really. I thought it must be him. At least, I did when I had thought it through. I didn't see him; it was Ann Tresize. She told me that there'd been someone asking for you in the shop. Said you'd been in Saturday and you were my friend. Told me all about that wedding suit as well.' The ghost of a wan smile briefly touched her lips. 'Very impressed with how much it had cost and the idea of having a wedding outfit like the gentry do. And now your brother will be here to see you wear it after all. You must feel very fortunate.'

She said it with such unconscious envy in her voice that Belinda, looking in the glass, realized that perhaps she was a lucky girl, at that. Even if she was obliged to give up her job and freedom and marry Jonah Lotts.

Jonah was a little bit inclined to sulk. And with good reason, too. It was a lovely afternoon – one of the nicest for the last few weeks – and instead of being willing to walk down to the sea, walk along the promenade and sit down on the wall and have a penny ice-cream like they belonged to do, Belinda wanted to drag him to the convalescent home to watch her brother in some dratted spoon race on the lawn.

It was supposed to boost the chaps' morale, or some nonsense of the kind. Jonah doubted it. Why, if he himself was wounded and had lost half a leg, and somebody suggested that he played childish games, he would have kicked them into the middle of next week with his one remaining one. And as for standing watching, drinking cups of tea, while well-meaning ladies stood around in shady hats and clapped, he would as soon have had his teeth drawn.

But there was no escaping it. Belinda was keen to be there, and Peter wanted it, and Jonah was very anxious to keep in Peter's good books for a while.

Not that he knew Belinda's brother very well. On the
contrary: he'd only met him once or twice. But this was the
same Peter who'd inherited that house, and Jonah had been
thinking about that quite a lot.

He'd been there with Belinda, after her gran had died. It
wasn't a huge place, but it was big enough. A kitchen and a
parlour and two small rooms upstairs – and a separate wash
house and privy in the yard. Bit dark and musty, but paint
would see to that, and there wasn't any damp or rot as far as
he could tell. It would do very well. Plenty big enough for
all three of them – much better than them cramming into Ma
and Pa's spare room, with Ma finding fault with everything
from dawn to dusk. And he wasn't being grasping, either,
when you came to think. Peter would need someone to be
there, wouldn't he? Stands to reason that he couldn't manage
with one leg, on his own. (Or perhaps 'stands to reason' was
an unhappy phrase.) And who better than his sister, to look
after him? All in all the sports day was a tiny price to pay.

Mind, it was still something of a trial – and not only for
the convalescents who were taking part. It was the kind of
occasion that Jonah hated most, with lots of county ladies,
just as he'd supposed, and elderly gentlemen in old-fashioned
coats who all turned to stare at them and then turned away.

Someone had roped off an area of lawn, and people were
grouped round it underneath the trees, sitting on garden
benches or picnic rugs. Jonah wished devoutly that he'd
thought of such a thing, and was ushering Belinda to an empty
group of chairs beside the grass, when somebody – a younger
man – came scurrying up to them.

'Not there, I am sorry. That is for the men and nursing
staff,' he said. He looked at Jonah, who was in his Sunday
suit – he himself was wearing a blazer and neat slacks and
some sort of fancy tie with crests all over it. He was carrying
a daft cream Panama straw hat. 'But thank you for coming.
We are glad of your support. Does the men good to have an
afternoon like this – as a bit of recreation out in the fresh air.
Nice class of fellow we have here as a rule. Of course, we
only take them if they are officers. I'm Leavis, by the way.
Soon be Doctor Leavis. I'm helping out a bit. Part of the
training and all that sort of thing. Do I take it that you have
a relative who's a patient here?'

'My intended's brother,' Jonah said, before Belinda could reply. 'Came up through the ranks.' The fellow's condescending smile was irritating him. 'But, as you say, a splendid sort of chap. Went as a volunteer when war was first declared.' He looked at the fancy get-up – more suited to a regatta then a hospital – and could not resist a jibe. 'You never thought of signing up yourself?'

'Did do, as a matter of strict fact, old fruit.' The smile never faltered but the eyebrows rose. 'Just starting my final year of training when this German row broke out. Threw it in and signed up right away – sense of duty and all that. Fancied taking a pot-shot or two at the Hun, you know the sort of thing, but when the army found out that I could read and write a bit they posted me to Stores, and I spent two years in Ordnance shuffling forms around. Then there was this paper sent around this year, calling back the medics who had volunteered instead of completing their final year of training over here. The government are trying to accelerate the course and rush us through and send us back again. There's a shortage of doctors over at the Front.' He did that cool appraising look again. 'So, that's my story. What about yourself?'

Jonah was already wishing that he'd never asked. For one thing Belinda had gone all moonstruck, and was gazing at the man as if he was a hero of the highest kind. And for another, the fellow had caught him unawares. He muttered something about how he 'worked in coal', and hoped that would be enough, but he saw Belinda stiffen and turn round with a frown. If he did not distract her, she would give the show away, and this wretched soon-to-be-Doctor Leavis would take pleasure in reporting him, no doubt.

'But, Jonah . . .' she began, but he had seen his chance.

'Look, here come the patients! Isn't that your brother there?' He took her elbow and swivelled her in the direction of the house, which had been turned over to the convalescent home.

'Yes, that's Peter!' She stood on tiptoe, waving, and the threat was over, for the moment anyway.

Jonah felt beads of perspiration on his brow. 'Jolly hot this afternoon,' he muttered, mopping at it with his pocket handkerchief – though it was not the sunshine which had made him sweat. 'Hope it's not too much for those poor blighters. Don't look too nifty, one or two of them.'

In fact they were a sorry sight, as they paraded out. One or two in wheeled chairs, many more on sticks and crutches; some without an arm, others with half their faces blown away. Empty sleeves and trouser legs told a sorry tale. How anyone could survive such things was more than he could tell. Yet most of them were smiling, and waving to the guests, and actually seemed eager for the nonsense that was to come.

There were many contests: archery and quoits, races for men with two legs and then for those with one – what the organizers styled a 'three-legged race' where the participants hopped on crutches, at a surprising speed. Then the famous egg and spoon race. One race was actually for men in wheeled chairs, each whisked around the course by a nurse in uniform. That group were pressed to have a photograph taken afterwards. The photographer posed them in a row, but while he was covering his head in a black cloth and fiddling with his big plates, they started laughing and had to be reproved and made to sit still for the few minutes it required. Five men with only eleven limbs between the lot of them. What was it, Jonah wondered, that could make them smile at all?

Jonah did not feel like smiling. He was bored and out of sorts and rather embarrassed by the spectacle. He was glad when it was over and it was time for tea, which turned out to be tiny little sandwiches that only teased your mouth, and dainty little teacups you were afraid to drop. At last Peter came hobbling over on his stick to say goodbye, and any minute now they would be able to escape.

'Enjoy that, Belinda? Thanks for turning up. Very jolly afternoon, I thought it was. Did you see me win?' He waved a piece of paper. 'Not that it much matters – they give everybody a certificate just for joining in. Just as well it wasn't next week. I'm going to have my new foot, and they say it's difficult to learn to walk again with them at first.'

'Oh, Peter, are you really?' She was gushing now, and Jonah forced a smile. It was to be hoped the artificial foot was not too much of a success, or Peter would not be needing people to look after him after all.

'Tin one, is it? That's what they do these days?'

Peter shook his head. 'They're going to try a wood one – they say it's easier, and I'll still be able to wear a boot and everything. Get it a whole lot sooner, I understand. If I'd lost any more of this confounded leg, it would have to be tin, but they are quite hopeful that I'll be all right with wood. Doctor Leavis thinks so. He's been extraordinarily helpful.'

Jonah bit back the comment that he'd found Leavis 'extraordinary' too, and just said, 'Well, good luck with it. I suppose you'll have to go. They'll be expecting you to go back to the ward?'

Peter rather looked as if he might demur, but before he could say anything Belinda butted in.

'Well, before you do go, Peter dear, there's something I want to ask you. If you want to find out information about someone who was killed – someone in the army – where would you apply? Someone I know has had bad news about a friend – saw it in the paper, just the notice of his death – and isn't satisfied with only half a tale.'

Jonah was impatient. 'Oh, come on, Blin, not now. Surely you can ask your brother at some other time. Can't you see he's tired – he's had a busy afternoon.' He took her arm with the intention of leading her away.

She shook him off. 'This won't take a minute. And I promised Maud.' Belinda could be stubborn when she put her mind to it.

He brother frowned. 'They write to the family, as a general rule. Tell them what happened. Make a point of it.'

'Well that's just the trouble. The family's disappeared. So where could she write and find things out, herself?'

Peter said slowly. 'Have to be Company Headquarters, I suppose. Try to get in touch with the commanding officer. Or failing that, she could try the regiment. Do you happen to know what outfit he was with?'

Belinda shook her head. 'I never thought to ask.'

'If he was a local lad she could try the Devonshires. Most of us Cornishmen started out with them – though it doesn't follow, necessarily. Once you've done your training, they can post you anywhere.'

'He did some special course, I think, about grenades.'

Peter made a face. 'In that case, he could end up any place at all. Look, if you'd like to tell her to come up and talk to me, I'll find out what she knows and see if I can help. No promises, mind you. And even if she does write, they may not tell her much. Sometimes they don't know what happened to a man themselves. It can be quite gory sometimes – lots of little pieces so you don't know who is who. Not a bit like the heroic stories you read in the press. You make sure she knows that, before she writes and asks. It might be kinder if she doesn't know.'

Blin flashed a smile. 'I'll tell her. That's very kind of you. I think it might be better if she did find out the truth. She's convinced herself there is some problem with the death notice, and she hasn't eaten since. Or slept, that I can see. She'll make herself quite poorly if she goes on like this. Better if she writes. However horrible it is, it puts an end to it. It can't be worse than her imaginings, and even if they can't tell her very much, at least she would feel she's done all she can. They will answer, won't they? She was going to marry him.'

'They should do, if she tells them that,' her brother said. He looked as if he had something else to say, but Jonah had lost patience.

'Come on, Blin!'

Even then she lingered long enough to say, 'I'll tell my friend to come and see you then. Hope your foot goes well.' She gave her brother's arm a squeeze, before she left at last.

Maud was a bit doubtful about going, when she first heard. 'I can't go calling on a man I've never even met. I know he is your brother and all that, but I can't just go into the ward and ask for him. What would the nurses think? Have to wait until we've both got time and you can go with me.'

Belinda looked impatient. 'If you want to write to the army, you want to do it now – catch the officers who knew him, before it is too late. You'll just get some bland official state-ment else. It's been weeks already – people get moved on.' She meant they might be killed, Maud realized, though the words weren't said. 'Anyway,' Blin went on briskly, 'you don't want to think like that. It isn't like it used to be before the war; there are lots of young ladies – proper gentry too – putting their names down on a list to volunteer to go and visit wounded officers, cheer them up a bit and bring them a few comforts. Someone in the booking office, just the other day, was saying how he had a brother in the post office. Seems an ordinary soldier, a private at the front, put an advert in the *Daily Chronicle*, saying he was lonely and away from home and would some friendly female like to write to him. And he had that many letters and packets and all sorts – more than three thousand in one delivery, some of them from titled ladies too – that they had to put a stop to people doing it because it was interfering with the mail. So no one's going to think it funny if you go up there, visiting a wounded officer – especially if you say his sister is a friend of yours. Anyway, I said you'd come, and he's expecting you. Visiting hour is in the afternoon. I said most likely Thursday, because it's half-day at the shop.'

Maud shook her head. 'Depends what private fittings are booked in that day, and what Madam wants for us to do with the display,' she said, though secretly she knew that she could easily be spared. There was neither the stock nor the business to keep them all occupied, the way that there had been a year or two before. 'Might wait, like I say, till both of us can go. Else, never mind what other people do, I aren't so sure it's quite respectable.'

But, of course, she did go in the end. Anything to find out the truth about Stan's death. There was still no letter from the Hoskinses, and whatever people said to try to comfort her, she was more and more convinced that there was something wrong. She was determined to write to the army and find out.

So, on Thursday afternoon she put on her best bonnet and her Sunday coat and set off up the hill towards Trevarnon House, though she almost turned back when she passed through the gates. She had been to a number of impressive homes, some of them belonging to wealthy families, but this was something on a different scale. The wide drive led through an avenue of trees to an area of lawn arranged in terraces, and beyond it she could already see the house, grey and imposing, with windows everywhere, more like a public building than a place where people lived.

A double flight of steps led up to the front door, and she was still hesitating as to whether she should go that way and knock, or whether she should find the tradesman's entrance round the back, when a pretty girl in a nurse's uniform came hurrying past her and ran up the steps.

'My stars,' she panted, pausing at the top. 'I'm late getting back.' She looked at Maud with interest. 'You coming in, are you? Looking for a patient? Tell me who it is, and I will

take you there. I'm so late back already, it makes no difference. Matron will have me on the carpet as it is – and it might
look better if I'm showing someone round.'

'I'm looking for a Captain Peter Richards.'

'Oh yes, I know. He got his foot today. I expect that he'll
be resting. I'll show you where he is.' And she led the way
along the corridor to a fine curved staircase with a balustrade.

She didn't ask Maudie what her business was, or any of
the other questions she had been waiting for, but clattered up
the staircase, talking all the while. 'They sent me to the station
to escort a blinded officer to the midday train, but it was half
an hour delayed, and by the time I'd got him safely in his
seat, the horse-ambulance had come back here to take another
case. I've had to come on foot. I don't know what Matron
will have to say, I'm sure.' She paused outside a door. 'Here
you are then, this is where he is. Who shall I say wants him?'

'Maud Olds,' she answered. 'I'm a friend of his sister – she
used to work with me – and I promised her that I would come
and see him when I could.'

The nurse gave her a little sideways, knowing smile. 'I can
see why you might want to. Lovely-looking chap. Must have
been a proper dasher when he had his legs – and so uncom-
plaining and cheerful all the time. Even charm the boots off
Matron, he could, if he tried. Well, you wait here. I'll go in
and make sure that he's in the ward. There's a concert for the
ambulant in the big room downstairs and they might have
taken him.'

Maud waited, shuffling from foot to foot, rather wishing
that she hadn't come. She felt uncomfortable, awkward and
very out of place. There were now bare walls and scrubbed
linoleum where there had probably once been expensive rugs
and works of art, but there was no disguising the grandeur of
the house. She felt like a trespasser.

She did not know whether to be relieved or not, when a
moment later the young nurse reappeared. 'You can come in,
Miss Olds. Captain Richards is beside the window in a chair.
Visit him by all means, but I am to tell you please not to stay
too long. He has had a tiring morning working with his foot,
and the nurse in charge says he will need to rest.'

Maud looked at the six patients crammed into the ward –
some propped on pillows, others up in chairs. There was only

one man by the window but she would have known him for Belinda's brother instantly, she thought. The same shaped face, the striking auburn hair, even the brown colour of his eyes as he glanced up and saw her, reminded her of Blin. There was nothing feminine about him, though, and he wasn't broad and muscular the way Stan had been, but he was tall and slim and rangy, his slim face etched with pain. Nevertheless, he met her with a smile.

'You must be Belinda's friend, Miss Olds?' His voice was pleasant, too: low and gently Cornish. She did not know what she was expecting – perhaps someone stand-offish with a lofty sneer. But this Peter wasn't anything like that. Reassuring somehow. She felt herself relax.

'That's right.' You couldn't shake hands with a fellow sitting down, so she made do with a smile. 'Belinda told you what I wanted?'

'Your young man was killed, I understand? You want to find out how? Blin warned you that it might be quite distressing, I presume?'

She nodded. 'Can't be any worse than it already is. Can't hardly sleep or eat for wondering . . .' She tailed off. 'It's very good of you to take the time to help.'

He grinned. 'Time is something that I have to spare, these days, though I can't promise that I'll be much help. I suppose you don't know what regiment your chap was in? Or, better still, the number of the division and brigade? If so, you could write to the commanding officer. That would be much quicker than the General Staff.'

A great weight seemed to have lifted from Maud's mind. 'Course I know.' She reeled off the information of his regiment and division. 'He was in B Company, I am almost sure.' She stopped. 'Here, what's the matter – what you frowning for?'

He was looking at her oddly. 'But that's the same outfit I was with myself. What did you say his name was, this young chap of yours?' There was something in his tone that made her catch her breath. 'Wasn't called Tregurtha by any chance, was he?'

She shook her head, relieved. 'There was a Tregurtha with them at one time, I believe. Went out underage. Stan used to write about him when he was first abroad – but when he came

home wounded he just said the boy was dead.' It was her turn
to stare. 'Why did you ask about him in that tone of voice?
Something funny about the way he died, as well?'

'Stan? You can't mean Stan Hoskins? Oh, dear lord alive.'

She had seized his hand, before she stopped to think. 'You
knew him. You must have. Don't shake your head at me. You
just called him Hoskins and I never told you that.'

He was looking at her face and there was sadness in his
eyes. 'You can't be the Maudie he used to talk about?'

'Of course I am. Maud Olds. I thought they told you, when
I first came in.'

'Not the first name, no. They just said Miss Olds. And
Belinda never said. I believe she might have mentioned your
name in a letter once, but I never for a moment thought . . .
Oh, dear heaven, how could this come about? What can I tell
you? I had no idea . . . I always thought Stanley was a Truro
man. So how did he come to have a sweetheart down here in
Penzance?'

Maud sat down on the window seat beside his chair and
told him the story about meeting Stan. It was soothing
somehow, remembering those times and being able to talk
about him naturally again. People were avoiding mentioning
his name, in case it might upset her – which it often did –
but it made it feel as if he'd never been.

'And now he's dead,' she finished. 'And you know all about
it, I can tell you do. And there is something peculiar. I can
hear it in your voice. Well, tell me, Captain Richards – I would
rather know.' He didn't answer, and after a moment she spoke
again. 'Something to do with that Tregurtha boy, perhaps?'

Peter shook his head slowly, but he wasn't saying 'no'. 'In
a way, it is.'

'What happened? Oh, don't tell me! Stan shot him, didn't
he? That's what he was saying when he came home last time.
"Could you ever be forgiven if you took a life?" he asked.
That's it, isn't it? Stan was a murderer, and I never knew. And
he didn't just get shot – they found out somehow, and they
executed him.' She had not meant it to happen but her voice
was getting shrill, and other patients were looking at them in
astonishment.

He squeezed her fingers. She had quite forgotten that she
held his hand. 'I suppose I'd better tell you. You are almost

right, in parts. But it isn't remotely the way you think it is. But, if I tell you, you must promise not to make an exhibition of yourself.'

She nodded dumbly, sick with embarrassment and dread.

'Then let me start by saying this. Stan was the finest soldier that I ever met. And the bravest too – he stood up for Tregurtha when Sawyer bullied him. I saw it, and I didn't have the nerve to intervene. So let me tell you, I admired him – and so did all the fellows in the company.'

'You really knew him well then?' The words were balm to her. 'He never mentioned anyone called Peter when he wrote.'

Belinda's brother smiled, and turned a little pink. 'There were a lot of Peters. They used to call me Charmer, in the regiment.'

She searched his face. 'You . . . you are his friend Charmer? And you're Belinda's brother! How come I never knew?'

'Never put two and two together, I suppose. Any more than we did on our part, over there. We didn't talk about our families much, only our interests and the girls we used to know.' He looked at Maudie sadly. 'I used to envy him. He was so proud of you.'

'You didn't have anyone yourself then?' Maudie asked, rather to her own surprise.

He shrugged. 'There was a girl once – before I went abroad – but she wrote and told me that she wasn't going to wait. Found herself another beau to marry, I expect.' He squeezed her hand again. 'I don't know why I'm telling you all this. It's Stanley that you want to hear about.'

'And the Tregurtha business,' she forced herself to say.

The dreadful story that he told her brought tears into her eyes. 'Poor little lad!' she murmured. 'And poor Stan as well. What a burden for him. And he never said a word.'

Peter nodded. 'Saved our lives, most likely. They'd have got our range for sure. And for Tregurtha it was the kindest thing. But it worried Stanley. All the time we were in hospital, I'd hear him shouting out. Always about Tregurtha. It drove him nearly mad.'

She nodded, clinging to his hand as if it gave her strength. 'But he had to do it, didn't he? Surely the army wouldn't punish him for that? '

He disengaged himself. 'No, it wasn't that. I don't know

how to tell you. And I wasn't there. I was in hospital with
this leg by then. I only heard about it afterwards, when one
of the men was passing through and came to visit me. Stan
was on a party, going to throw his bombs and take the ruins
of a building where the Huns had been. Seems there was a
barrage, and the group got blown apart . . .' He paused.

Maud held her breath, almost afraid to hope. Had Stan been
killed in action after all?

He had dropped his voice now, and she had to lean forward
to hear what he said. 'There was a lad – they called him
Beanpole Smith – who was out there with them. He'd become
the butt of Sawyer's bullying, just the way Tregurtha was
before – and he was out there, on his own, right in the line
of fire. I think Stan saw the same thing happening again –
that's what he said later, in his own defence. And he'd been
knocked over by the German shell, besides, so his brain was
probably half-addled by the blast. Anyway, the long and short
of it is that when Sawyer gave the order to advance, Stan ran
the other way.'

Maud felt her blood run chilly in her veins. Her voice came
from somewhere miles and miles away. 'Deserted?' She almost
whispered it.

His smile had vanished now. He was angry, you could see.
'That's what they called it – or rather Sawyer did. He reported
it and put Stan on a charge, although he didn't have to. No
one would have known. Sawyer was the only other one to
make it back alive – there were snipers waiting in the ruins
who killed the lot of them. Except that Sawyer managed to
save his own wretched skin. He made his report and they
court-martialled Stan and found him guilty on Sawyer's
evidence. I'll tell you something, Maudie. They may have had
their reasons, and done it by the book, but the wrong man
was shot that morning. He was worth ten of Sawyer – and
we all knew that.'

She found that she was shaking. 'So I was right,' she
murmured. 'I knew there was something. I just knew there
was. I see why his mother was so frightfully ashamed, and
put it in the paper that he 'died of wounds'. Well, I suppose
he did. Poor Stan. He was no coward! How could they do
that to him? He'd been wounded once, and gone back to fight
again.'

'According to the man who told me this – who was there to give evidence on Stan's behalf – it was cited at the trial that one of the doctors had declared Stan fit before but he had exhibited "symptoms of disturbance" which kept him from the war. They made it sound as if there was nothing wrong with him, and that he was simply unwilling to return.'

She shuddered, remembering Stan's dark moods of terrible despair. 'And after all he'd been through. I can't believe it. It simply isn't fair.' But she did believe it. The certainty and horror gripped her mind and heart and an icy desolation flooded over her.

He took her hand again, as if they were old friends. 'I warned you that it might be painful – though I couldn't guess how much.'

She nodded. 'Well, thank you, Captain Richards. At least I know the truth. And I heard it from someone who was fond of Stan. That counts for something – more than you might think. We know he wasn't guilty. Not in spirit anyway.' She got up from the window seat, and found she was almost swaying with the shock of it. 'That nurse is coming over here. I think I've stayed too long. I was told not to tire you, and I'm afraid I have.' She attempted an apologetic smile but it trembled into tears.

Unsmiling, like a formal declaration in a book, he said, 'I would deem it an honour if you would come again. It makes a link with Stan. If you can face it, I would like to hear all about the family and the farm and everything. But of course we could talk of something else if you prefer.'

Come again? It struck her into panic. 'I don't know . . . perhaps I will . . . I don't know what to say.'

'Then don't say anything, Miss Maudie Olds. You have enough to bear. But if you could stand to come and visit me, I would appreciate it more than I can say.'

# Five

Wilfred hesitated outside the door of Madam's shop and peered through the glass. Not too many customers, which made it easier – though the lettering on the windows – 'Alterations and Fittings carried out' –worried him a bit. It suggested that there might be female persons in there taking off their clothes, and lurking in dressing-rooms in just their underwear.

But, he told himself, he would go through with his errand now he had come this far. He had been debating this meeting half the week. He wasn't one for interfering, as a rule, but he couldn't stand by and watch Maudie fade away. Bad enough when she first went to Truro and got the news of Stan, but this last week or two she'd become like a wraith. Hadn't slept or eaten as far as he could see, and her eyes were red and swollen – 'from working in poor light' was all that she would say, and all his blandishments couldn't get anything further out of her. She had even refused twice to come for Sunday tea, saying she wanted to be on her own.

And now her pretty friend Belinda was upset, because she wanted Maudie to come and see her wed, and had come to Belgravia Street yesterday to talk her into it, thinking perhaps Maudie wouldn't like to ask for time off. Only, of course, Maud was not there to persuade.

Well, he was going to sort it out. He'd asked for time himself, gone in to the stationmaster, bold as brass – they didn't like you leaving the premises in your lunch-time as a rule – but there had been no problem, and so here he was, feeling conspicuous in his uniform.

So why was he still hesitating outside the door? Stupid really, he'd been here many times with Maud, but never to go in. Well, you wouldn't would you? Not a woman's shop

– not unless he was accompanying your wife. But even when Maudie's mother was alive they'd never come here. 'Why would I want to buy things ready-made,' she used to say, 'when I could make them for half the price myself?' Clever with a needle. Maud got that from her.

But he wouldn't think about all that. He took off his cap, stuffed it underneath his arm, took a deep breath and walked into the shop.

Madam bustled over to him straightaway.

'I'm Wilfred Olds. I'm Maudie's father,' he began.

'I know who you are, and I am very glad you've come. I was contemplating whether I should write to you or not. Come into the office. I suppose it's about Maud?'

He nodded and followed her, much relieved. The ornamental door with 'Office' on the glass, the aspidistra and the straight-backed chairs, and even the desk with its ledgers, filing spikes, ink stand and typewriting machine had all been carefully chosen to impress, but they were a lot less daunting to a simple working man than all those frocks and bonnets, and tiers of shelves and boxes full of gloves and corsetry.

In the office a tall, thin woman was sitting at the desk copying up a list of figures into a ledger-book. She glanced up as they entered and seemed about to speak, but at a sign from Madam she rose at once and left, taking her task with her. Madam immediately sat down in her place, and gestured for Wilfred to sit down opposite.

'Now, Mr Olds, I'm glad that you've called in. As I told you, I was wondering if I should write to you, to ask you to take Maud home and keep her there awhile. I don't think she is well. She isn't eating – at least not any of the food that is on offer here. I provide three meals a day for all the girls, of course, and usually she has an average appetite, but I doubt if she has swallowed more than a spoon or two of anything put in front of her in the past ten days. And to be frank with you her work has suffered too.'

This alarmed him further. 'She isn't getting careless? That's not a bit like Maud.'

Madam shook her head. 'She's a good little seamstress and her work is excellent, but several times lately I have come into a room and found her simply staring blankly at the wall. And on Friday afternoon, when she should have gone out to a client's home for a private fitting, she came and asked me if I'd send someone else. Well, of course I couldn't, she's the senior girl, and besides the customer had asked for her by name, but when she did go – according to the lady in question – she was vague and unsmiling and had to be told twice. Not good for business, Mr Olds, that sort of thing. Especially in wartime, when times are very hard. The takings of this shop have halved these last twelve months and I can't afford to keep on a senior girl at ten and six a week if she isn't really doing what she ought to be.'

Wilfred felt a wave of anger rising in his chest. What did this woman mean by finding fault with Maud? And it wasn't half a guinea if you took off bed and board! But somehow he managed to curb his tongue and say, quite evenly, 'Are you telling me that you're dismissing her?'

Madam made a deprecating gesture with her hands. 'No, not that exactly. Just a temporary measure, while she gets over this. You might regard it as a sort of unpaid leave. I'll gladly have her back – just as soon as trade picks up again – though if she wants to try elsewhere I'll give her a character, of course.'

And that is what Maudie might be forced to do, he realized. If this was not dismissal it was the next best thing. Trade might not 'pick up again', as Madam said, for years. He felt like voicing his anger, but he couldn't scupper Maudie's chance of returning if she wished to, by speaking out of turn. 'You know that my daughter has had a dreadful shock? Losing her young man, and everything?' And then, on impulse, 'Is it a wonder that she's a little vague? Perhaps you would have felt the same if Mr Raymond had been killed.'

Madam was looking at him oddly, and her voice was cool. 'Mr Olds, I do not wish to be unkind, but thousands of people have had a dreadful shock, and somehow the business of the country must go on. Don't think that I'm unfeeling. I know what it is to lose someone in the war – I had a son who was lost at Mafeking. But all the same, I had to carry on, just as your daughter will have to, in the end. In the meantime, she is better off at home.'

He was nonplussed by that story of the son, and his anger faded into sympathy. He said, rather gruffly, 'Should I take her now?' They'd have his guts for garters when he got back to work, but he'd deal with that problem when he came to it.

Madam gave him a professional smile. 'I've paid her until Friday, but if she wants to go with you I won't insist that she works out her time. If she should decide to hand her notice in, I promise you it won't cause much remark, or go against her in the future when she's more herself. Lots of girls are leaving jobs and going to factories, or volunteering to go and work the land.'

He nodded slowly. He had heard of this before. It was in the paper that big houses ought to send their staff, and the government was already setting up a register of names, just like they did for calling up the men, and was threatening to post young women into essential work – those who weren't married or had families, of course.

'It's not like it used to be before the war, you know, when people took a job and stayed there all their lives. No one will think it odd if Maud goes somewhere else,' Madam was saying. 'There are lots of places vacant, with the men away – crying out for women with her intelligence and skills.' She paused, and looked down at her small, plump hands. 'But of course, it's up to Maud herself what she decides to do. She is up in the workroom. Shall we have her down?' And without waiting for an answer she went out to send for her.

Maud looked dreadful as she came into the room. There was not the faintest hint of colour in her face, her cheeks were pale and sunken and her eyes were dull. She listened expressionless to what Madam had to say, as though no news had the capacity to touch her any more.

'I'll go and get my things then.' That was all she said, and even as they walked up Market Jew Street afterwards he couldn't get another syllable out of her at all. He stopped at the corner of the Arcade Steps. 'It's no good, Maudie. There is something wrong. You know it and I know it. Tell me what it is. I am your father. I'm ordering you to speak. How do you expect me to help you otherwise?'

Perhaps it was the appeal to obedience that did the trick. Maudie turned suddenly to him and said, 'I'd better tell you then. I didn't want to say. I didn't want anyone else on earth to know.' He saw that there were bright tears standing in her eyes.

'I won't tell a soul,' he promised gently, 'especially not Aunt Jane.' He had hoped to make her smile, but there was no response. 'Let's go in this teashop and find a quiet spot.' It was an extravagance, of course – he hadn't been in a teashop since his courting days – but it was worth it to see her look of gratitude and they found a quiet corner away from listening ears. He waited until the girl had brought a pot of tea and a horrid rock-cake made of National Flour, then he leaned forward.

'Stanley?' he said, and she poured it out to him.

For a minute he could not believe his ears. Stanley, shot for cowardice – it was impossible! Yet you could see that it made sense of everything – why Mrs Hoskins didn't write to Maud, and why they had simply packed their bags and gone if they thought one of the neighbours had found out the truth. People were not kind to the families of cowards and deserters, when their own menfolk were obliged to stick it out and run the daily risk of being blown to kingdom come.

He looked at his daughter. She was really crying now. Silent tears were flowing down her face, but she made no move to stop them or to wipe her eyes. He was relieved to see it, in a peculiar kind of way – it was better than her retreating into that private shell. He wanted to goad her into life again, and after a moment's thought, he found a way. 'You aren't going to let them destroy you as well? You owe him that, at least.'

She stared at him, astonished. 'What do you mean by that?' But she no longer sounded lifeless.

He tried to press the point. 'They killed him, unjustly – we know it must have been. But how does it help Stan if you give up as well? I know what I felt when your mother died, but you have got to go on living – on his behalf as well – experience things for his sake. He would want you to.'

There was a long silence. Maudie didn't speak, but she was breaking little bits of rock-cake off and eating them. She didn't seem to notice that she was doing it, but he was heartened that she'd found a little appetite.

At last she said, 'I don't know. It's been so awful, I can't think of anything at all.' She toyed with her teacup. 'And now Madam's turned me off. What am I to live on? Where am I to go? Aunt Jane won't want me in Belgravia Street.'

'You leave your Aunt Jane to me,' he said, with more confidence than he felt. Maud was back in the real world then. That was a good thing. 'And I'm glad you told me. It's an awful burden to carry by yourself. But it's Stan's secret – no one else need know.'

She picked up the one tiny sugar-lump – all they provided nowadays – and dropped it in her tea. 'Perhaps someone ought to write to the army and make a case for him. They can give a pardon, can't they, even if he's dead? It doesn't help poor Stan, of course, but think what a difference it would make to his mother if they did.'

Wilf was a bit alarmed at this development, but at least it showed a willingness to tackle life again. 'You going to write then?'

She was sipping tea. 'Don't know where to write to.' Her face brightened a little. 'But I know someone who might. The man who told me – Captain Richards, up at Trevarnon House. If he is still there, that is. Since he's got his foot now they might have sent him home.'

'Well, go and ask Belinda. She'd be sure to know. She was up to Belgravia Street asking after you – all about her wedding. She'd be glad to have you call. You can go down there when you've had your tea, perhaps. In the meantime, I'd better take you home. I'll be in trouble down the station as it is.'

'Why don't I come with you?' Maud pushed her cup away. 'Save you time, and perhaps I could see Belinda while I'm there. She's still working on the tickets, isn't she?'

He nodded. 'Till she gets wed, in any c—' He broke off suddenly. A brilliant idea had just occurred to him. Perhaps he could put a word in at the station on Maud's own behalf. But he didn't say a word. Better not to rush her – let her come to it herself. Enough that she had volunteered a sort of plan. 'If you want to wait for me afterwards in town,' he said, 'I'll see you underneath the clock when I've finished work, and we can go home together and tackle Aunt Jane then. I'll take that bag for you.'

She shook her head. 'I'll wait on the station.'

And that is what they did – though he didn't half get a wigging when he got back to work. Thirteen minutes late! He was very lucky they didn't stop half a crown out of his wages over it – and what on earth would Jane have said to that!

Belinda was astonished to see Maudie walking in, right in the middle of the afternoon. It wasn't even half-day closing at the shop, and here she was, as bold as anything, making her way up to the booking grille.

'Where you off to, this time of the day?' she said, by way of greeting. 'Madam sending you off somewhere on some special job?'

Maud shook her head. 'I'm taking unpaid leave – I've not been very well.'

She was looking awful, Belinda thought. Pale and haggard – not herself at all.

'Not going up to try to talk to Stanley's folks again?' she said, and then wished she hadn't.

Maud's face had closed, like a shop blind coming down. 'Not going anywhere. I don't want a ticket. I came to talk to you, just for a minute, if you've got the time.'

Belinda looked around a little nervously. The office superintendent was working at his desk and all the other clerks were occupied as well. 'Well, here, have this timetable, pretend to look at that. Anyone looking will think you want a train. Can't have them thinking that I'm wasting time on private conversations.' She pushed the booklet over and peered at it herself, pointing with a theatrical forefinger to a random page.

Maud scarcely glanced at it. 'I wanted to ask about your brother. Is he still up at the convalescent home?'

Belinda nodded. 'Be there a while yet. He's got his new foot and he was doing well, but now he has got an inflammation in the stump.' She grinned at Maudie. 'I heard you'd been to see him. Did he help at all? Able to give you the information you wanted?'

Maud raised tired eyes and looked at her direct. Belinda thought she'd never seen her friend look so forlorn. 'More than I expected. He was very kind. He was a friend of Stanley's, did he tell you that?'

'He did say they'd been together for a time, but that he was away in hospital at the time your Stan was killed, so he didn't really know the details.' She shrugged. 'He didn't say a lot about it, otherwise – only that you'd been to visit.' She grinned at Maudie. 'You made quite a hit. He keeps on asking when you're going to come again.'

Some of the strain had gone out of Maudie's face. 'I'd half-decided not to, but I think I will. Need some more advice about where I ought to write.'

Belinda frowned. 'I thought you said you had the information now? I presume it was horrible – since you haven't said. He did say to warn you it might not be nice.' She held up a hand. 'Don't tell me if it's awful, I don't want to hear. Only give me nightmares. I have them as it is. Bad enough thinking about poor Peter's foot. Did I tell you Jonah's got his papers and is going to have to go? Soon as we are married – though he's planning to appeal. You can't imagine how upset he's been.'

'When is the big day? It must be coming up.'

'It's a week on Friday. Chapel do, of course, and quite a small affair. Just the family and the Polkinghornes. I was going to try to talk you into asking for the morning off to come, but if you're taking leave already . . .' She broke off. A woman had come in and tried to join the queue, and Belinda had to serve her with a return to Paddington. She wanted the tea train with a hamper, and a first-class reservation facing to the front in the women-only carriage, so there was a lot of writing up. But at last it was ticketed, and Belinda turned back to Maud.

'Well, Madam, have you decided which train you will take?' she said loudly, for the benefit of the departing customer. Then, when the listening ears had safely gone, she said, 'This here wedding. Please do try and come. Ten o'clock it is. There'll be a bit of something afterwards in the chapel hall. Sandwiches and that. Jonah's mother has arranged to get a bit of ham, and she's managed the ingredients to make a saffron cake – though heaven knows how it will turn out with this National Flour: all this chalk they're putting in it, nothing seems to rise. And thanks to Billy Polkinghorne there'll be some sweet treats too – he's promised some soft toffees and a bar of chocolate. So there'll be quite a feast.' Maud still did not answer so she added wickedly, 'Besides, my brother Peter will be there.'

Maud said, rather crossly, 'Don't be so silly. Why should I care if he is there or not?' But Blin noticed that there was a tinge of colour in her sallow cheeks. 'All the same, I'll come – if you would like me there.'

'I suppose,' Belinda said suddenly, struck by an idea, 'you wouldn't come around one night and help me with a tiny alteration to my suit? I think the hem is just an inch too long.'

'I suppose I could do,' Maud said slowly, and next day she did, and while she was busy pinning up the hem, she talked to Belinda about the visit she had made up to see Peter in the afternoon.

'Of course Aunt Jane has had me scrubbing floors, and then keeps on finding fault because I haven't done it right. I tell you I was glad of an excuse to leave the house.' She was kneeling on the floor and she looked up at Blin. 'She makes me feel a nuisance, and I suppose I am. Father has had to turn out of his bed for me and is sleeping in a chair – but obviously it can't go on like that for very long. I'll have to find something, if I don't go back to the shop. Here!' Belinda gave a little start. 'If you don't hold still I'll never get this straight.'

'But I've just thought of something,' Belinda said, still fidgeting with glee. 'After next Friday, I won't be living here. I'll bet Miss Simms would have you – and be glad of it. She likes a bit of company, and she speaks well of you. Like me to ask her, would you?'

Maud looked up so suddenly she upset the pins. 'You know, it just might be the answer,' she said thoughtfully. 'I could go up to Belgravia Street and have my tea, perhaps – Dad and Tully would like that, anyway – and come back here to sleep. But I don't know. How would I pay for it – I won't be earning, without Madam takes me back.'

'Well, how don't you go down and try for my job, then? You've got good writing – tidier than me – and you're much more organized. It would suit you perfectly. And they know your father. They'd have you like a shot.'

'Oh, I couldn't possibly.' Maud didn't look at her. She was using a magnet to pick up the scattered pins. 'They'll be looking out already and have somebody in mind. No point in my applying. And it is far too soon to make up my mind for certain that I won't go back to Madam.' But there was something in her voice that made Belinda think she would.

Belinda's wedding day dawned fine and clear, but sharp and chilly with a breeze in from the east. Maud, at Belinda's invitation, went down early on to help her get ready and pin up her hair.

The famous costume – which did look much more fashionable with the altered hem – was rather lightweight for the temperature but Belinda pooh-poohed all notions of a coat and could not be persuaded even to a vest, because, she said, the extra thickness round the hips might spoil the line.

She didn't half look pretty though, when it was time to go, in her smart two-piece costume with a matching blouse, boots polished like a mirror, hair swept up on top, a posy of wildflowers clutched in her right hand and a bunch of little rosebuds pinned to her lapel. More like a poster outside a moving-picture house than the real live person Maud had known for years. Maud felt her eyelids pricking, but it was joy this time.

She had taken some pains with her own appearance too. Only her ordinary Sunday best, but she had pressed the skirt and blouse, and put some brand-new ribbons on her hat in honour of the day. And before they went downstairs and out into the street she did something she would not have done a week or two ago. She stood before the mirror and copied Belinda's technique – pinched her cheeks and bit her lips to make them colour up. It was only that she wanted to look nice for Blin. Nothing at all to do with Peter Richards being there.

She had been up to see him at Trevarnon House again. Just once, to ask him about her little plan of writing to the army. He had been very kind – heard her out and listened to her plans – before suggesting gently that she wait a year or two.

'I wouldn't make the plea until a peace is signed,' he said. 'I know the way they think, these generals. They won't give pardons while this war is on – afraid that they'll encourage other people to desert. But when it's over – if it ever is – it might be possible, if you can find someone who will testify to Stan's good character.' He looked at her, his brown eyes very dark. 'I would be prepared to do that for you – if you think that it would help. Of course, it would mean that you and I would have to keep in touch. I would be happy to do that, if you will agree.'

'If it would help Stan's cause . . .' She knew that she was blushing, though she didn't quite know why. She changed the subject swiftly. 'How is the walking now?'

He waggled a booted leg at her. 'I was doing well – learning to walk as fast as billy-oh! But then I got a bit of trouble where they strap it on. Chafed the wound stump something terrible, and then I got infection in it, and that put me back. But it's coming on – hardening up and healing very nicely now, though a wood foot is supposed to be the easiest of all.' He saw her wincing, and he gave a smile. I am sorry, Miss Olds – Maudie – I go on too much. I may call you Maudie, mayn't I? I think of you like that – because of Belinda and Stanley, I suppose. Anyway, I didn't mean to keep complaining and make you wince like that. But there are so few people I can talk to now – the staff are very good, of course, and so are the other men, but most of them have people who come and visit them. I just have you and Blin – but she always comes with Jonah and he doesn't want to stay. And you . . .'

He didn't finish. 'You don't visit often' – that was clearly what he meant. She flushed again, a little disconcerted. She felt a little guilty that she hadn't come before. 'I'll come again, I promise,' she murmured. Then she was embarrassed and she rose to go. 'Next week sometime, I don't know exactly when. There's a job that I've applied for and there'll be an interview – and if I get it, they might want me to start.'

He smiled. 'The job that Belinda is doing now, in fact? She told me you'd applied. Well, good luck, even if it means that you can't visit me. I shall see you at Blin's wedding, I expect, in any case. She tells me you have promised that you will try to go.'

'I will,' she muttered. 'Try to come, that is.' Why should that make her go all strange and pink? 'And now, if you'll excuse me, I must hurry off. I have arranged to meet Miss Simms later on this afternoon, to talk about the possibility of my taking Belinda's room.'

His smile and 'Goodbye Maudie' had stayed with her ever since.

And here he was now, at the chapel door, in hospital uniform, but looking very smart. He was walking with a stick now, rather than a crutch, and he fell into place beside her as they went inside. Jonah and his parents were already there, stiff and uncomfortable in their Sunday clothes, and Maud heard his mother's disapproving sniff.

'That's Belinda's friend.' The whisper was quite loud. 'Look at the state of her, with carmine on her cheeks. Must have, mustn't she, to be as pink as that!' And Maudie gave the lie to that by blushing redder still. She sat down in a pew, and Peter sat beside her, quite naturally, as if it was the expected place for him to be. Then the Polkinghornes came in – fat little Billy and his skinny wife, and their sickly baby who whimpered plaintively, until her mother gave her a sugared cloth to suck – and the little wedding congregation was complete. The bride and groom went shyly to the front.

It was all over very quickly, and half an hour later Jonah and Belinda were man and wife at last. Jonah did not look as happy as he might have done, but of course he had received his papers and might have to go and fight straight away.

Billy Polkinghorne was sympathizing loudly with his plight. 'You can appeal. You might get out of it. I was lucky that way – it didn't come to that. They called me up all right, and I went before the board, but they wouldn't take me – said my heart was bad. 'Cause I'm fat, most likely.' Which, as the new Mrs Lotts said to Maudie afterwards, didn't really comfort Jonah very much.

Then it was time for some sandwiches and cake, which hadn't really risen, though it tasted well enough. Belinda took her baggage and got into the cart, which had been scrubbed and decorated with a paper bow, and she and her new family trotted down the street, back to the Lotts' house where she was going to live.

Peter took out a pocket handkerchief and waved them out of sight. 'That Jonah wanted to move in with me, you know,' he said to Maud, conversationally. 'It was hard to persuade him that I was saying no. I might take Belinda, while he's overseas – when they let me out, I shall be glad of help and I think she'd rather be over there with me – but I'm not having Jonah, especially when I am not there myself. I know the type too well. If I once let him in my house I'd never get him out.' He turned and grinned at her. 'Besides, you never know. I might find a bride myself.'

He'd flustered her again. She buried her face in the posy that Blin had given her. 'I expect you will.'

'I've got something to offer,' he said. 'I'm young, and relatively fit – apart from this damn foot. I own a house already and I have a skill. I can earn an honest living, missing foot or not. You don't need both legs to be a carpenter. And it's an honourable trade. I can think of someone very special who was a carpenter.'

It took her a minute to work out what he meant. 'Peter!' she said reproachfully. 'That's disrespectful. You shouldn't talk like that!'

He misunderstood her, and said with quick concern. 'No, of course I shouldn't. It is far too soon. But one day, perhaps, you might consider it? In the meantime, let me walk you home.'

'I only meant . . .' she started, but then changed her mind. It would sound as if she was accepting what he'd said to her. She'd apparently accepted his invitation too, without quite noticing, as they seemed to be walking down the street together now. She changed the subject quickly. 'Did you know I'd had a letter from Stanley's folk at last? Said they'd heard from Granfer that I'd been at the farm, and felt they ought to write and tell me about Stan.'

He squeezed her arm, as though he were her brother and not Blin's. 'And did they tell you? Everything, I mean?'

She shook her head. 'No, only sent that cutting from the paper. And they gave no address. But they did send me something else as well. It was with Stan's things apparently, when they sent them home. Something that I sent him, but I was glad to have it back . . .' She trailed off again. 'Nothing of any value, like the present he gave me. Only a piece of paper with a dried flower inside.'

Peter stopped and looked at her. 'I remember that. Stan showed it to me once. He always had it in his pocket, nearest to his heart. And there was writing on it.'

She nodded. 'I was the one that wrote it. "From Penvarris – with Love." Just a silly thing. I picked it on the cliffs, to remind him of the places where we used to walk.'

'So it wasn't silly. It was very meaningful. I would have treasured it, if I'd been in his place. Now, this is your street, so I'll say farewell for now. But I'll see you again. I know you're working at the station from next Monday on, and that you're moving into Belinda's old room at Miss Simms.' I'm sure I'll find a way to meet you now and then. Perhaps you will consent sometime to take a stroll with me? And then one day we'll walk out on the cliffs, and you can show me where you got that flower from. Not now, but one day, when your heart has healed. You'll find that I'll be waiting.' And, raising his hat politely, he turned and walked away.

She watched him go and found that she was smiling through her tears.

# Epilogue

## May 2007

'Come on, Peter,' his mother shouted up the stairs. 'Turn that laptop off now and get yourself to bed. You've got school tomorrow and it's nearly ten o'clock. What are you doing anyway? Watching DVDs again?'

'I'm doing my homework,' Peter said, aggrieved. She'd come upstairs now, like she always did, to fuss him from the door. 'Doing this project on the First World War. I'm just downloading something from the internet.'

'Well, you should have done it earlier instead of wasting time playing with your Facebook or whatever it's called.' She started picking up stray socks and T-shirts and putting them in the laundry basket where they ought to be. He hated it when she did that – and he knew exactly what she was going to say next. 'Look at the state of this place! When are you ever going to tidy up this room?'

'I'll do it when I've finished. This is quite interesting.' Anything to deflect her from nagging him again. 'I think I might have found an ancestor of ours. Look, there he is – among the list of wounded officers who were treated at Penzance in some convalescent home or other. Peter Richards – same as Dad and me. Former civilian occupation: carpenter. And here he is again, married in 1917 to someone called Maud Olds and running a joinery business in Clarence Parade. That would make sense, wouldn't it? Wasn't Maudie the name of Dad's great-grandmother? The one in the picture in the dining-room? At his parents' wedding, with all the rest of them?'

She shook her head, still picking T-shirts up. 'You'd have to ask your father. He knows who they all are. That picture was taken in 1962 – and most of the older generation had passed on before I met your dad, so I have no idea. But I think there was a Maudie, so you might be right. Let's have a look at that list you found.' She leaned across and squinted at the screen. 'Captain Peter Richards. Yes, I think that's him. Lost an arm or something, but he must have done all right if he set up that joinery. If it is the one, he died in the bombing during World War Two, but she was still living in the eighties. Still sewing baby garments when your dad was small. Yes, I'm sure the name was Maudie, when I come to think. They had a big family, I know. Seven or eight of them, I think. Your great-grandfather was the second son – and there's always been another Peter in the family since.'

'Yes, that's weird. That's something else I found on another website about the local school. Like, here's a historic photograph of all the children up to standard three.' He moved the mouse and brought the picture up. 'There's Peter Wilfred Richards – that's Great-Granddad then – and obviously that's his older brother standing next to him. It could be a clone of him, they're so alike. But you just read the name Stanley Lionel Hoskins Richards. Imagine calling someone Hoskins as a middle name. Sort of like a surname. But when you Google that – like this – the name turns up again – Stanley Lionel Hoskins – in the list of people who were shot at dawn and were given that official pardon only recently. And the same dates and regiment as Peter Richards, too. You reckon it's connected?'

'Shouldn't think so for a moment. Why would anyone want to call their son after someone who was shot for cowardice? No, it was a common enough name. Most likely just coincidence. Now, you're wasting time, and it's after ten o'clock. Put that stuff away. It's not even really what you should be working on.'

He closed down the computer. 'Interesting though. Weird thing, coming across your own name in a list like that. Makes you wonder what your ancestors were like.'

'And that's only half your ancestors – just on your father's side. What about my family? You didn't happen to find anyone called Lotts, I don't suppose?'

He yawned. 'I didn't look for them. But I will do if you like. Tomorrow evening, if I have the time, what with all the homework stuff I've got to do.'

She rescued his pillows from the floor, patted them to fluff them up and put them on the bed. 'No, doesn't matter. Don't waste your time on it. You probably wouldn't find any record anyway. Nobody on my side was very interesting. No one was an officer – not in either war. And nobody was wounded, as far as I'm aware. Just ran a coal merchant's for years and years, and then went into selling gas appliances instead. Not much of a story, on the Lotts side, I'm afraid.'

But Peter would look tomorrow, he had decided that. Amazing to find a name you knew among a list like that – sort of linked you to it, in a funny kind of way. Hard to imagine that they were people just like you, except they were living a hundred years ago. Pity you could not step back in time to see what it was like.